Chapter 1

A shock of bitterly cold wind blew the fine rain directly into Zoë's face causing her to gasp involuntarily. She wrapped her cardigan tightly around her body and looked left, then right.

As had been the case for most of the day, the pathway lacked the presence of shoppers and she had found that each hour had crept by tiresomely. The day had not seemed to reach a point where any significant light had been able to break through the heavy pewter sky, which had only heightened the air of pessimism further.

Stepping back inside, Zoë bolted the door firmly against the late February bleakness. She could see the cobbled path glistening in the orange glow from the Victorian style lamp that hung from the shop opposite. Two girls suddenly appeared pressed together under an umbrella as they hurried past taking small, swift steps in their thin, ballet-style pumps. They were talking animatedly, their words caught and thrown by the wind and were seemingly unconcerned by the wet seeping through to their bare feet. The subject of their conversation was inaudible to Zoë, but as she watched them pass by she realised she felt envious of their carefree, fatuous demeanour.

She turned and rested the back of her head against the door and surveyed the small boutique that was once her parents' but now belonged to her. It felt so much a part of who she was and after having spent most of her childhood listening to her parents deliberating about different aspects of their livelihood, her own instincts now seemed honed to realise what was best for the

1

business. She loved the ambience of the old building with its quirky layout and solid textured walls. Stood in the centre of one of these in the small upstairs room which was now used to keep overflow stock, was a heavy, antiquated fireplace surround and despite the chimney having been boarded up many years ago, a draught would still chill the room on particularly cold days. Traces of previous unknown occupants remained here especially – where ingrained marking on the walls and floorboards had been painted over but not entirely concealed and Zoë liked to think that her own impression would also be left for future residents to ponder over.

In comparison the modern malls that no city seemed to be without now, felt impersonal and austere to her. Rails crammed with stock that was creased and too frequently soiled as a result of slipping on to the floor and harsh, white lighting that divested the brain of recognising the time of day.

But it was obvious that there was a demand for the shopping centres that were popping up in every town and city. The incessant need to consume made simple with the longer opening times, multi-storey parking and high street chains situated together in one area. She'd feel her mood plummet entering the fluorescent lit walkways as she was swept along by the sea of bodies moving from store to store.

Stepping up to the window display area she turned off the coloured spotlights that had recently been installed. There was still a faint smell of varnish coming from the model figures that her boyfriend had crafted out of wood for the new display. She ran her fingers over the smooth wood at the neck of the model, pausing over a dense knot that gave this form its unique identity and she again felt the tinge of joy that these beautifully constructed figures gave her.

Gage had worked on them during the evenings with Zoë watching his precise, confident actions. He'd applied all his concentration to the carefully sculptured models, with his large hands moving gracefully over the wood and his forehead furrowing as he brushed dust from the surface before once again picking up his hand plane. Moments like these were precious to Zoë, with no outside distractions from friends or family they were content just to be in each other's company.

Today being Saturday, she had hoped for some fruitful sales to compensate for the rest of the week's poor trading. Instead the day had dragged on, crushing this desire and leaving Zoë with the oppressive feelings that she had been harbouring for the last couple of weeks. Her usual buoyancy had been replaced with a terrible pressure, which had made her withdrawn and sullen. The uncertainty of her recent decision to introduce different styles into the boutique lay at the heart of her anxiety.

She had been to a local trade show put on by a couple of university graduates and had been excited and inspired by their innovative designs. She had bought a small collection and was thrilled with how it instantly refreshed the look of the boutique. But now standing in the dim evening light, she no longer felt the thrill, just ambivalence and foreboding.

Amber came through to the front of the shop carrying two over-sized mugs of tea. She gripped the rim of one as she held it towards Zoë, offering her the handle and burning her own fingers in the process.

'I think I'll change the window display before I leave tonight. Maybe I was a little premature putting the new stock in, after all it's hardly spring-like weather and I don't want the clothes to look tired by the time people are looking for new pieces.'

Amber watched her friend's pensive expression and wondered if she was able to ever truly absolve herself from the concerns of the small business. She was glad that she didn't have to worry about such things and could go home at the end of the day with a mostly clear head.

'Zoë, leave it – we can do it together on Monday if you really feel the need. I insist that you go home and forget about it until then.' Zoë turned and smiled knowingly at her.

'You insist, eh? So this would have nothing to do with the guilt you would feel leaving me here alone?' Amber raised her eyebrows in mock astonishment,

'If you would rather stay behind fretting instead of enjoying a cold glass of wine at home, well that's up to you. But seriously Zoë, I've had enough for today – and you're right, I don't want to leave you here alone.' She watched as her words seemed to puncture a hole in Zoë's resolve.

'OK, I hear you – I suppose it does make more sense to come back on Monday with a clear head. I don't expect that Gage would be too impressed if I stayed behind either as it's my turn to get the take-away and he's not at his most tolerant when his hunger pangs begin kick in.'

'That's settled then – let's finish up here and go.'

A little while later, they stepped out into the alleyway that ran alongside of the boutique and were immediately hit with the aroma of Indian food from a neighbouring restaurant. Both women hurried to their cars which were parked to the rear of the shop in a typically run-down car park. Industrial wheelie bins from each of the business premises stood waiting to be emptied. The stench of rotten food that emanated from some of them was enough to make people cross over to the narrower path opposite at times.

Faded graffiti clung to weather-worn walls and a towering block of flats stood to one side overseeing all activity below. Children's voices and babies' cries could be heard throughout the day, whilst later the sound of slamming doors and calls to people below echoed around the car park.

After waving goodbye to Amber, Zoë pulled away in her car, wishing she could assuage the uneasiness which she knew would be lingering around her for the majority of the weekend.

As accustomed as she was to the route home, she drove heedlessly along the familiar roads. Roads which she had walked first with her mother, and later her friends as she began to experience the first steps of independence. The exhilarating sense of autonomy she had longed for was everything she'd desired. Zoë had always been sensible with her new found independence for fear of losing it again. She made sure to be home at the specified time and used her common sense in making decisions, even if it meant temporarily losing face with her friends. These friends were in awe of her never having been grounded before though, something she was very proud of.

Their favourite pastime was sitting in the park observing passers-by, but predominantly the older teens whose ease and wisdom of the opposite sex fascinated them. The girls, whose high-heels sank into the grass as they strutted across to meet their boyfriends at the far end of the field, held their interest greatly. More often than not cigarettes trailed from their brightly polished fingertips and as they walked their small, quilted, gold bags bumped in unison against their denim-clad hips. The boys, with their casual persona enjoying the sense of dominance they held at that time, would stand in groups waiting to be approached. Their open displays of affection would both enthral and disgust Zoë and her friends, but they were always secretly disappointed on the occasions when they were not around to entertain them.

A flashing light further up the road filled Zoë's car with a mix of blue and red hues, the rain had smeared her windscreen slightly, but up ahead she could see a cluster of people spilling onto the road. As she gradually slowed to a standstill behind the queue of stationary cars, Zoë began to feel anxious about what horror might lay ahead.

A policewoman was directing the traffic through, and Zoë began to move forward, but to her dismay, the car in front of her stopped and the policewoman began directing the congested traffic from the opposite direction through. As she waited, curiosity got the better of her, so releasing her seatbelt she slid her body across to the passenger seat. Here the reason for the delay became apparent. A mangled bicycle lay in the road with its cracked, back reflector catching the lights from all the activity around. She could see the hi-vis jackets of the paramedics as they tended to the casualty on the ground, and was shocked to see the subject's bare foot exposed in the headlights from the car ahead.

Feeling shamefully intrusive of their cataclysmic situation, Zoë moved back to her original position.

The rain began to fall harder and she wondered if the anonymous figure on the ground was conscious to all that was happening around them. Could they feel the cold rain on their uncovered skin and the mounting trepidation that hung in the air? Zoë began to question why their foot had not been covered and thought troubled her as she waited helplessly. She wished that Gage was there, at least then she could have expelled some of her nervous energy through talking to him – he was always calm in an emergency and his poise steadied her. Now her feelings of inadequacy were amplified as she was forced to sit and witness this person's horrific turn of fate.

When she had been about six years old, her mother had spent some time in hospital. Zoë remembered standing staring up at the ugly, tower block that had too many windows and wondering which one held her mother captive. An uneasy feeling in her tummy had crept up into her throat and she had feared that she would be sick all over her new black, patent shoes.

Her father, carrying a small bouquet of pink roses, had clasped her hand and led her through the main entrance before ushering her into a small, humid lift. As they ascended, Zoë had thought about how empty and strange their home had felt without her mother. Her father had been extra attentive and talkative towards her, but his voice had sounded strangely synthetic. He had bought her a soft, rabbit toy from the local shop, even though he usually complained that she had too many cuddly toys. It had floppy, patchwork ears and a green velvet bow. Each evening when he read her a bedtime story, she would listen to his soft, mollifying voice and hold the small bunny under her chin, breathing in the smell of the new material that smelt so unlike all her others.

But his concern floated around him like a delicate ribbon of smoke from a struck match. When he thought that she wasn't paying attention, he would sit staring out of the window – looking but seeing nothing. Song after song would play on the radio that continuously hummed in the background, but he wouldn't go out to tend to the garden or sort through the post that had begun to pile up on the side.

On entering the ward, Zoë had scanned the bright room until she had spotted her mother sitting up in the bed nearest the window. Her hair had been longer then and it had hung loosely around her shoulders with her fringe clipped back, revealing her pale face. She had looked incongruous surrounded by the frail and elderly. Zoë had been frightened by the vacant stares and bird-like fragility of the older women, so she had focused her attention on her mother, avoiding letting her gaze slip to the other mounds lying around her. She remembered how her face had lit up as she had beckoned her over, but the rest of the visit was hazy apart from when they had left having been given the news that her mother could go home the next day. Zoë had felt much lighter as they walked the curved corridors back to the lift. She had been enjoying listening to the rhythmic sound of her heels hitting the tiled floor when a nurse had stopped in front of her, beaming widely. The friendly nurse had commented that Zoë would make an excellent nurse in the future with her speedy walk and Zoë had felt a huge surge of pride and importance. For years after, when asked what she wanted to be when she was older, her answer had resolutely been that she wanted to be a nurse.

If this had become a reality, she would not have felt as inadequate as she did now, having to sit without being able to offer any kind of help to this unknown person.

Others passing by also seemed distracted from their own troubles for a while, local residents stood with their neighbours sharing in the horror that was enfolding on their own doorstep.

Pulling slowly forward, Zoë turned her head as she passed the now foiled-covered figure. She realised that she would probably never find out what had happened here – momentarily so close to the occurrence, but never to hear the end of the story. As she continued down the road she felt suddenly cold and tired, eager to get back to the sanctum of her home.

Chapter 2

Gage had secured a contract with a local building developer to construct the kitchens in a small plot of executive builds in the city. Expectations of the completed homes were high and with Gage being able to offer bespoke requirements to clients, he had come highly recommended by a fellow developer. He was popular due to his affable personality, commitment and patience that he showed with each new demand placed on him by his customers. He was not arrogant but had strong self-belief when it came to his ability in carpentry, so this new contract was not causing him too much concern. The fact that he was able to use his creativity to support himself was never taken for granted, and he felt compassion for some of his friends who had to work long, unsociable hours just to make ends meet.

Being ahead in his schedule, Gage had left the site early planning to surprise Zoë by preparing the evening meal. He stopped off at the local supermarket to buy the fresh vegetables and chicken for the stir-fry he intended to make. Impulsively he picked up a mixed bouquet of purple freesias and white roses that were placed close to the entrance of the store. As he put them into his basket he felt a tinge of guilt as he would usually make this type of purchase on the high street in support of local trade – he knew only too well the importance of this.

By the time he left the supermarket it was fully dark and a fine mist of rain had begun to sweep across the car park. As he crossed over to his van a cold wind pulled at the carrier bag gripped in his hand, dislodging the carefully positioned flowers and lifting them into the air, before dropping them a little way behind him. He hurried back to where they lay, quickly placing his foot on the stems before the wind had a chance to take them again. As he lifted them up he saw that one of the roses had been spoiled. Its ethereal petals were torn and the outer layer was only held in place by the cellophane that they were wrapped in. Slightly irritated, he pushed the bouquet into the opening of his coat and headed over to his van.

Determined not to allow anything to spoil his jovial mood he turned up the radio and thought about his latest project. He was feeling really satisfied with the ways things had been progressing and had received some positive feed-back from his clients that had ended his day positively. Now he also hoped to lift Zoë's mood as the concerns of the boutique had recently seemed to be causing her greater angst resulting in her becoming distracted and unusually withdrawn. He knew how driven she was and how she wanted to maintain the success of the family business, but he felt that sometimes she pushed herself way too hard.

Zoë was not good at hiding her emotions, her facial expressions and body language would always betray her. When she met people for the first time, Gage could always tell if she had warmed to the new acquaintance or not. There was undoubted sincerity in her smile when she met someone she liked, which she could not simulate when meeting someone she did not. Her eyes would widen and sparkle and the recipient would feel that she was wholly absorbed in their conversation. She would focus on them alone and not allow herself to be distracted by activity around her. Her ability to listen intently added to her charming appeal all the more and people often found that they divulged more than they had at first perhaps intended.

However, when she found herself in the company of someone that she had little tolerance for, be it their political beliefs or social conduct, she could not force a disposition to please. She would disengage herself from the conversation gracefully, but leave the person in no doubt of her sentiment. It was for this reason that there were people who adored Zoë, whilst others avoided her.

Gage had first seen Zoë when he had been at the boutique taking measurements for some boxed shelving that was becoming popular at that time. It had been her idea to introduce a more interesting way to merchandise the stock and she had convinced her mother, Stephanie, who was then still the manager, to have shelving built along the wall where they would contain folded t-shirts and knitwear.

He had been asked to provide a quote by Stephanie, who had been given his number by a friend of a friend. Much of his clientele had been built up in this way during the early days and he was grateful for it. Zoë had arrived at the boutique a few minutes after Gage; she had marched in with her arms enveloped around a pile of folders, and had smiled briefly at him before disappearing through to the back of the shop. He had never experienced such an instant attraction to anyone before and had felt suddenly uncomfortable and awkward in having to be at such close proximity to her. When she reappeared, she had removed her light jacket and had begun inspecting some papers on the desk before she'd looked up and smiled at Gage, more broadly this time. He'd felt as if on one hand, all his senses had been heightened, but on the other, that the strength in his muscles had dissipated.

As he'd taken guarded glances at Zoë as she'd moved around the boutique replacing clothes to their designated rails, he'd been all too aware of the uncomfortable air that would ensue if she'd happened to catch him watching her. With this in mind, he'd continued taking surreptitious looks when she'd been facing away from him. He'd noticed that she had a habit of shaking her head to move stray segments of hair away from her eyes as she'd moved from rail to rail. She'd moved quickly and had been totally absorbed in the task at hand, her manner seeming to be abrupt until she'd pause to smile in acknowledgement of a customer entering the boutique. When this happened, her persona shifted to the accommodating, effervescent sales woman hoping to entice her subject into making a purchase. Gage would learn that under the right circumstances, Zoë would usually succeed in this mission. Gathering up armfuls of clothing, she would cajole the customer into the fitting room, obtaining information about their needs as she did so, to create the ideal outfit. As each piece of clothing was tried on, Zoë would give honest and constructive feedback, not straying from their side until she was certain that they were feeling the exuberance that they had been seeking on entering the shop.

After taking a considerable amount of time measuring up, Gage had forced himself to make his approach. To his complete horror he'd found himself to be reddening as he stood in front of the desk waiting for Zoë to look up at him. Sweat had formed in his palms and armpits which he knew would soon become apparent in his tight-fitting t-shirt. He'd wanted to turn and stall the moment in an effort to compose himself, but it had been too late. Zoë had looked up promptly and shaken the hair from her forehead, pulling a shorter strand behind her ear and holding it there as she stared into his eyes. He'd found it impossible to hold her gaze for too long and so had looked past her as if trying to locate Stephanie, who he'd said he had a few questions for, before being able to complete the quote. Zoë had poked her head round the door of the back room and Gage had taken the opportunity to observe her without caution. She had been wearing black tailored shorts that stopped at the knee and a fine, cream top that showed the smooth contours of her body. She had been balancing on one leg with the other raised off the floor as she'd relayed the message to her mother and he'd noticed that she had firm calf muscles that were in contrast to her fragile-looking ankles. She was considerably shorter than any other woman he had dated and before she returned her attention back to him, he'd marvelled at how tiny the shoe that hung from her foot was. He'd been struck by the irony that this petite woman utterly terrified him and had reduced him to a sweaty mess.

The infatuation had grown from there.

Gage was preparing the vegetables and as he sliced into a red pepper he couldn't resist devouring some of the slices raw; the combination of the crunchy skin and juiciness of the interior were too tempting for his empty stomach.

The radio was playing loudly and so he failed to hear Zoë come through the front door. In the hallway she removed her ankle boots and socks and grateful to be finally free of their constriction, she flexed her toes backwards and forwards. Padding through the unlit lounge to the kitchen at the back of the house, she saw Gage's large frame hunched over the kitchen worktop, he was blithely singing along to a song on the radio as he concentrated on his task. She stood watching for a moment and felt envious of his ability to let go, to be content living in the moment and not allow himself to be weighed down by problems that he could not immediately resolve. She knew that tonight, she would be unable to fully relax as thoughts of the boutique would somehow filter through and demand her attention. Gage could seemingly put his concerns to one side and return to them when necessary and Zoë wondered where this negative energy was held mute in the meantime. She couldn't help but to wring out all the possibilities of a certain predicament until she was happy with one of the solutions – or so drained that she fell asleep.

It was one of the qualities that had first attracted him to her – he displayed a serenity and ease that she herself rarely felt. It wasn't so much that she didn't possess the ability to relax, but almost that if she did, she'd never be able to get back up to speed and therefore lose everything she'd strived for.

Thinking back to the day she'd first encountered Gage, she recalled his presence being overpowering. Being accustomed to feeling confident and prestigious in her role in the boutique, she had been confused by the sense of awkwardness that Gage had instilled in her that morning.

After a while, she'd had to admit to herself that this feeling stemmed from pure lust. She could not deny that his broad shoulders and sculpted muscles had made an impression on her and had deliberately kept her eyes averted from him, afraid that he would see right through her. When he'd actually approached her, she'd been relieved to hand him over to her mother, certain that she would have tripped on her words and embarrassed herself if she'd had to confer with him for too long.

'I thought I was getting take-out tonight?' Zoë stepped into the brightly lit kitchen and stood behind Gage peering round his elbow at the sliced peppers and courgettes on the chopping board.

'Blimey, Zo – I could've lost a finger! What are you doing sneaking up on me like that?' Zoë couldn't help grinning at the fact that she'd caught him out.

'Your singing must have drowned me out – by the way, don't stop on my account.' Gage smiled good-humouredly refusing to be drawn into her game.

'I just fancied cooking – why don't you jump in the shower while I finish this? He pulled her to him and wrapped his arms around her slender shoulders. She let herself collapse against the contours of his body breathing in the familiar scent of wood shavings, spicy deodorant and the uniqueness of him that could not be labelled. When they had first begun dating she would frequently press her nose to his skin to breathe him in, and although Gage would tease her by comparing her to a mangy cat, he'd been secretly delighted.

'There was an accident on Heath Road tonight, a cyclist had been knocked off their bike … it was awful.'

'Really?' Gage pulled away a little and looked down at her with his eyebrows raised. 'Not the best weather to be biking in though is it? Was it serious?'

Too late Zoë realised that she didn't really want to discuss it anymore – she couldn't convey her feelings to Gage adequately about how the short experience had touched her so acutely.

'I'm not sure – but the paramedics were still there as I left and the police were closing off part of the road.' Gage rubbed her back soothingly and she felt her muscles loosen as she leant back into him.

'How were things at work – did it pick up at all?' Zoë disengaged herself as gently as she could, not wanting to show the irritation the question had posed.

'No, not really, but I've been thinking about widening our advertising as with having the new stock from the show, I think we could attract more students. If I aim it towards that demographic hopefully it will expand my market presence further, and with the pieces being more select, it should hold more appeal to them. I'm going to speak to Amber about perhaps putting a show on one evening – free Prosecco and nibbles might entice people through the door.' She groaned inwardly to herself – she'd only just walked through the door and already she was talking about the boutique.

'Well you can keep the Prosecco, but I'd definitely be interested in the nibbles,' he smiled playfully, 'go and have a shower, this is almost ready.'

As she walked back through to the hall she switched on the corner lamp and saw the flowers placed in the middle of the set table. She turned to Gage who was watching her and let out a small laugh at his theatrical wink and sheepish grin.

A couple of hours later as Zoë had just finished rinsing her plate at the kitchen sink, she felt Gage's hands gently clasp her hips and his lips brush the side of her cheek. His hair was still damp and smelt faintly of coconut; warmth effused from every part of him encasing her in a bubble of tranquillity. He untied her towelling dressing gown and pulled it down to expose her smooth, lightly freckled shoulders. She let her mind drift as he dropped butterfly kisses along the top of her back before snaking his hands into her hair to unveil the nape of her neck. Here he pressed his lips to her skin that was as light and vulnerable as the inside of a shell. He twisted her round and his eyes fell from hers to the sheer, cream camisole that lifted and supported her breasts perfectly to enhance her alluring curves. He kissed her lips, increasing the pressure gradually until Zoë had to put her hands back to support herself against the worktop. An intense heat had spread throughout her body and she could no longer tolerate her feet enveloped in her slippers or the gown still hanging from her arms. She pushed Gage away from her to release herself from the redundant items. The cool tiles beneath her feet sent a shock through her body, accentuating her already erect nipples further. Gage stood facing her and took in the curves and softness of her petite frame. He loved that she had an edge of fragility about her but also possessed a confidence and strength that many envied.

Under the glare of the spotlights and Gage's appreciative scrutiny, Zoë began to graze her fingers against his chest and taut stomach that contracted as she did so. His mouth was on hers again, this time with more urgency and the low groans that escaped from his throat sent a rush of colour to her cheeks. He picked her up and carried her through to the lounge where he lowered her on to the sofa. She let herself float on the sensations that overcame her – her mind completely liberated from thoughts of everything for a while.

Sunday morning allowed frail rays of sunshine to edge through a slit in the curtains that had been hastily drawn the night before. Zoë had woken first and enjoyed a few moments' procrastination before making plans for the day ahead. It pleased her that there was a faint promise of spring in the air, the winter had begun early and had dragged on mercilessly, but on Tuesday the new month would begin.

Thoughts of the boutique began to push to the forefront of her mind, but lying in their bed watching as the curtains lifted in the cool air, she rationalized that nothing could be done until the following morning. She would challenge all her recent misgivings and face them head on – her voracious determination had seen her through difficult periods before and would do so again. Beside her Gage slept almost silently with his back facing towards her, she slipped out of the bed and reached for her dressing gown and careful to avoid stepping on the squeaky floorboard, she left the room.

Taking her coffee through to the living room she glanced at the clock, it had just gone half-past eight and they were expected at her parents' house for lunch at one. Her mother had promised to bake one of her rhubarb crumbles for Gage. Zoë hoped that she would have the power to resist as of late she had noticed that some of her clothes nipped, and her once taut stomach had developed more of a soft, roundness to it. Years of dancing had kept her in good shape, but now it seemed the lack of time to spend on this had begun to catch up with her. She was also fast-approaching her thirties and although she tried to eat a healthy diet, her habits at the boutique were sometimes erratic. Often she would snack on convenient readymade foods rather than to eat a substantial lunch. As she headed towards the bathroom, she made a mental note to start running again and to perhaps do a HIIT class with Amber – she was always talking about the benefits of this type of training.

Pulling into her parents' gravelled drive some hours later, she looked across at Gage who was wearing a long-sleeved white shirt with the cuffs folded back and a slim fitted pair of jeans. It amazed her that she still felt as attracted to him now as she had done five years ago when they'd first met.

Zoë had ended a relationship to be with Gage which had been painful to do as her boyfriend had done nothing to deserve the abandonment. She had felt such remorse at her actions but knew that the relationship was stuck in a rut and had definitely become unbalanced. Ethan had been so relaxed and easy-going when they had first met, but later had become insistent about them spending more time together. Zoë would come up with different excuses to avoid this until it became apparent to them both that she just didn't need him like her needed her. Then Gage had come on the scene and she hadn't been able to deny the feelings that he stirred in her.

Stephanie Shaw stepped outside to meet them, beaming brightly as she held something close to her chest.

'Surprise! We've been waiting for you to arrive – look isn't she delicious!'

'Oh Mum, let me see! Where did you get her from?' Zoë kissed her mother quickly on the cheek and then pressed her nose into the silky, tortoiseshell fur of the kitten held in her arms. Its marble eyes were alert with inquisitiveness and it began to fidget, catching its tiny claws in the fibres of her mother's fine blouse. It suddenly emitted a piercing meow, making Zoë and her mother laugh with delight.

'Your father and I were coming home from Cambridge the other day, when we spotted a notice at the entrance to the farm down the road. I swear, I didn't speak a word, he turned in without any coercion – and I'll tell you something else – he's completely smitten, Zoë!'

'Awww, how many are there?'

'We got the last two, a boy and a girl. The other one is a lazy little thing, it's probably still curled up on Ed's lap – he's been completely immobile for the last hour!' Gage approached carrying a bottle of wine smiling warmly at Stephanie before leaning down to greet her with a kiss.

'Gage, you look gorgeous as ever – come on inside before this one escapes or rips my blouse to shreds, I'd forgotten just how sharp their claws are – they're like needles!'

Her parents' house never failed to enthral Zoë. Set slightly back from a quiet country road, it stood on a rising that gave it an impressive sense of magnitude. Magnolia trees towered, waiting to expel their resplendent blooms alongside cherry trees which framed the perimeter of the vast garden. In the springtime when the blossom would fall on to the grass beneath, Stephanie would absolutely forbid Ed to rake it up citing that it would only last a few weeks. This went against his tidy nature, but he knew that on this particular argument, he was beaten. The blossom would lie like a delicate carpet of pastel pink until the edges curled and browned, and it was only at this point that Ed would dare to clear it.

They followed her mother through the dark hallway. On the walls hung black and white family photographs that, when she was younger had embarrassed Zoë as being the only child, she dominated the collection. Cousins that had now become estranged also featured and Zoë always felt a mixture of guilt and sadness when reminded by the images of this fact. Everyone was busy with their own lives and the harsh truth was that distance and time meant that none of them had the inclination to instigate contact again.

Many of the photos had been taken by her father during family outings – there was one Zoë standing rigid in the frothy sea displaying a shocked expression at the apparent chill of the Norfolk coastline. Another of her, taken around the same time, wrapped in a towel with her damp, golden hair curling around her cheeks, the day's pursuits showing in her weary face. But her favourite was one that had been taken at a family wedding when she had been aged about eighteen – she and her mother caught unaware, laughing ebulliently, Stephanie hanging on to Zoë's shoulder in the effort to stay upright. It caught her mother perfectly, highlighting the fact that she was always the life-and-soul of the party and loved being in the company of others.

On entering the sitting room, Zoë breathed in the comforting aroma of home cooking and her stomach gurgled in anticipation. She looked across at her father who was sitting in his favourite chair in the far corner. A book lay on the arm with his glasses folded neatly on top and a black and white kitten was curled up tightly on his knees.

'Hi Dad, I have to say that you're looking extremely comfortable there.'

'Well, I've spent the morning running around with a piece of string – think I deserve a rest in all honesty!' Edward grinned archly at his daughter and Gage, displaying the perfectly neat teeth that Zoë had inherited.

He was an extraordinarily orderly man with a small frame and surprisingly smooth skin for a man in his late-fifties. He always dressed smartly in shirts and coordinating jumpers and trousers which Stephanie would tease him for, Zoë could not ever recall a time seeing him in disarray. He seemed unflappable and able to deal with situations using logic and noble judgement, people trusted him and this quality had served him well in his career as a business man. Zoë held him in great esteem and had striven to gain his approval in all aspects of her life, although this had not needed to be laboured for as Edward had been proud of Zoë from the moment she was first placed in his arms.

Over lunch, Zoë shared her plans for the boutique with her parents. Edward was fully aware of the current situation as Zoë sent him weekly emails detailing the takings and general welfare of the business. He was not overly concerned by the recent dip in figures – experienced as he was in retail he understood the peaks and troughs, but also recognised the need in Zoë to share her unease with them both. He waited until she had finished speaking and then gave his response.

'Zo, you know we've never doubted your ability or judgement, if anyone can make positive changes to the shop, it's you. Your intentions sound great, you've got good contacts, and of course the tenacity of a dog with a bone.' His eyes shone with pride and mischief as he said this. 'But your mother and I are a little concerned that you're not allowing yourself time off mentally.'

Stephanie stood and began clearing the empty plates away, the abundance of silver bracelets on her arm slid down and jangled together as she did so, rousing Gage from his torpid state. The warmth of the room, together with the wine, food and soothing tones of Zoë and her father's voices had made him comfortably drowsy.

'You should both get away this year, my lovelies – take that holiday to Florence you've always wanted. I could help out in the boutique – you know how I like to keep my foot in the door and Amber would love it too,' she laughed. Zoë smiled as she watched her mother carrying the plates through to the kitchen, she'd cleared them all in one taking, deftly balancing some on her forearm, with gravy swilling precariously, but not a drop spilt. It was certainly true that Stephanie had more than enough vigour to work in the boutique for a fortnight or so, but Zoë just couldn't contemplate going away at the moment, she had too many plans to enforce.

'I'll keep that in mind thanks, Mum.'

Stephanie returned with a glass dish containing the promised rich, rhubarb crumble, the juices were still bubbling at the bottom and Zoë felt her willpower dissipate almost immediately. She eventually opted for a small portion with a tiny amount of cream and savoured the sweet, viscid texture of the crumble which had cooled slightly under the splash of single cream.

A couple of hours later, they said their goodbyes in the late afternoon dim light with the distinct smell of burning wood hanging in the cool air. Gage breathed in a lungful and stretched extravagantly as he waited for Zoë to activate the unlocking of the doors.

'Thanks for lunch, Steph – spectacular as always. Feel like I'm set up for the week now.'

'Absolutely my pleasure, darling, oh hang on – I made you a crumble to take home with you – I'll just run and get it.' Turning quickly, Stephanie ran back to the house, her long Indian, cotton skirt swishing round her ankles as she moved, but just as she reached the door, Ed came out holding a foil-covered dish, which she hastily took from him.

'Better not leave this behind, it's too much temptation for one man – I'm beginning to develop a paunch!' He laughed and patted his stomach.

'You and me both, Dad!' Zoë called back.

'Bye my darlings, have a safe journey back – and Zoë, think about what I said, won't you?' For some reason the note of tenderness in her mother's voice made Zoë feel as she had when she was a child watching her mother leave through the school gate, as she waited in line for the school day to start. The combination of dread and longing which had often plagued her during her first days at primary school, came back to haunt her briefly.

Gage sifted through the tired collection of CDs that had been left in her glove compartment for the last few months, searching for music to suit his genial mood for the journey home. Pulling out of her parents' drive Zoë looked in her rear-view mirror and just glimpsed her mother going back inside the house. She felt a little sad that their relationship no longer held quite the same intimacy it had when they had worked together. Her mother's young out-look on life and her candid attitude meant that Zoë had always been able to speak freely to her as she was not easily shocked or affronted. With her asinine sense of humour and cordial personality, Zoë's friends would often confide in her also and although Zoë was proud of her, she was also secretly jealous of the attention her mother gave to others at times.

As they left the sanctum of the country lanes and joined the expanse of the dual carriageway, the thought struck her that maybe she had been too demanding of her mother. Being the only child she had taken for granted the fact that she didn't have to compete for attention from either of her parents. This thought made her a little uncomfortable, but since she didn't really have anything to measure it by, she could only hope that this was not the case.

Gage had already told her that when they were ready for a family, he would like at least two children, so perhaps she would find out then.

Chapter 3

The early morning mist had cleared quickly and although the breeze was still cool, the omnipotent rays of the sun warmed everything in their path. Zoë felt uncomfortably warm in her heavy coat and scarf. This morning she had picked up her coat still expecting the winter's chill to be present, but now walking from her car to the boutique she realised her mistake. Already she could feel the unpleasant sensation of her deodorant sticking in her underarm and attaching itself to the delicate blouse she wore. As impatience superseded her discomfort though, she refrained from stopping to rearrange her clothing – Zoë had begun recognising the character flaw that had first presented itself as a child, more and more these days. Her nan had used to mutter that Zoë was always *champing at the bit*, a phrase that she had not fully understood until she had asked her mother the meaning. She certainly understood it now.

Once inside the much cooler building, she dropped her folders on to the desk and removed her coat before hanging it on the hook beside the door. She noticed that the lining had begun to come away a little and the once rich, plum colour had faded considerably. She admitted to herself that it wouldn't see her through to the next winter which she regretted as it suited her perfectly.

Finding clothes to fit her well had been a life-long arduous task. Petite ranges carried limited styles and although useful for staple items, did not provide individual pieces that Zoë liked to wear. Gage found it amusing that she could buy shoes from the teen's section and teased her mercilessly when she did so.

A tapping on the front door alerted Zoë to the fact that Amber had arrived. She laughed as her friend put her face to the glass and with mock irritation mouthed for her to hurry up. Pulling open the heavy door, the equanimity she had been feeling alone in the boutique began to dissipate. Once the doors were flung open to the public, she would again be at their mercy and unless sales improved, the terrifying prospect of failure would resurface.

She watched as Amber crossed the floor with the poised manner that only the confident possessed. Her chestnut curls rippled as she moved and then as she tilted her head to search for something in her bag, fell across her cheek in loosely coiled segments. After greeting each other Amber began absentmindedly relaying the events of her weekend, 'I always do it. I go out with these expectations of what the night will be like, and then it turns out that the best part of my evening was getting ready! Honestly – if I'd have known the night was going to be that bad, I'd have stayed in my bedroom with my wine and music.'

'Surely it wasn't all bad – what about the band you mentioned?'

'Argh, they were all right, but they just played the usual covers and it just got boring in the end. I have to say that the drummer was very nice though – it's just a shame that his girlfriend thought so too.' Zoë folded her arms and slowly shook her head.

Having accompanied Amber on numerous occasions to bars and clubs, Zoë could envisage aspects of how the night would have unfolded. The men's flagrant stares as Amber slipped through the masses eager to reach the heat and oblivion of the dance floor. There, she would be in her absolute element, her long limbs moving in unity, graceful and fluid as she danced without inhibition. She herself loved dancing too, but always felt at a disadvantage due to her height – it seemed that more often than not her cheek was in the perfect position to be poked by a flailing elbow or hand. The feeling though was unparalleled, as one tune mixed into another, Zoë would feel euphoria take her over and in that moment nothing else would matter. A mix of complete exhilaration and abandonment and when she and Amber would catch each other's eye, if was if they were as one, fused beneath the flashes of white strobing light. The air that would carry the heaviness of innuendo and bravado was tolerable to begin with, but as the evening drew on somehow it turned into desperation and would leave Zoë feeling hollow and out of place. She couldn't comprehend how some people were determined to just have sex with anyone, and if by the end of the night they'd failed to *pull* someone they were actually attracted to, they'd settle for whoever was at hand. How many times had she heard the phrase 'complete moose' being thrown around, by men usually, to describe a person they'd had sex with? It turned her stomach to think that people had such little regard for others and could use them for their own sexual gratification.

Amber though, would be in total control and her cool and confident manner gave her supremacy under the luminous lights. When after one too many drunken advances, they made it out into the night air, Zoë would have an emptiness in her stomach and muffled sounds in her ears. Privately Zoë questioned how much longer this type of evening would hold its appeal for Amber.

'Come on, there must have been at least one moment that made it worth the effort? Did you meet anybody interesting?'

'Oh you know what it's like Zo – by the time we got to the club most men were too drunk to hold a conversation, the decent ones were in groups with their partners and the rest were just after a quick shag. I gave up looking for anyone serious in a club ages ago. It was more the atmosphere that was drab though, I couldn't even lose it on the dance floor. Perhaps I'm just past my prime and it will all be downhill from now on.'

'I doubt that very much. Why don't you have a party? You'd have all of the benefits and none of the negatives,' Zoë suggested.

'Yeah, maybe . . . with a barbecue too now that the weather is improving.' Zoë watched the suggestion ticking over in Amber's mind as she went through to the back to put her bag away.

Out of each corner of the boutique, music emerged from the carefully positioned speakers and Zoë began her daily routine check of her stock. It felt dark in comparison to the brightness outside, but she knew that by mid-morning the sun would be cast in their direction to bathe the shop floor. She loved to listen to the occasional sound of the old wood in the building softly creaking under the sun's attentive glare.

Zoë could see shoppers beginning to appear in the narrow street outside and prayed that some of them would make their way into her boutique. The intoxicating smell of ground coffee from the vegetarian café opposite wafted through the open door and she watched as an extraordinarily tall, dark-haired man emerged from within. He sat himself down at the metal table placed outside and awkwardly pulled his long legs in beneath him. A young waitress that Zoë saw frequently as she made her way to and from the boutique, stepped out carrying an espresso cup which she placed down in front of him. He said something to her that made her smile before she swiftly turned on her heel and returned back inside, her long thick plaited hair smacking her back as she did so. Zoë couldn't help laughing to herself at how tiny the cup seemed in his hand as he took a sip of his coffee. He was casually looking around as people bustled past and his gaze fell on the upper level of the boutique which he seemed to inspect until a woman with short, blonde hair appeared and stooped down to kiss him on the lips. He pulled himself up and they stood looking at each other for a few moments, smiling broadly as if they shared a secret, until the woman broke the gaze and gestured in the direction from which she had just come. Together they set off on the cobbled street. Zoë wondered what the day held for this striking couple – perhaps a little house-hunting or a trip to the theatre or cinema. Whatever it was, they hadn't looked time-restricted and Zoë felt slightly envious of them as she returned to her work.

'A fair few people about.' Amber stood in the window replacing a bag on the model with one that hadn't sold as well.

'Let's hope that some of them make their way here,' Zoë smiled back at her.

The type of customer that the boutique attracted was diverse in nature. Firstly there was the impulsive buyer who would be drawn in by a particular display in the window or perhaps seduced by the quaintness of the shop. They would be pleasantly surprised to find an article of clothing or possibly an entire outfit without premeditation and their thrill of the unanticipated purchase always gave Zoë a great sense of gratification.

Next, was the all-important regular that would pay a visit to the boutique as part of their weekly routine. A habitual character who would make a single purchase at each visit, however small, occasionally to be returned on the subsequent visit.

They enjoyed the recognition that they received from Zoë and her staff and would make repetitive small-talk which Zoë enthused but Amber politely tolerated. As well as being able to lift Zoë's sometime pensive mood, these customers were an excellent source of free advertising and had attracted others to the boutique by word-of-mouth.

A rare treat was the customer who had little time or enthusiasm to supplement their wardrobe. Shopping was seen as a necessary evil and an invasion of their precious time. Large intervals were left between sprees and known shops would be returned to each time to lessen the fuss of the deed. They were grateful to find well-constructed outfits on display to take some of the labour out of the task for them. Although Zoë did not want to be seen to be exploiting this type of customer's weakness, she knew that if she recommended certain accessories to complement the chosen articles, that they would rarely be rejected. As clothes were hastily pulled on and then handed back to Zoë still warm from the heat of their bodies, two piles of either rejected or accepted items would mount up on the desk top, giving Zoë a flush of colour as her exhilaration grew. They would be thrown down in obvious disregard for the task and in eagerness for it to be over. Zoë found so much pleasure in separating and precisely folding each piece, placing the chosen items into the brown, paper carrier bags. Even the buyer would seem to find this part of the process therapeutic as they watched Zoë smoothing and folding the garments. Some small-talk could be exchanged now as they relaxed in the knowledge that the process was coming to an end, but their card would be held in hand ready to complete the transaction and make their escape.

One Saturday afternoon, shortly after Zoë had taken ownership of the boutique, a cross-dresser had walked in and begun inspecting the clothing on the side wall. There were several customers in at the time, but Zoë immediately noticed a woman, who appeared to be in her early-fifties, throwing distasteful looks at him. Her obvious intolerance grated on Zoë and she felt suddenly protective of the man who was dressed in an ill-fitting skirt and blouse. On his feet he wore pointed flat shoes that elongated his already large feet. As she'd approached him he'd looked at her with a hint of uncertainty and when she'd enquired as to whether he'd needed any assistance, he'd simply replied that he was enjoying looking at all her beautiful clothes. He had spoken in a soft, hushed tone and Zoë had been touched by the integrity in his voice. When she had turned her attention back to the garments that she had been displaying on the front rail, she had felt a presence at her side. She'd looked up into the pinched expression of the woman who was blatantly disgruntled and listened as she'd spouted her protest at Zoë for allowing the man to remain in the shop. With a calmness that she hadn't felt she'd informed the woman that he was indeed welcome in her boutique and at this the woman had huffed and stormed out.

In the weeks that followed, Zoë had various trade shows and buying trips to attend. Having returned late one Friday afternoon, she walked into the boutique to find a queue of customers at the till and instantly, the fatigue she'd felt travelling back seemed to lift – all her efforts were beginning to pay off.

Takings began to improve and Gage noticed the difference at home. Instead of coming home to find Zoë in a preoccupied daze, he'd find her in the garden deadheading flowers or soaking in a deep bath as the scent of rosehip and jojoba trailed down to greet him. In the evenings she would sprawl herself across the sofa with her eyes lazily absorbing whatever was on the television screen. On one such evening, Gage lifted Zoë's legs and tucked himself beside her. He took her wrist in his hand and began to trace the tiny veins on her arm, enjoying the pliable softness of her. The nature programme on the screen was following the plights of the penguin.

'Have you given any more thought to us going away?'

'I have, it's just I don't think now is the best time. I want to ensure that the new supplier I've taken on was the right decision for the boutique, it's a big thing for me and I want to see how the stock is received before we go off anywhere.'

'I'm just afraid that there's never going to be a good time – can't you see that I just want you all to myself for a week or two?' Zoë felt a familiar warmth unfurl in her chest, she reached up to cup his cheeks feeling his stubble graze her fingers and pulled his mouth to hers. She kept her eyes open as she kissed him gently, watching his eyelids flicker and his frown slowly ease away.

'You do have me, Gage,' she whispered. He pushed himself up and began to kiss her with greater urgency – all thoughts of holidays temporarily abandoned as he pushed his hands under her top and ran his fingers across her skin. She marvelled at her response to his touch as she pulled up his t-shirt and felt the heat of his torso against her. Somewhere in the distance she heard a baby penguin squealing for its mother.

The stock from the new supplier was due and Zoë drove to work feeling excited at the prospect of merchandising and promoting the new collection. This was a new era for the boutique and she felt that she was finally making her own mark on the business. Being aimed at a younger market, Zoë planned that students, especially, would be targeted in her promotional campaign by offering them a ten per cent discount at the upcoming college fashion show. She had ordered a range of different styles in small quantities and hoped to appeal to the individuality of youth. The accessories she had chosen were like nothing that the boutique had held before – bright African inspired necklaces and bracelets and a variety of statement headbands made from brass that she had thought unusual. Zoë had been thrilled with the brass designs in particular, the delicate rings had really caught her eye and both she and Amber were going to wear them in the boutique to hopefully induce sales.

As she waited at the traffic lights, she glanced around at the array of people en route to wherever it was they had to be. A smartly dressed woman caught her attention – she was wearing a simple long-sleeved cream blouse beneath a black fitted dress that stopped just above the knee. In the crook of her arm she carried an expensive-looking caramel bag and was walking with purpose to her destination.

Earphones hung down from the ears of many – the now ubiquitous sight of coloured cords trailing across the bodies of those hooked into their own private soundtrack and avoiding eye-contact at all costs. Two women stepped out in front of her, one with afro hair and beautiful matt skin and the other with sleek blonde hair, but both sporting the signature black, heavily lined eyes. Zoë imagined them dressed in her new lines and felt a flutter of excitement in her chest.

The lights turned, but as Zoë was about to pull forward, a homeless man that she had seen on numerous occasions around the city, stepped out and ambled across the road. His thick, brown hair was so badly matted together that it hung in rope like sections and although his beard hid most of his features, his sharp, green eyes still shone out beneath his bushy eyebrows. He turned to look at no one in particular and laughed as the cheap bottle of cider that he held in his stained fingers, tilted and left a sticky trail behind him. Zoë watched him reach the curb safely before she continued on her journey.

Just before lunch, the delivery finally arrived and she and Amber made a start on unpacking the stock. Zoë had taken advantage of it being the Easter break and had Aidan, her Saturday assistant, in doing a few extra hours. He was doing a fashion degree at Norwich University and had proven to be a great asset to her, not only for his enthusiasm towards the boutique, but also for the humour he saw in most situations – he was fun to be around.

While they tore into the packaging and hung the items on a rail ready to be steamed, he looked after things downstairs.

'This is really nice stuff, Zo – I absolutely love this material,' Amber enthused as she hung a delicate, silky camisole top on to a hanger. Placed by Zoë's foot was a box of the brown luggage labels that were attached to each of the items in the shop. The design was simple – an empty black hanger with *Her Boutique* inscribed in silver pen across the centre. It was moments like these that reminded her of the thrill she had felt when she first took over the boutique, two years earlier.

As she sat carefully writing the prices on the labels in white chalk pen, contentment and a pleasant feeling of optimism washed over her.

'I knew you'd love it, Amber – I feel like it's Christmas morning!'

'It's going to look so good at the show on Wednesday night. Do you know how many models you'll have yet?'

'I spoke with the organiser, Lara, yesterday on the phone and she said that we'd have three models doing two runs each. She's given me their sizes so we just need to pick out the six killer outfits!' Amber had heard about the event being held at the local college through a friend and Zoë had readily agreed to take part. She was feeling a little anxious about it now though as she'd expected that the models would have come in to try the clothes on before the show, but that wasn't going to happen apparently.

'I just hope it will be all right – it seems a bit unorganised to me.'

'Stop worrying, Zo – it will be fine. Lara's done a few now and from what I hear they've been very successful, so let her worry about the details. I'm really looking forward to it – I never get to go to the London shows with you, so this is the next best thing.'

'Oh, don't make me feel guilty – you know I like you here to keep things running smoothly!'

'I'm only teasing, you know I like being boss for a few days,' she grinned.

Stephanie had originally employed Amber to work as a Saturday Assistant, she had been aged eighteen, two years younger than Zoë who, initially, had not known what to make of the confident, brazen and not to mention, very tall woman sharing the boutique with her. Luckily, Amber turned out to be much more than a work colleague though, and she and Zoë's friendship blossomed quickly. When Zoë became too intense, Amber managed to bring out a more insouciant side of her – laughter came easily to Amber and she didn't take life too seriously. Her loyalty to not only the boutique but also to Zoë made her invaluable.

'How are the plans for Saturday night going – do you need a hand with anything? Just don't ask me to bake though – you know that's not my strong point.' Zoë knew that Amber would have everything organised, but felt it only polite to ask.

'No, it's all sorted, thanks. Gage helping with the garden bits will be a huge help, but I was going to ask that, if it's not too busy I could leave half an hour early?'

'Not a problem – I'll ask Aidan to stay later, just in case.'

A scraping sound in the loft woke Zoë earlier than usual. She listened as the starlings whistled gaily to each other as they cavorted backwards and forwards in the eaves. She smiled to herself as she imagined them hopping about in little boots – it always astonished her how such small birds could make so much noise.

Drawing the curtains back, she took a moment to watch the clouds moving across the salmon sky. Although hidden she could see the sun's rays trying to permeate the obdurate shield where the cloud cover was thinnest. April was proving to be generous with its deliverance of sunshine this year.

Gage turned over in his sleep and tendrils of his brown, wavy hair fell onto his sleep-creased cheek. She waited for his breathing to fall back into a steady rhythm before quietly slipping from the room to have a shower. As the warm water drummed against her back, she lathered the sweet-smelling shower gel in her hands and traced the outline of her body. Her preoccupation with managing the boutique and her concerted effort to eliminate the junk food from her diet had resulted in the loss of pounds that had taunted her every time she'd struggled to button her clothes at the waist lately. She looked down at her nails and saw that they were torn and uneven and that the skin on her knuckles was desiccated and rough – winter and all the physical work in the boutique had definitely taken their toll. She would need to find time later before the party to tidy them up a bit. The thought that she could nip out at lunch time to visit a nail salon fleetingly crossed her mind, but she dismissed it immediately. She quickly dried herself feeling the cool breeze from the window brush against her skin and then slathered some moisturising cream on, paying particular attention to her hands.

'Morning my beauty!' Gage sauntered into the kitchen just as Zoë was collecting her things to leave. He wore only his hipster shorts and Zoë took a minute to take in his physique before he pulled her into a hug, his body warm and scented with sleep.

'You don't have to go out just yet, do you?' her voice was muffled by the closeness of Gage's chest, but she didn't want to let go of him until she had to.

'No, I've got the whole morning to myself. I'll drop by Amber's later to drop off the wood for the chimnea and set the lights up as promised, then meet you back here. I've booked the taxi for eight – is that OK with you?' Zoë sighed as she picked up her bag and started to make her way towards the door.

'Yeah, that's fine.'

'Why the sigh?'

'Oh it's nothing – I just wish I'd had a bit of time to at least get my nails done or something, I feel decidedly unglamorous right now.' Gage caught up with her and placed his palms up against the door, trapping her in between.

'Turn around,' he said sternly. Zoë did as she was asked and looked up at him with a small smile playing on her lips. He kissed the side of her face and then lightly bit at her ear. Despite herself, Zoë squealed and laughed. 'You can stop all that rubbish talk. I will see you here later looking gorgeous as you always do.' She knew from his mildly menacing tone that although he was playing, there was also a message to be heeded.

It turned out that the fashion show had indeed created good publicity for the boutique, during the day Zoë was excited to see groups of students huddled round the rails talking animatedly to one another. They took it in turns to try on the clothes they'd seen modelled at the show and their excited chatter charged the boutique with a new exhilarating energy.

Aidan was in discussion with a pretty red-haired girl about whether the short, khaki-coloured dress she was trying on would look better with military-style or Converse boots. Zoë smiled as she watched him giving his earnest opinion as the girl twisted one way and then the other, looking at her reflection and obviously enjoying the experience and attention that Aidan was giving her. He certainly had a gift when it came to selling. There was no pretence or falseness, he gave honest opinions and made the customer feel relaxed with his undeniable charm and humour. Laughing now at something the girl had said, his long, brown fringe fell across one side of his face and he flipped his head back to reveal his deep green eyes. No sign yet of the lines that would inevitably appear by their sides from his ever-present smile. They came to a mutual decision regarding the shoes and the girl went to the desk to pay.

'Next!' Aidan called out to the girls waiting in line, before turning to Zoë and giving her his biggest, goofy smile.

Before she knew it the afternoon had almost passed and as she was writing out new labels to attach to the waiting stock, she felt Aidan sidle up to her.

'Right boss, I'll be off then.'

'Oh hell, I meant to ask if you'd mind staying a bit later tonight, but with it being so busy it completely slipped my mind!' Zoë could tell from the apologetic look forming on Aidan's face that this was not going to happen.

'Argh, sorry Zoë, you know I would – but we're all heading off to that festival tonight and I'm being picked up in an hour, I'm already pushing it as it is.'

'Aah I forgot it was this weekend – look, don't worry about it, it's died off now anyway, I'll be fine.' She hugged him quickly and pushed him through to the back. 'Have a great time and whatever you do, don't forget your hand gel, those toilets are seriously revolting!'

Half an hour later, following a discussion about outfits and alcohol choices for the evening, Amber collected her things and made for the door. As she did so a man and woman entered the boutique carrying an array of designer bags. Amber stepped back and smiled to allow them through then signalled to Zoë to ensure that it was still all right for her to leave. Zoë nodded and waved her off, as long as she could cash up on time, she could leave everything else until Monday just this one time.

The woman smiled as Zoë greeted them and then flicked through the stock on the rail nearest the door. The man regarded the boutique with a kind of mild interest, looking round at the structure rather than the content. Zoë felt proud of its heritage and appreciated the fact that he seemed to notice the boutique's quaint qualities. His gaze suddenly fell on Zoë and so she smiled warmly. Without returning the gesture he approached his partner, who now had several items draped over her forearm. Zoë heard him speak in a deep, hushed tone and saw from his body language that he was not happy about something. Feeling a little uncomfortable, but also aware of the fact that it was getting late, Zoë made her way over to them.

'Would you like me to put those over on the desk for you while you carry on looking? I can see that you have your arms full.' The woman, who she could see now, was probably in her late forties, smiled appreciatively at her.

'Yes, that would be very helpful, thank you. I'm actually looking for an evening dress, nothing too dressy though – something that I could wear to dinner and a show.' Zoë nodded as the woman spoke, grateful that she was more amiable than the man who accompanied her. 'Sorry, I know it's a bit late, it's just we're going on holiday on Monday and I've been searching for most of the afternoon, without luck.'

'Well I certainly have some more individual pieces – let me show you what I have in the corner there.' Now seated on the edge of the display area she heard the man sigh, 'Amanda, remember the parking ticket.' Amanda's face fell and her pretty features were masked momentarily behind her obvious irritation.

'I just want to quickly try a couple of these on, I won't be long – and actually, if we hadn't spent as much time in the pub at lunch time, we wouldn't be having this problem.' She laughed lightly to disguise the heat in her comment, but it was ineffective as their animosity remained present in the air like the smell of wet dog.

Feeling uncomfortable at their open display, Zoë stepped away and moved over to the side wall to pull out the dresses she had in mind for her irritated customer. She wished that she could distance herself further from them but presently unable to escape the heavy atmosphere, she resolved to make the sale and get rid of them as quickly as possible. She held up two dresses to show Amanda who responded with a grateful look and moved over to her. Lifting one of the dresses, she collected the material up in her hand and then let the silky fabric fall across her fingers.

The man pointedly checked his watch and made an impatient huffing sound as he crossed one long leg over the other. As disconcerting as his behaviour was, Zoë could see that if it were not for his permanent scowl he could be quite attractive. As he sat hunched over with the look of disapproval planted to his face though, she couldn't help thinking that he looked like a stone gargoyle and may at any moment spout water from his mouth. He appeared to be the same age as his partner, although he had an unfortunate high-hairline that left a significant part of his forehead exposed, whilst the rest of his thick hair was cropped short. Dark, broad eyebrows framed his penetrating eyes that made Zoë want to look away whenever they were cast in her direction, which she now noticed was all too often.

He jumped up suddenly, 'I'll be in the car. Don't be long.' He turned abruptly but as he reached the door, stopped when he heard Amanda speak.

'Look – why don't I just meet you at Nina and Dan's? It will only take me about fifteen minutes to walk from here.'

'Fine,' he pulled the handle sharply.

'Wait – you can take the bags with you though,' she called out. He turned quickly and scooped up the bags that Amanda had left by the front rail.

Was this how they lived? Zoë wondered to herself as she placed the two dresses on the hook in the dressing room for Amanda to try. While she waited for her to re-merge, Zoë turned the door sign to 'closed' and dimmed the lights in the window. Thankfully, it wasn't long before she heard the sound of the curtain rings being drawn back against the metal bar. Amanda stepped out in the navy satin dress that she had selected for her and looked at her reflection in the full mirror. Despite her impatience to finish up for the night, she couldn't help feeling thrilled at the soft look of appreciation in the other woman's eyes – she had done that, she had made her feel good about herself when moments earlier she had looked to be feeling pretty rubbish.

'That's just perfect – it hangs beautifully on you,' she smiled encouragingly behind her. Amanda swept her dark, glossy hair up into a messy bun at the top of her head and peered at her reflection further before looking back at Zoë. In that moment she knew that the sale was certain.

'It *is* perfect – I'll take it. Could you just help me with the zip though? it's so delicate, I don't want to pull too hard. She turned her back to Zoë allowing her access to the fastening. As she pulled the zip down she exposed a small cluster of moles which together formed an almost diamond shape on her smooth, ivory skin.

'Actually – I've just spotted those white trousers.'

'The linen ones?'

'Yes, they'd be handy to take – could you grab me a pair in a size eight, please? I won't try them now as I'd better get going.'

After bidding her a lovely holiday, Zoë saw her out and locked the door. Thoughts of the evening ahead filled her mind as she completed the end of day duties. She was tempted to leave the sweeping and come in early on Monday, but then berated herself for her slackness – she knew she'd feel better having left everything completed. Moving quickly around the boutique she thought about the couple again. She pondered on what fulfilment they each got out of the relationship – Amanda seemed smart and confident, and although Zoë had initially found her to be a little guarded, she had displayed warmth and gratitude when Zoë had assisted her. She knew that she'd only seen a snapshot into their lives, but the man – Zoë couldn't quite put her finger on what triggered her sense of unease, but he was certainly dull and insolent – what did Amanda see in him? The way he had spoken to her and in public too, not caring about the kind of impression he gave to observers. Zoë had seen a ring on her wedding finger when she'd been trying on the dress, perhaps it was just a bad patch in their marriage which she had been witness to.

She swiped her judgemental thoughts aside and reasoned that she could have just caught them on a bad day as others could have done with her. Who knew what kind of opinions had been formed about her as she had gone about her day-to-day business? – the woman at the bank who took her deposits occasionally when she was short of time and eager to get back to the shop; the guy she gave her coffee order to as she mentally checked off her to-do list, they didn't know her and she didn't show any of herself to them, but it wouldn't stop the opinions forming anyway.

Manoeuvring the brush under the chair placed by the door, she felt it knock against something hard, so giving it a sharp push she saw a dark green bag slide out on the other side. Crouching down to take a closer look, she found that it contained a shoe box that had a neat, gold logo inscribed across the middle. It wasn't a name she recognised and looked quite expensive. Realising who it must belong to she took it through to the back room and placed it beside the fridge.

On re-entering the boutique, Zoë jumped at the sound of a loud knock on the glass of the door. Seeing Amanda's husband standing there she cursed under her breath as she'd already set the alarm and eager to get going now, resented giving up any more of her time to him. Punching in the code she signalled at him to wait a moment, to which he smiled apologetically in return. She pulled the door open slightly and poked her head round to face him. He was looking surprising embarrassed and sheepish about the situation and as he spoke ran his hand down the back of his head and neck.

'I think I may have left a bag here . . .'

'Yes, I just found it while I was cleaning up,' Zoë answered quickly, 'if you just wait a moment I'll grab it for you.'

She let go of the door and let it fall back against the latch as she jogged through to the back. Retrieving the bag from where she had positioned it minutes before, Zoë heard the sound of the latch catching in the front door and then the scraping of the heavy bolt.

Distracted and confused by what she'd just heard, she stopped and stayed deadly still. The threat slowly began to register in her mind as simultaneously her body responded to her fear. Every muscle stiffened and locked into place and a sudden whooshing invaded her ears momentarily muting the sounds around her.

Then his slow, measured footsteps echoed through to her consciousness. Still she couldn't move her body. Her legs were paying no heed to the adrenaline that raced through her veins urging her to react. She remained facing away from the door, bent over slightly from where she had lifted the bag from the floor. Thoughts of self-defence classes she'd had a school flashed through her mind, but were replaced by doubt. Surely he was just being presumptuous in locking the door? Perhaps he thought that he was being helpful and was going to collect his bag and go?

She could no longer hear his footsteps, but could sense his presence. The smell of him was seeping through to the small room. His strong, woody aftershave – one she felt she'd smelt a hundred times before, and the faint aroma of pub food.

A tight squeezing sensation began in her throat, as if incoming air was trying to push through at the same moment as exhalation. Even if her mind was unable to accept the situation – her body had begun to do so.

The back door was only a few steps away and having finally woken to the fact that she was in danger – she moved. Like a jammed spring having been released from its obstruction, she shot forward throwing the bag behind her as she went. But it was too late. A violent blow struck her between the shoulder blades, taking the air from her lungs and sending her lurching into the table in front of her. Her hip crashed into its sharp edge and she cried out in pain before she landed face-down across the top. The grains of the ancient oak wood blurred beneath her vision as her head bounced against the hard surface.

Struggling to breathe from the force of the blow and rising panic, she spun round to face her attacker. Supporting herself on the edge of the table she kicked out with everything she had, her static foot slipped slightly on the floor, but she caught him on the side of the hip with a satisfying blow. Her thin shoes did nothing to protect her toes from the impact and she felt the nail on her big toe split sending a sharp, stinging sensation across the sensitive pad. He swayed off balance slightly and Zoë propelled herself towards the back door.

'You little bitch!' he growled as he stretched out one hand and grabbed the material of her cardigan. She heard the seam tear as an explosion of pale yellow buttons scattered to the floor. With his free hand he grabbed her waist and thrust her back so she was leaning against the table, her fight only fuelling his rage further. She felt the wooden legs shift beneath her making a course scraping sound against the floor as if in resistance to the sudden imposition. Now that she was inches from his face she could see his open pores and the tiny red blood vessels in his manic eyes. His breathing was surprisingly controlled as Zoë found herself gasping for air and fresh liquor of some kind oozed from his warm breath.

With a swing that she did not foresee, he slapped her with such momentum that her neck snapped to the side and she fell back knocking a mug off in the process and scattering ceramic shards across the stone floor. Involuntary tears clouded her vision while all the time the words rang out in her head: *this can't be happening, this can't be happening…*

'Get the fuck away from me!' her voice sounded unfamiliar to her, horror and desperation changing her vocal tone into someone she did not recognise and despite her effort to challenge him, her fear remained evident to them both.

'I'm going to have to shut that dirty mouth of yours – we don't want anybody coming snooping do we?' he whispered in her ear. The menace was enhanced as he spoke through gritted teeth with the hardness of his cheek bone jutting into the side of her face.

Throwing her weight to one side Zoë tried to roll herself off of the table but was halted by her attacker's unrelenting determination to keep her down.

'No, no, no,' he spoke calmly now, as if to an upset child. Before she could react further he used his hand to cover her mouth. He studied her intensely; his face inches above her as he switched his eyes deliberately backwards and forwards from hers.

Watery blue eyes that she would never be able to forget. That would remain solidified in her memory, extinguishing some other precious moment from the library of her mind.

She began to take short breaths through her nose and felt her lungs struggle to inflate properly as she bore the weight of him upon her. Glinting dots descended down across her eyes and her head ached deeply from the effort of retaining her breath.

Terror – it had consumed her, this stranger was in command now.

Her skirt was pulled up to her waist in one swift action. She felt her thin tights being ripped at the thigh and his unfamiliar fingers touching her there as he tugged further at the ethereal nylon. Ladder-lines shot down her legs as a larger opening was forced exposing her thighs and underwear to him. Zoë made a deep frantic cry from her throat that scraped at the soft tissue there and choked her further. She tried to kick out, but the attempt was futile, even with one hand forced down on her mouth, the weight of his body and his immense strength kept Zoë pinned to the table. She was whimpering now and pleading with any greater-force witnessing, that the ordeal would end soon.

Hanging from the ceiling was a light that lit the small back room which could remain gloomy even on the brightest of days. It had a cream-coloured shade that was made of cotton and small glass beads that hung from the bottom that twinkled when they caught the glare of the bulb. Focussing there, Zoë could see the faint gossamer webs floating between the beads and dust patches that darkened parts of the transparent material.

A tearing pain between her legs forced her eyes shut and a long, low groan to escape her. She immediately felt the pressure being reinforced to her mouth – though she hadn't thought this possible and her skull ground further into the table top.

He consumed her now and there was nothing she could do about it – her lungs were full of him, his breath and stale perspiration.

'This is what you wanted, isn't it?' he hissed. She forced her eyes open again and stared back at him in an act of defiance at the words he had just spoken, and when she could bare it no longer, looked back towards the light. Its brightness burned through the thin fabric and she kept her eyes locked there until, when she closed her lids again, vivid, orange blotches had formed. They floated across the darkness like coloured wax from a lava lamp and now she took herself back to when she was younger, leaving the horror of what was happening behind.

She imagined herself in the sanctum of her childhood bedroom, surrounded by soft velvet toys, over-sized cushions and the warmth of her long-haired black cat as he slept curled up in her lap. She would watch the lamp fascinated by the graceful blobs that would form and separate like cells before her very eyes. Her father had once tried to explain the science, but she had not been interested, to her it was magic.

The sink tap to her left dripped a consistent rhythm, the drops splashing into an ever increasing pool into the empty bowl beneath. She counted each one as they fell.

Above her now, she felt his weight begin to lift from her. As he took his hand away, he dragged it across the side of her cheek with a look of disgust etched across his face. Free from the constraint, she turned her head and breathed as deeply as she could without making too much sound. She did not want to have to look at him, but could hear his own erratic breathing begin to calm as he fumbled with his clothing.

Every second held a taut tension – what was he going to do next? After a long moment of silence in which, despite her desperate efforts, she had not been able to control the tremors that had begun to wrack her body, she heard his steadfast steps moving away from her. The familiar sound of the bolt being drawn back finally reached her ears closely followed by the click of the door closing.

She waited a few more seconds until she dared to move and then gingerly sat up using her elbows to support herself. Ignoring the sharp pain than shot through her pelvis and up along her spine, she curled herself forward and edged off of the table. Her legs felt like dead weights but she knew she had to get to the door – that was her priority and nothing else mattered at that moment.

Shuffling through the boutique, she grabbed on to each rail as she passed to help her reach her destination. The people walking past outside were a blur as she finally managed to secure the door.

The violence of her trembling caused her teeth to crash together and made her movements awkward, but she somehow made her return to the back room.

She stared at the table, subconsciously noticing that the angle was wrong. The pieces of broken ceramic on the floor had dark patches of coffee splayed between them already drying on the stone tiles. Taking in each detail, she knew that she had to stay and absorb the pain, if she fled now as she wanted to do, she might not ever be able to return to her boutique again – she wouldn't have the strength to walk back into the terror that she was feeling now. It needed to be faced head on.

Her sobs came from deep within her; they forced their way up from her stomach in erratic convulsions that once again left her gasping for air. She folded, her legs giving way beneath her, and lay on the cool tiles allowing her body the freedom to do what it needed.

After a while the feeling of numbness filtered through her as if she had suddenly been attached to an IV drip with anaesthetic being pushed through her veins. In the small bathroom she examined her face. An abrasion marked the thin skin to the left of her forehead and there was swelling beside her right eye where she had taken the force of the slap. Mascara was smudged beneath her puffy eyes and had left a dry residue that she gently dabbed with a make-up wipe to remove what she could, before splashing her face with cold water. Without warning the contents of her stomach rose up and splattered across the porcelain basin before her. She remained leant over until certain that there was nothing left to come up.

The sound of her mobile vibrating against the kitchen worktop made her jump and as she grabbed a handful of toilet tissue, the roll fell from its holder and trailed across the floor in front of her. She stepped over it and hurried to reach her phone that continued to intercept the silence. As she suspected she saw Gage's face fill the screen and took a steadying breath before she answered, 'Hi . . .'

'Hey, are you all right? – I thought you were going to try and leave off a bit earlier.' Hearing his voice, Zoë felt a lump rise in her throat.

'Yes I was, but I've had a stupid accident and had to come back and tidy myself up a bit.' She heard him tut and let out a quick breath.

'What happened, Zo?'

'I tripped on the cobbles – wasn't paying attention,' she laughed lightly to try and appease his concern, 'took a bit of a knock to my head and cheek, but I'm OK, really.'

'I'll come and get you – you might have concussion or something!'

'No, no, you don't need to do that, I'm fine, it's just a cut – I'm leaving now.'

'Well, please be careful, Zo – see you in a while.' She hung up quickly and got on with cleaning up the remnants of her ordeal.

Before leaving, she tore off the lacerated remains of her tights and screwed them up into a tight ball. As she stepped out into the watery sunshine, she threw them into the bin but catching her nail on a strand of the nylon the bundle began to unravel and hung from her fingers suspended above the bin. Irritated, she ripped them away and inspected her hands that were now in a worse state than they had been this morning. On her ring finger, dry blood stained the curve of her nail.

A girl from the Indian takeaway was leaning against the side door of the premises, smoking. As Zoë passed her, she looked up from her phone and smiled briefly, but Zoë could not bring herself to return the gesture and with her head bent down, walked quickly to her car.

Chapter 4

Parked outside their house, Zoë remained seated in the car listening to the ticking of the engine as it began to wind down from its journey. A cat was rolling in the road before her, enjoying the last of the sun before it disappeared behind the row of houses. It stretched out its white paws exposing its soft, downy tummy before rubbing its back against the heat of the asphalt beneath it.

She knew straight away that she would not tell him. That she could not tell anyone. Gage knowing would only cause more problems and complications – and she wanted to just forget. If she could push it back to the furthest corner of her mind by concentrating on her work and family, in time the memory would fade. She wasn't stupid and knew that it would take time, but she was strong of mind and self-disciplined and these virtues would save her any further anguish of divulging the sickening details to anyone else.

An unpleasant mix of lower stomach pain and a stinging sensation in her bladder made her want to pee urgently and she knew that she could no longer put off going inside. The cat suddenly startled by the shouts of children running down the street, jerked up abruptly and with ears pinned back and its body slunk low to the ground, padded towards a garden wall and disappeared to safety.

To her relief, Gage was on his phone when she got in. She pulled herself up the stairs, feeling a stab of pain in her hip with each lift of her leg, but aware that she needed to get to the bathroom before Gage saw her, she quickened her pace.

Within moments she was standing beneath a warm jet of water. Her insides were swollen and the shower gel stung when she covered herself in its sweet lather, but she continued to foam the silky gel between her palms until every part of her was coated. Everything ached and as she ran her hands across her body she felt new bruises forming on her soft, pale skin. She would have to wear a long sleeved top under her dress now to hide the blemishes. Momentarily she thought about phoning Amber and saying that she was unwell, but quickly dismissed this idea realising that it would probably require more energy than actually going. Amber would only be disappointed and try to persuade her to change her mind by using all kinds of emotional coaxing. Gage would insist on staying home with her and then it would just be the two of them and she wasn't ready for that intimacy yet, she needed noise and a throng of people to smother the panic that intermittently threatened her. Each time it occurred, she felt a tightening in her jugular and a pounding in her ears and suddenly the act of breathing, this previously natural bodily function became a panicked, arduous task.

Downstairs, Gage was finishing the call that had been from his sister, Meg. She was the same age as Zoë and had a ten month old boy with her partner, Dale. They had not seen much of each other lately, both being weighed down with different kinds of responsibility. Gage felt a pang of guilt at the realisation that Jack would be walking soon – the months had passed quickly since he and Zoë had visited only hours after he had been born.

Climbing the stairs he called out: 'That was Meg – she wants to sort out a get together for Mum's birthday.'

Twisting the bedroom door knob, he felt the resistance of the lock. They never locked the doors, only when they had company.

'Zoë?'

The floor boards made their familiar creaking sound from the other side and then Gage heard Zoë pulling the lock back before she appeared in the doorway wearing her dressing gown. Her face was bare of make-up making the red abrasion on her head and the swelling under her eye more obvious. But it was the look in her eyes that startled Gage. She looked slightly stunned, like a cornered injured bird being eyed by a skulking cat.

'Bloody hell, Zoë, why didn't you tell me it was that bad? You made it sound like a slight trip!'

She turned away from him and he followed her into the room.

'It's really not that bad, Gage, please don't make a fuss. It will look better when I have my make-up on.'

'Here, let me look.'

Gently angling her face to the light he inspected the marks, tutting as he did so. A hollow feeling settled in his stomach, as if he had taken a blow himself. It was a stark reminder of how much he loved her and hated the thought of her being hurt.

'Do you feel alright? Maybe you should be checked over for signs of concussion?'

Irritation bit at her, she couldn't help it. Of course he'd be worried, it was only natural, but she felt too tired to deal with all of this now.

'No, it's OK, really. I'm fine. I need to get ready though, if you want to do something for me, you could make me a cup of tea.' She managed to smile up at his concerned face and felt a wave of remorse at her irrational anger towards him. She must keep calm and show him that everything was normal; a silly fall was all it was. Luckily the initial shock of seeing her seemed to wane and he left her to get ready as he went down to the kitchen to make her a drink.

A little while later, Zoë was sitting looking at her reflection in the mirror. She was pleased with the results, the concealer and foundation hid the redness and her eyes no longer looked as bloodshot. Taking a few calming breaths she went down to join Gage.

'You look absolutely gorgeous.' He kissed her on the head before gently running his thumb across her cheek bone. 'Come on then let's get going, all the hot-dogs will be gone if we're not careful and you know how I love a hot-dog.' He smiled mischievously at her and she knew she had a part to play now, to hold up a shield between herself and those around her.

Through the window behind him she could see the voluptuous white clouds standing motionless in the watery aero blue sky; they looked like mountains. As a child she would stare at them from her bedroom window listening to the music that floated up from the lounge where her parents were relaxing, and imagine that she lived somewhere hilly. Somewhere so unlike the flat lands of Norfolk.

Taking his hand in hers, she returned his smile, hiding the stab of pain the action induced.

'Let's go.'

They did not have to travel far and moments later their taxi pulled up outside the terraced house that Amber shared with two others. Both junior doctors were working the night shift, so Amber had the place to herself and had spent the last couple of hours arranging tea lights and moving furniture to accommodate her guests.

Zoë and Gage walked down the dark uneven passageway that ran alongside the house. The noise of Zoë's heels hitting the ground was accentuated by the enclosed arch around them and reminded her of metal being struck by a hammer. With each step she took it seemed to get louder and the reverberations punctured her ear-drums setting her nerves on edge. She gripped the neck of the wine bottle she held even tighter, the delicate tissue it was wrapped in felt crumpled and rough in her closed fist. She focused her attention on Gage and noticed that he had put some product on his hair which made his waves appear darker and stiffer.

A waft of cool wind picked up her hair from behind and blew some strands into her face. She froze. The now familiar scent of him caught in her throat. How was it possible that she could she still smell him? She had washed every part of herself exhaustively and had generously sprayed herself with her favourite perfume. Having reached the bottom, Gage had turned to see Zoë halted a few steps back from him.

'Zoë, what's up – have you forgotten something?'

As quickly as the scent had appeared it left again and was replaced with the smell of barbecuing meat.

'No, it's OK, I thought I'd left the door unlocked, but you did it didn't you?'

'I did. Now come on, I'm gasping for a drink.' He reached out and gently pulled at her hand until she was alongside him. Still feeling unsure about the possible side-effects of the bump to her head, he was going to suggest that neither of them drank too much tonight.

The long, thin back garden had a trail of lights enclosing its perimeter creating a feeling of occasion. Clusters of people were grouped in circles drinking and enjoying the freedom that the weekend brought – being able to give themselves over to hedonistic pleasure for as long as the evening stretched out.

Zoë spotted Amber at the bottom of the garden. Her long legs were wrapped in denim and further accentuated by the height of her heels. A cropped orange top showed off her toned stomach and enhanced the streaks of red in her hair, finishing her effortlessly polished look off perfectly. She glanced over towards the two of them and beamed a welcome at them, raising her glass as she did so. Gage strode over towards the barbecue as Amber disengaged herself from the group she had been amongst and headed to meet him.

'Jake got it going, but I'll leave you in charge, just save some food for the rest of us, Gage.' Amber playfully patted his stomach and turned to Zoë.

'Hey you!' she hugged her tightly. Zoë felt herself flinch and Amber pulled back slightly but still held her in an embrace. The smile slipped from her face as she noticed the swelling near Zoë's eye.

'What on earth have you done, Zo?'

'I tripped outside the boutique – you know how clumsy I can be. But it's fine, honestly. Don't start him off again.' She inclined her head towards Gage.

'You poor thing. Come and get a drink and grab a seat by the chimnea.'

The lie, although hadn't come naturally, was beginning to become easier. In her mind's eye she could see herself leaving the boutique with her folder and jacket supported in one arm, while the other hand searched for her phone that had slipped to the bottom of her bag. Distracted, she mistimed the step of the curb and fell forwards, her head hitting the rough brick of the Indian take away and then rebounding to knock the other side of her head. Yes, this all fitted with her injuries and would explain the bruises on her body too.

Turning the chargrilled sausages over to cook on the other side, Gage felt his stomach rumble. The bottle of beer he was drinking sat heavily in his stomach and was making him belch more than usual. He looked for Zoë and located her sitting further down the garden with a glass of wine in her hand facing a man he didn't recognise. He seemed to be quite animated as he spoke and kept sporadically pushing his black framed glasses back against his face. The sun had long left the sky now and Zoë had her arms folded across her body and was leaning towards the warmth of the chimnea as she listened to him. Her face was illuminated by the glint of the miniature lanterns strung around the garden.

He loved that face. The way her oval blue eyes watched him when he spoke –gently mocking him when he said something she felt was ridiculous, searching his when she needed reassurance and guarded when she tried to conceal how she was feeling. Their slow deliberate movements were mesmerising and when coupled with her seductive smile he was absolutely rapt. No one had ever come close to making him feel the way she did.

Sometimes it frightened him.

Everyone that loved somebody else was just as vulnerable, of course. Those that bore themselves wide open to hurt, disappointment and rejection knew the risk they took. But, ultimately none of this measured against the intoxicating pull of infatuation.

A song that had been popular the previous summer was playing and the volume was suddenly increased as people danced along. Bodies moving liquidly, with ease as the effects of alcohol loosened their inhibitions as was hoped. Zoë suddenly realised that the friend of Aidan's who was sat beside her was laughing at something he had just said to her. She smiled back at him as genuinely as she could. He was oblivious to her vague response and seemed happy to talk at her, rather than elicit a response from her. She was actually grateful to him though. To onlookers it seemed that she was engrossed in conversation when actually she was waiting for the wine to take her to a state of oblivion. To obliterate the images that kept nudging their way into her thoughts.

Over by the barbecue, Zoë could see that Amber was now by Gage's side plating up the food he had cooked. She was laughing at something he had said and had placed the palm of her hand on his shoulder. They looked good together; Amber almost matching Gage's height, both having the easy-going demeanour and self-possession that was deemed attractive. She wondered fleetingly whether they were attracted to each other, although she had only ever seen banter-style flirtation, she knew that it was human nature to find others appealing even when in the most secure of relationships. It seemed that it was totally acceptable to adore actors, musicians and television stars that were completely out of reach and therefore a harmless fantasy. But what happened if it was someone you saw regularly? There wasn't a switch that you could flick that turned off these emotions. She only knew that even if she did take a second look at a stranger on the street, perhaps with an alluring smile, intriguing eyes or a sexy stride, that there was a contentment within her since she had been with Gage – that he had smothered any possible desire for others.

She needed to get some water as the scorching in her bladder seemed to have been intensified by the acidity of the wine. Excusing herself she made her way to the house.

Someone had turned on the light in the kitchen and an orange glow spread out into the yard exposing a crate spilling over with empty beer and wine bottles. Zoë side-stepped this and hovered by the kitchen door which was blocked by a group of oblivious students deep in conversation. They were completely unconcerned by others around them and continued with their drawn-out monologues as she waited for a gap to intercept. Finally she edged her way round them, too impatient to stall any longer.

Many of the candles that had been placed on the kitchen sides had burnt themselves out and there was a trail of cooled wax which lay solidified across the worktop where a tea light had been knocked over. Zoë tried to lift it with her thumbnail before realising that the ripped edges that remained there would have no effect on the stubborn substance. She searched for something more effective in the drawer but could only see large bread and carving knives. Wiping off the remnants of butter from a knife in the sink, she started to push at the edge of the wax. A large piece flipped up leaving no trace underneath, but a small part required some scraping and Zoë persisted until just the displaced flakes sat in a pile. She swept the dry pieces into her palm and dropped them into an empty crisp packet that had been left lying on the worktop.

Finding only an empty bottle of still water in the fridge, Zoë helped herself to a glass from the cupboard and filled it with water from the tap. She watched as bubbles formed across the slightly cloudy surface, before gently bursting again.

'Excuse me – can I just get to the tap?'

Zoë turned, startled from her reverie and looked up into the face of a large framed girl with expertly winged eyeliner. She had round, cartoonish blue eyes and when she smiled at Zoë her thin, red painted mouth revealed neat, white teeth.

'Sorry.'

'You were in a little place of your own there – literally miles away!' she threw her arm up over her head to illustrate the matter. Zoë felt herself shrink in the face of this exuberant character and moved away quickly to avoid further interaction.

Tightly gripping her tepid glass of water, she waited outside the bathroom, wincing at the sharpness of the pain stabbing in her pubic area. She tried counting the abstract diamonds in a picture hung on the wall to try and take her mind off of her discomfort.

'Zoë, are you alright?' Amber placed her manicured hand on Zoë's shoulder and tilted her head round to look into her face.

'Argh, I seem to have a touch of bloody cystitis. I don't suppose you have any of those dissolvable sachets, do you?'

'Oh that's the worst – I'll have a look in the kitchen cupboard for you, but I don't remember seeing any recently. There is definitely some ibuprofen though and I always find that they help a bit. You're really not having a good day, are you, Zo?'

The bathroom door was abruptly pulled open and a thin woman with short, straight, straw-coloured hair emerged. She was wearing a checked, red shirt and tight black jeans tucked into flat boots. As she passed Amber and Zoë she gave a slight nod and tucked her hands into her pockets as she loped down the stairs.

'A friend of Aidan's – did you see how perfect her skin was? Like pure porcelain,' Amber said. 'Anyway, let's get you sorted out – you go in before anyone else sneaks in.'

Zoë sat on Amber's bed waiting for her to return. A sickening empty feeling washed over her. She felt as if she was disconnected from reality and that even though she was aware of those around her, she was unable to act as she normally would. Her head felt hollow and light, yet her body was heavy, with every movement hampered by some unseen tether.

'Look what I found!' Amber came sweeping into the room holding a tall glass with a deep pink liquid in it. 'No sachets, I'm afraid, but some angel's brought cranberry juice as a mixer. Now, get it down you and these too.' She held out her palm to proffer the two perfectly round tablets that were lying there.

'Thanks.' Zoë lips curved upwards but the smile didn't make it to her eyes. 'This will teach me for holding myself all day – must make time to pee in future.'

'Is everything OK, Zoë, obviously, apart from the cystitis? You don't seem yourself. I thought you'd still be on a high from all those customers today.'

The beseeching way that her friend was looking at her bore into her resilience and for a moment she considered unburdening herself. But staring back at Amber with tear welled eyes she found that the right words would not come.

'I'm just being stupid. It's probably part relief and part exhaustion getting to me. Go back down and enjoy yourself – I'll drink this and see you outside when I've finished.'

Having convinced Amber, she was left alone again. She berated herself for her moment of weakness. She just had to hold on as time would make everything so much easier and she knew it would be for the best in the long run.

Laughter and raucous shouts outside reached her through the open window. She stood up and made her way to the purple-veiled pane. Gage was now sitting further down the garden chatting to a man and woman Zoë didn't recognise. He was gesticulating enthusiastically, the way he did when he was explaining matters to do with work. Probably touting for business she mused with a pang of pride. Thudding footsteps coming up the stairs interrupted her thoughts.

'I leave you alone for five minutes and you're all over him! If that's what you want just say, I've told you before, I don't need this shit!'

'It's not what I want, I want you, Lisa. Please calm down – I was only talking to him and as far as I know that's not a crime!' The girl's voice rose steadily as she tried to accentuate her point.

'Why him though? You know he likes you and he sees it as a personal challenge to take you away from me, the dick!'

'We are going to fall at the first hurdle if you carry on this way. I hate all this possessive crap. You have to trust me.'

It went quiet so Zoë took her chance to leave the bedroom. The girl from earlier looked up at her as Zoë slipped into the bathroom again. Thankfully she didn't seem too bothered about her hearing their conversation or perhaps she'd assumed the music was too loud for their words to be heard.

This time when she emptied her bladder she found it to be less uncomfortable and almost cried with relief at this small reprieve. Before making her way back downstairs she tucked the cranberry juice carton into her bag.

As she went down the first few steps she saw that the couple were still sat on the landing, now with their foreheads touching and hands pressed together in their laps. Squeezing past, Zoë noticed a flush on the cheek of the otherwise flawless skin of the girl in the checked shirt. So many problems and complications relationships caused, she thought fleetingly as she made her return to the garden. She was met by Gage at the back door and as she got closer she saw that he held an empty beer bottle in one hand and a cigarette in the other. A streak of annoyance skimmed across her – he knew how much she hated him smoking.

'Hey you – I thought you'd done a runner.' She could tell from his stance that he had consumed quite a few more drinks than she had. 'How're you doing, you feeling alright?'

'Yeah, I'm fine.' She dismissed his concern as gently as she could.

'Let's go and sit down for a bit.' He steered her towards the now vacant chairs close to the glow of the chimnea. Having stacked on more of the chopped wood he'd brought over earlier, Gage stepped back and enjoyed the heat of the blaze. The conversation that he'd had with Amber's neighbours a little earlier had left him feeling slightly uneasy. They had got talking and when Gage had told them what he did for a living, they had said that they were looking for someone to renovate their spare room. They had liked the idea of bespoke reclaimed wood flooring and shelving that Gage had suggested and as they had spoken further, the woman had gone on to divulge the more personal details of their lives. She explained that they had hoped for a baby, but after several years of trying and two failed IVF attempts they had decided that they couldn't go through it again. For a long while she had blamed herself thinking that if she hadn't been so absorbed in her career they would have had more time on their side. Now though, they had vowed to put their disappointment to one side and move on with their lives. Therefore, the room that they'd always hoped would be full of soft toys and nappies needed a new identity. Her love of reading had inspired her to start writing herself and although nothing could take away the feeling of having lost something she'd never had, her life now once again had a purpose. The husband had watched his wife as she had shared this sensitive information and Gage noticed the look of mournful resignation that sat almost comfortably upon his face – he really had given up hope.

'It's the age old story; you think you have all the time in the world and that these things won't happen to you. But of course they can, and do,' he said. Gage suspected that this was still a relatively new decision for the pair and that the amber coloured drink that he was holding in his hand had made this disclosure easier. The woman shook her dark, wavy hair and smiled brightly. The fine creases beside her eyes were accentuated by the action but only made her look even more attractive.

'Are you here with anyone?' she had enquired

Gage had told them about Zoë, pride and warmth flooding through him as he explained what she did and how they had met.

Watching Zoë now, he realised that he had fallen into the trap of assuming that time and good fortune were theirs for the keeping too. He nudged her foot with his to get her to look at him. She appeared not to notice and continued to stare into the flames that occasionally tongued their way through the gridded metal window. His second attempt though brought her attention back to him.

'What are you thinking about?'

'Nothing really – I'm just relaxing.' She answered quietly.

An idea popped into his head. Beer and the intimate details that had been disclosed to him earlier making him eager to share this thought with Zoë. Ignoring the niggle that lamely attempted to push through the alcohol induced mist, he leant forward and took Zoë's hands in his.

'Zoë, you know how we've talked about marriage and starting a family? Well, what do you think, should we start thinking about having a baby?'

Looking at him with a bemused expression, Zoë slowly took her hands away from his. In that moment, a medley of rejection, disappointment and anger fisted their way through the joy he had fleetingly felt. He suddenly understood that having a child was what he wanted most in the world. Her reticence began to irritate him. She hadn't said a word and just sat staring down at her lap.

'Please say something, Zoë. I know I've had a drink and could have put it more eloquently, but I thought you'd at least want to talk about it. Maybe feel a bit excited by the idea.'

She couldn't meet his eye. She'd seen the look of enthusiasm slide from his face as his words hung in the smoky air between them. How could she respond to this when she felt nothing but fear and emptiness? There were so many words spinning around in her head desperate to leave her mouth, but instead she swallowed them down along with the bile that stung at the back of her throat.

'Gage, I just can't talk about this right now.' She paused for a moment, the agitation evident on her face. 'In fact I think we should go home.'

He shook his head fractionally. Jaw set rigid and avoiding all eye contact with her, he went to retrieve his jacket that had been so casually flung on the back of a chair only hours earlier.

They stood awkwardly beside each other as they waited to say goodbye to Amber who was enveloped in a large group. They were all smiling and laughing as they listened to a short, stylishly dressed man relaying an obviously funny event. Gage felt envious of his carefree demeanour, something he himself had felt earlier in the evening. Their own stiff body language was in stark contrast to the group enraptured before them and as if they were emanating a negative energy, the man stopped speaking and looked in their direction. Amber followed his gaze as did the others with smiles still planted on their faces. Gage stepped forward to hug Amber.

'Argh, you're not going are you? It's not that late.' Her voice sounded a pitch higher than usual and she swayed slightly as Gage released her.

'It's my fault, blame me, Amber,' Zoë said.

Amber took Zoë's face in hers and kissed her on the lips making an exaggerated mwoah sound as she did so.

'Hope you feel better, Sweetie,' she whispered in Zoë's ear.

They walked away from the party, both feeling deflated and

confused.

Back to back, but not touching, Gage and Zoë waited for sleep to release them from the uncomfortable silence that had settled between them. It was not long before Zoë heard the rhythmic heavy breaths from Gage's side of the bed. Drink always made him a noisy sleeper and sometimes she would go to the spare bed to ensure a good night's rest. She didn't want to leave him tonight though, even asleep his presence was reassuring and she needed that right now. After a while she couldn't ignore the fullness in her bladder and although the stinging had eased, she dare not risk aggravating it again, so she edged herself out of bed and after relieving herself, made her way down to the kitchen. She had never been afraid of the dark and the glow from the slatted blinds allowed enough light for her to reach the kitchen before finding the dimmer switch there. After drinking a large glass of water she returned to bed and closed her aching eyes.

Woken suddenly, she felt confused and uncertain of what had disturbed her. Gage was still by her side where his breathing had reached crescendo point. She turned over and tried to settle again but when she closed her eyes she saw him. His face above her, the dark arches of his brow drawn together as if in concentration. The drumming of the leaking tap echoing in her ears once again. The smell of him was all around her – filling her nostrils and causing a swirling in her stomach. It was as if the scent had been stored in her thalamus ready to evoke terror whenever it pleased.

'This is what you wanted…'

A bead of sweat trailed from her throat and ran along the side of her breast as her heart fought with the sound of the dripping tap for supremacy in her ears. She opened her eyes and fixed them on the luminescent figures of the clock radio beside her;

tracing the numbers over and over again until the rhythm of her heart returned to normal and her muscles began to unclench. This is the hard part, she told herself; it had to get easier, people got over traumas all the time and she would too.

The clock, now dulled by the brightness of the room, declared that it was just after ten a.m. She could already sense that Gage was no longer in the bed even before she turned her head. There was a gap in the curtains where he had probably looked out to see what kind of day it was and the strip of sunlight that was now evident gave Zoë a sense of hope of what the day might hold.

She found him in their small back garden sipping black coffee. His wavy hair was flattened down on one side of his head and his face still looked swollen with sleep.

'I'm so sorry, Gage. I love you so much and do want a child with you. Please forgive my reaction last night – all I can say is that it was a strange night for me.' She watched him as she waited for his response. He lifted his eyes from the patch of ground he had been staring at.

'Forgive your lack of reaction, you mean,' His eyes teased hers. She loved that about him – how he never held a grudge with her.

'Perhaps I overreacted. I just felt so happy and wanted to share it with you. We obviously weren't in the same place. You'd had a busy day and I should have realised that – let's go out for lunch and make up for it.'

Her heart flooded with love for him and his eagerness to put things right again. She must not mess today up, she thought to herself.

Scraping the metal chair back on the uneven paving beneath, Gage settled himself down in the pub garden. He felt the warmth of the sun on his back and although he had a slight thudding in his head, he was feeling pleasantly content. He looked across at Zoë who was still inspecting the slightly dog-eared menu in her hand, even though they had already ordered at the bar. The glare of the sun exposed the dark green hue that had formed below the marginally raised bump on her head and the red welt beneath her eye. She looked as though she'd been slapped, he thought fleetingly. He was worried about her. In recent weeks, although busy at work, she had seemed less anxious at home. Now he feared though, that she was slipping back. Today might be a good opportunity to talk things through with her, before any worries had a chance to escalate, he thought.

Through a speaker risen up on a tripod next to them, sudden distorted sounds blasted through making Zoë actively jump. After a moment a woman's lilting voice broke out announcing her first song choice. Gage looked around to locate where the voice was coming from, but couldn't see anyone outside. He made a mental image of what she could look like; blonde, short bobbed hair, nose ring and heavy eye make-up, he guessed.

A lad in his late teens appeared beside them and placed their food in front of them. The logo of the pub was printed on the left pocket of his creased t-shirt. He almost flung their cutlery down in his haste to get back to the kitchen.

'Thank you, very much.' Gage said sardonically to the already out of earshot waiter as he raised his eyebrows at Zoë. She appeared not to have noticed though and was picking the mushrooms out of her risotto and arranging them in a neat pile on the side of her plate.

'I'll have those.' He removed the offending slippery fungus from her dish and she smiled at him.

Another song began after a short burst of applause that Gage completely mistimed, almost dropping his fork as he joined in just as everyone else had stopped. Zoë would normally find this kind of goofy behaviour hilarious and mock him mercilessly for it. But she hadn't even looked up from her plate of barely touched food, Gage noticed.

'Is that good?' He shouted above the singer's Irish-tinged voice.

'Yeah, I'm just not that hungry really, I sneaked a bag of crisps while you were in the shower,' she lied.

Today should have been really lovely, she mused. It was rare that she didn't feel some kind of pressure attributing to the boutique, but last week, sales had been amazing and she should have been able to bask in that success. But instead, she couldn't wait for it to be over; was literally counting off each minute until she could phone the STI clinic tomorrow morning. The thought had struck her when she had been in the shower this morning – what if he'd given her something? Who knew what kind of things he got up to? She'd had another panicky episode in the bathroom when the thought had dawned on her. He could visit prostitutes for all she knew or even worse practise casual sex. She presumed that prostitutes used protection, but there was no accounting for these faceless individuals that she had conjured in her mind. It was as if just when she was feeling that she was in control of her life, the universe had conspired to bring it all crashing down around her ears again.

Gage had decided not to drink after over-indulging the night before, but after having eaten his lunch he was feeling more like himself again and so went to the bar to buy a bottle of beer. There, he saw the same lad who had brought their food over to them earlier. He was moving with agility and speed from one area of the bar to another, serving impatient customers who were waiting with their notes raised in their hands watching his every move. He felt a jolt of guilt at his earlier annoyance at the worker who was obviously being exploited by his employer.

When it came to Gage's turn to be served, the lad held up his hand.

'Sorry sir, just bear with me a moment, I'll be back in a second.'

Gage nodded his head and watched as he went through a door behind him and reappeared with two plates of food. He wove his way through the mass of drinkers and disappeared out to the beer garden. The door at the back opened again and an older woman emerged. She couldn't have been more contrasted to the previous worker – her movements were slow and slothful and her full figure impeded her ability to bend and reach the low refrigerator holding the bottles. She had an air of superiority about her though and Gage suspected that she was 'the some-one' who was implementing the exploitation.

'Who's next?' She enquired, sweeping her hooded eyes across the line of people standing at the bar. Before he could respond, the lad was back with his eyes cast in Gage's direction.

'What can I get you?'

Gage carried his bottle of cold beer and Zoë's orange juice back to their table. The singer was taking a break and standing by the door furthest away from where they were seated. Gage was happy to see that he had at least got some of her appearance correct: heavy eye make-up, blonde hair, but shaved on one side and a septum piercing instead of a nose stud. He smiled to himself and then noticed that Zoë was looking up at him.

'Like the look of something?' she asked with a half-smile.

It was one of their jokes – if either of them was caught looking at another person they would use this phrase as confirmation that they had been seen.

'Ha ha, Zoë. I'm glad that I've got your attention now though. You've been miles away.'

'Not miles, just a few yards maybe.'

Realising that she was running out of excuses for her apathetic behaviour, she thought that she had better make an effort to at least appear normal.

'I'm looking forward to the fashion show in London on Tuesday. Hopefully I will be able to pick up some new contacts for the boutique – you haven't forgotten that I'm staying the night there, have you?'

'No, it's in my diary. It's going to be a busy week for me too. The site manager is pushing for completion even though we weren't initially able to start the project on time. I might have to do a few late nights.' Gage stated this as a matter of fact with no hint of resentment or annoyance, even though it probably meant that others had not been pulling their weight in getting work completed on time. She loved this quality about him, the way he just got things done and avoided pettiness and finger point-ing at all costs.

'Zo, what I said last night…I think we should at least discuss it. I know that I just sprung it on you out of the blue, but I thought that it was something that we both wanted. I'm not wrong am I?'

He spoke quietly but Zoë could hear the earnest back-drop to what he was saying. She kept her face even, whilst inside she was screaming at the injustice of it all. Discussions about starting a family and weddings should be the most happy of occasions and she did not want this time to be tainted by the sickening abuse she had endured. Fury rose up in her now, but not being able to share it with anyone, it stayed rigid in her throat. He was an ever present companion in her mind now and one that she couldn't eject. He followed her everywhere. He was in the shame she felt, the anger that she had no outlet for and now he sat between her and Gage like a king upon his throne.

'You of all people know how I hate surprises.' She tried to lighten the air between them that threatened to unbalance the equilibrium. 'Of course, you aren't wrong. I just need time to get used to the idea. It was always something that was in the future but with no set date. Now it sounds like you want to put a date on it and one in the near future at that.'

Gage felt a stab of disappointment at Zoë's response. It was as if a switch had been flipped in his brain and now having a child with her had become something he wanted to make a reality rather than a thought. He knew not to persist with the conversation now though, she was right, he knew how she hated surprises. He'd let her think about it in her own way and time.

'Let's see how things go in the next few months, give you time to get comfortable with the idea,' he smiled suggestively.

Walking back home in the pleasant sunshine, they passed an elderly couple tending to their front garden together. It looked immaculately kept with beds of flowers that had obviously been given forethought of where each should be placed. Deep pinks and soft candy coloured petals were sat beside intriguing shaped leafy plants in various shades of green. Zoë felt it was like looking into a window of their relationship, the care and pride that they applied to each plant was a reflection of how they nurtured each other. They worked impassively, each concentrating on their own area, but also seeming aware of each other's movements.

A dandelion caught in the light breeze sailed by them and Gage leapt forwards to catch the delicate puffball in his hand. He turned back to her and held out his fist triumphantly.

'Make a wish,' he smiled.

When she was younger, she used to play this game with her father and whoever caught the dandelion got to make a wish and then release that wish back into the wind. It took her years to realise that her father was letting her win the catch each time – he'd only ever seriously intervene if it looked as though the puffball was getting away and then he would stride forward with an agility that somehow surprised Zoë.

Even though she knew it was utterly ridiculous, she still did it and made the wish – that she could forget. Gage slowly unfurled his hand but the white fuzz was completely squashed and had stuck to creases of his palm. He had to blow it off and it dropped in a small clump to the ground.

Under the comforting flow of the shower, she felt relieved that she had made it through the day. It had not been easy, but she had done it. After tomorrow, she could put it all behind her. Forget it ever happened and look forward to the future.

She just needed to get the all clear at the clinic. She felt the dipping in her stomach again though when she thought of the different possibilities. She'd never had a sexually transmitted infection before, was always so careful. How dare he put her in this situation? Feeling the tightening in her throat again, she grabbed her towel and sat on the edge of the bath. She controlled her breathing by releasing long, gentle breaths through her mouth until her throat felt more relaxed. She pushed the anger back down, she would have to deal with that at a later date, she knew that, but hopefully by then it would have subsided into something she could manage more effectively.

She joined Gage on the sofa where he was watching a comedy satire programme that they always watched together and lay her head on the arm rest. The audience's laughter was the only thing that broke through to her consciousness as she let torpidity wash over her. She was unable to make sense of what the panel were saying and felt utterly exhausted, her limbs felt sapped of energy as if she had spent the day swimming against a high tide.

Gage reached for her leg and began massaging her calf with his eyes still on the screen. She looked over at him and let out a grateful sigh as his fingers gently kneaded the soft tissue and muscles below her knee. Letting her eyelids close, she felt her body surrender to the need to relax further as the sound from the television faded further away from her.

Just as she was drifting off, she felt Gage's fingers snaking their way further up to her thigh and before she could say anything, he had lifted himself above her with his arms locked on either side of her shoulders. She felt the hardness of him as he scooped down to kiss her and panic rose up through her inhibiting her movement and speech, but in her head she screamed the words, *Oh God, no!* Gage must have seen something in her eyes because he pulled back and regarded her as if trying to read writing on a piece of paper that was held too close.

'What is it, Zoë? is it your bruises – did I hurt you?'

He sat back on his heels with his hands cupping her knees. Through his thin cotton trousers she could see his erection that poked out like a metal pole in the centre of a tent that had drooped on both sides. She turned away.

'No, sorry it's just that I'm so tired. I think I'd better go up and have an early night, you don't mind do you?'

He looked wounded for a moment, but quickly disguised his emotions using humour that they both knew was feigned.

'Yeah, of course, don't worry about it – this will wait,' he joked, as he pointed to his now deflating penis. Before he could say anything further, she pecked him on the side of the mouth and retreated to the bedroom.

Gage sat staring at the flashing images on the screen as he struggled with his feelings of rejection. After the way Zoë had reacted last night, he had wanted to make sure that things were resolved between them, especially as she would be going away this week. An uncomfortable feeling of uncertainty settled around him – was she shutting him out? He couldn't put his finger on what was troubling him, but the weekend had been very strange and he felt as though Zoë was pushing him away, hiding herself from him. He was accustomed to her anxieties and moments of self-doubt, but he had always been able to reach through to her somehow. For the first time, this felt like a barrier that he had no way of manoeuvring around.

Chapter 5

Having woken early after a fractured night's sleep, Zoë was eager to get to the boutique. She needed to make that first step back into the room because if she couldn't do that then everything else would be futile. She couldn't allow him to infect the place that she loved and had worked so hard to keep. It was hers. The anger began to rise within her again, but today she was going to use it to her advantage to make it through.

She left Gage a note, hoping to start the new day on good terms, beside the freshly filled kettle. She placed his favourite mug alongside it with a teabag and spoon. Knowing that this simple act would please him, she felt a small knot in her stomach and longed to hold him. She thought back to the night before, how scared and repulsed she had felt at the thought of having sex with him – her Gage who put her before everything and who wanted to spend the rest of his life with her. Physically, it was out of the question anyway, she still felt sore and torn, her body tender from the violent invasion. *This is the hardest part, it will get easier,* she reminded herself. Each small step she took would distance her from him and she would gain control once more. With this thought in her mind she stepped out into the hazy stillness of the early morning.

Sitting in her parked car metres away from the entrance to the shop, Zoë felt butterflies flitting around in her stomach. It was almost as if she were about to go into an interview situation. In the flats that stood beside the car park she could see a curtain edging out of a half open window on one of the highest floors, she watched as it billowed victoriously in the breeze. The sound of a dog barking was interrupted by the calls of children who, half dressed in their school uniform were taking turns to do tricks on a scooter. Everything looked the same, but everything felt different.

After taking a few calming breaths she got out of her car and began walking with a determined stride to the side door of her boutique. As she neared the entrance she felt her legs weakening and the now familiar tight choking sensation in her throat. Spots danced across her vision as if she had stood up too quickly and didn't have enough blood pumping to her brain. Needing to steady herself she continued walking past the door and out on to the main cobbled pathway.

Opposite, the café had its door held open a crack with a sturdy block of oak. The sign on the door was turned to show that they were still closed but Zoë could smell the aroma of coffee and baking that had escaped through the opening. She leant against the window frame and looked across at Her Boutique – a place that she had always thought of as her second home. Slowly, her breathing began to feel easier and her vision returned to normal.

An image of her mum suddenly came to her mind. She was standing at the counter of the boutique, but her ever-present smile had been absent and instead a vacant expression haunted her pale, hollow face. Zoë remembered how she hadn't even seemed to notice her standing at her side observing her unusual behaviour. She had felt afraid and had sensed that something was being hidden from her; something of great magnitude and she feared that her mum would never return to the way she had been before.

A pigeon flew past swooping at eye level and landed with un-gainliness on the cobbles, it had a quick surveillance of the area around it and then began pecking at the ground. Her eyes rested again on the boutique and she realised that other than checking the displays in the window enclosures, she never stepped back like this and viewed the front of the building. The solid wooden slab that stretched across the top of the door and had the name and logo carved into it looked unique and sophisticated. She and Gage had spent an evening comparing different ideas and sketches. When he unveiled the finished piece, Zoë had actually cried. It far outweighed any expectations she had envisaged and she had thought it was beautiful. The day that Gage had fixed it into its new position had marked a moment when the boutique really had begun to feel like hers.

Turning her head to breathe in the scent of freshly baked scones, she was transported back to the Saturday afternoon visits to the bakery she had taken with her father. She remembered how after spending the morning in the boutique colouring or practising writing out her times tables, Ed would take her hand and together they'd walk the short distance to the pastry shop. They would discuss what treats they'd have and Ed would always tease her by saying: 'So, the usual egg custard for you, Zoë, and a big cream cake for me, that's right isn't it?' she would giggle and exclaim that she hated egg custards as she laughed up at him and caught the twinkle in his eyes. She never tired of his silly jokes.

The Devonshire cream and jam splits had been her favourite and she had found the sight of them bewitching as she gazed longingly at them through the bakery window. She still felt the same excited anticipation she had felt as a girl when she spotted them now, although now she didn't allow herself the luxury of consuming the calorific treat, they remained a childhood indulgence. The two of them would always take something for her mother too, usually a scone or Eccles cake; Zoë could never understand why she would choose such a plain cake when there were such other tantalising varieties to choose from.

Thinking of her mother again brought her focus back to the present. She too had worked so hard to make the business a success – even after all she had been through. She retraced her steps back round to the side door and without giving herself time to think she pushed the key in the lock.

Once inside, Zoë switched on the light. The table stood dominant in the small room as it always had, but now seemed to give off an intimidating air as if it knew the significance of its presence. A slight shudder ran through her as the heavy feeling of nausea settled in her stomach once again. The tap dripped lazily producing a dull thud as it hit the basin below. She swept into action, turning on the music system and lighting. Before leaving the house earlier, she had picked up the scented candle that had been burning the night before and placed it in her bag. She lit it and placed it on the desk and as she moved around the boutique she felt calmed and comforted by the sweet vanilla and raspberry essence that reminded her of home.

Just as she was making a list of jobs that needed to be done whilst she was away, Amber banged on the door with her elbow. Zoë rushed to unbolt it and Amber came crashing through with her arms full of plastic containers holding food.

'Morning, Zoë – whatever happens today we're definitely not going to go hungry!'

She tottered through to the back room and Zoë heard the containers topple on to the table.

'Seemed a shame to waste this food, some of it hasn't even been opened, I'll put it in the fridge,' she called out.

Zoë looked at the clock and realised that she only had to wait another twenty-five minutes until she could call the clinic. She felt nervousness clawing in her stomach again but knew she had to try and appear normal in front of Amber.

'How did the big clean up go?' she asked brightly.

'It was okay, I left it until the afternoon as Han and Claire were asleep in the morning and to be honest, so was I!'

She lifted her nose in the air and gave an exaggerated sniff.

'It smells gorgeous in here by the way,' she moved closer to Zoë, leant in and scrutinized her face, 'the bruise has come out more, but the bump has gone down, that's good.'

'Yeah, should be gone in a few days,' Zoë smiled.

'Were you OK yesterday- has the cystitis gone?'

'I think the cranberry juice did the trick, it's much better, thanks.'

Zoë felt that Amber was going to question her further, so she made an excuse to go up to the stockroom. Out of her pocket she pulled a piece of paper with the clinic's number written on it and placed it on the side under her phone.

Ten minutes to go.

She busied herself by size-ordering the over-stock for something to do with her hands. Her ringtone suddenly rang out amidst the music playing downstairs. She grabbed for her phone, seeing Gage's smiling face in the screen.

'Hi Gage, is everything alright?'

'Yes, everything is fine. I just wanted to say good morning to you, it felt weird you not being here when I woke up.'

'Yeah, sorry, I woke early and decided that I may as well get on with things here seeing as I'm going to be away for a couple of days.'

There was no clock in the room and Zoë began to feel jittery and was anxious to end the call.

'Well as long as you're OK, I'll leave you to it. Will you be home normal time? I'll probably be a bit late, unfortunately.'

'Yes, I'll be back normal time, send me a text when you're leaving and I'll put dinner on.'

'Alright, see you later.'

'Bye, Gage.'

She ended the call and checked the time; one minute. Pressing the digits on her screen, she felt the pulse in her neck pulsating rapidly. She waited for the call to connect. The engaged tone sounded briefly before the screen returned to the call page.

'Damn it!' she hissed. The call not being taken felt ominous and her anxiety shot up another level.

She pressed redial and again got the engaged tone.

'Zoë, do you want a coffee?' Amber called up the stairs.

'No thanks.'

Her fingers felt thick and awkward and she almost dropped the phone trying to retype the digits just in case she had dialled incorrectly the first time. Maybe if she redialled it would change her luck and the call would be picked up? She waited. Again she was disappointed and suddenly infuriated also why weren't they fucking- well picking up the phone? She booted a half-empty box of discarded plastic hangers and it slid across the floor making an unpleasant clattering sound that ricocheted around the room.

Anxiety now having been replaced by fury, she hit the call button again. After a short pause she heard the call connect and the phone began to ring.

'Good morning, Westgrove Clinic'

'Hello, can I make an appointment please?' Her voice sounded strained and alien to herself.

'You can, but I need to ask you a few questions, first, is that alright?'

'Yes.'

She wanted to shout that no, it was not *alright*, none of it was in fact *alright*.

'How long ago was your last sexual contact?'

Zoë could feel the frown on her face deepen and her impatience increase. A prickling sensation crept up her back. *There was no sexual contact,* she wanted to scream, *he fucking raped me!*

'Saturday.' She replied quickly.

'Well, what I can do is book you an appointment for four weeks' time as you need to wait to ensure that you get reliable results. Any further tests that the doctor may advise you to have, can be discussed with them when you come in.'

'Four weeks!' Zoë couldn't comprehend what she was hearing.

'I can't wait that long.' Even as she spoke, she knew that she sounded desperate and barely recognized the person shouting down the phone.

'I'm sorry but there really wouldn't be any point in you coming in any earlier. Four weeks is a good average for the time required to wait. If you need to speak to someone urgently, please make an appointment with your GP.' The woman sounded sympathetic but professional and had obviously had this conversation many times before.

Zoë wrote down the date and time of her appointment on the paper alongside the phone number that she had held in her hand and ended the call.

She went over to the window and gazed down at the café where she had been standing earlier, ready and eager to make the call that would help her on the road to forgetting. Now a huge stretch of uncertainty lay ahead that would impede her healing and leave her in this unbearable static state. She felt a hot aching in her throat and ears, the sensation that usually occurred with tears, but her eyes remained dry. A rage unlike she'd ever experienced seemed to be building and gaining momentum like a determined athlete sprinting down a track.

'You alright, Zoë?' Amber called from the doorway looking concerned, 'I thought I heard you shouting.'

Pressing her hand to her head and smoothing down her hair, Zoë turned and faced Amber.

'Argh, it was just this supplier, they've let me down on some stock that's all, they keep fobbing me off and it really got to me this time.'

'That's not like you, Zo. Are you sure you're OK?'

'Yes – honestly. Although, Gage and I did have a bit of a disagreement at the party, perhaps that's playing on my mind a bit as well.'

'I thought you two were a little off with each other when you left.' Intrigue and concern flashed in Amber's eyes as she stepped closer to Zoë.

An overwhelming tiredness washed over her as the adrenaline, present moments earlier seeped from her body. It seemed to press into her bones leaving her muscles devoid of energy and her brain without sufficient glucose to function properly.

'I just feel a bit confused right now.'

'Perhaps these couple of nights away will do you good – give you some space to think...? Don't be too hard on him though, Zoë – there aren't too many Gages in the world.' Amber laughed to try and lighten the mood and make Zoë smile again. 'Hey, guess what? I'm meeting someone for a drink tomorrow night. He works at the hospital with Hannah and Claire funnily enough and was at my party as a plus one, you might have seen him, tall, dark, handsome,' she grinned mischievously.

They walked back down the steps to the floor below and Zoë was relieved not to have to talk about herself anymore. She listened as Amber chatted excitedly about her date, Theo.

Even though the rectangular patch of earth that lay before him was a mass of uneven clumps, Gage could envisage what it could become. Mentally he placed a shed in the far right corner and a plum tree that would produce its pink blossom to signal the arrival of spring, halfway down the left side. He would add a stony area for tubs and shrubs to inject colour and fragrance, and of course some bespoke wooden benches carved by his own hands. He sipped at his steaming black coffee as he thought about the next part of his job this morning. Thom would be here any minute to begin on the electrics. They had done many jobs together and worked efficiently each being familiar with how the other worked. Through the constant banter existed a friendship that Gage valued greatly, they each knew that they could depend on one another, whether it be for an odd job or advice on whatever was troubling them on a particular day .

After speaking to Zoë on the phone a little earlier, he was feeling slightly easier about the atmosphere that had nestled between them over the last few days. She had sounded back to her usual self and eager to get on with things at work. He'd make sure that this weekend would be different, they had the meal for his mum's birthday on Sunday and it would be good to surround themselves with family – he was really looking forward to it.

Rosa, his mother, had always been there for him and Megan as they were growing up. Their father worked away a lot and it was often just the three of them on a day to day basis. No matter what the weather was like, Rosa would take them to different parks and forests during the weekends. He and Meg particularly liked to ride their bikes round and round the large pond in one of the parks in the centre of Norwich. Rosa would sit and read or sketch, frequently looking up to keep a protective eye over her children. Gage loved the sense of freedom as he pedalled furiously, lapping his younger sister as she manoeuvred her smaller bike more carefully around the curves of the pond.

Once, he'd taken a wooden sail boat that his grandad had made for him, to sail on the water. He had kept it on a shelf in his room for weeks – had marvelled at the smoothness of the varnished pine body of the boat that his grandad had carved from offcuts. He would run his finger along the perfect angle of the bow and gently change the angle of the sail that had been made from a fine linen fabric. Meg was under strict instructions to never touch it and it was for this reason that it was kept on the highest shelf in his bedroom, even he had to stand on a stool to reach it.

On this particular day, after his grandad had questioned him on numerous occasions on the telephone on whether he had taken the boat out yet or not, he decided to take it with him to the park. It was a hot day, the air smelt strongly of decomposing algae and Gage could see a green scum that had settled towards the centre of the water. He looked at the perfect creation in his hands; he would need to be very careful not to let it out of arm's-length.

Having watched Meg set off with her doll, Daisy, sat in the front basket of her bike, Gage began the serious business of sailing his boat. He'd had to plead with his mother to keep her away from him while he concentrated on this as Meg had wanted to put some small plastic passengers on the deck, so they could go sailing too and had got upset when he had told her no. Gage had been annoyed and told her to stay away – this was his boat and not a toy. He had leant over the concrete wall enclosing the water and placed the boat close to the edge. Gently tapping the stern with his finger he watched as the boat floated a few inches away from him parting the water ever so slightly as it did so. He felt a swell of pride and contentment as he pushed it again and sent another ripple through the stillness of the pond. A family of four had stopped to watch him and he noticed that the two boys were looking on with awe. They were each holding a brightly coloured butterfly net and small plastic beach buckets that looked brand new – Gage could see the sheen of the yellow buckets reflecting in the light.

The sun shone down on to the back of his neck where his T-shirt didn't quite cover the delicate skin there, but he didn't care, he was engrossed in his sailing. The pond had become a huge ocean, the algae an island that he, the captain needed to avoid at all costs. He steered his boat around the lily pads that floated in his path, imagining them as other vessels that shared the same sea.

He had almost done a full circle of the pond when he heard a scream followed by a familiar cry. Looking up he'd seen his mum running towards Meg who was lying on the ground. Her bike was tilted on top of her and Daisy had been propelled out of the basket, her short yellow curls now having slipped from the bands that Meg had placed in bunches that morning. He grabbed his boat and ran the short distance towards them. Meg's crying had now reached its peak and her cheeks were red and wet with tears. The edge of her blonde fringe was stuck to her forehead with sweat and appeared to have turned much darker than the rest of her hair. Their mother was wiping at her knee which was an angry red and had bubbles of blood oozing from the wound. Gage had picked up her bike and doll and carried them to the metal seat nearby. Meg had been carried over by their mum and her sobs had begun to subside as she sat on her mum's lap, her head nestled in the crook of her neck as she was rocked to and fro. Gage had stared at his sister's inflamed knee and had known how he could make it better.

After hobbling over to the pond's edge, she watched as Gage had returned his boat to the water. She squealed with delight as he let her set the boat off across the pond and Gage had looked up at his mum who was standing behind them. She had looked at him and smiled with such pride that he felt he would cry. When he glanced back he saw that Meg had pushed the boat again, this time though it had veered off towards the centre of the water and was sailing towards the periphery of the green algae that he had so carefully avoided. It was now out of arm's-length for even their mother to retrieve. Gage felt a panic rise up as he watched his boat stop to a halt in the green sludge. One of the boys who had been watching him earlier came running over with his green net flailing over his shoulder. Without speaking, he threw his net into the water just catching the edge of the boat but unsuccessfully bringing it any closer. Gage wanted to take the net from him as he was slightly taller than the boy and knew that he could reach his boat more easily, without causing it any damage. The boy threw the net out again, this time capturing the top of the sail within the green netting. Gage couldn't watch as he dragged the boat back to the water's edge – he already knew that the cream linen would now be covered in green splodges from where the boy had been fishing earlier. With reluctance he thanked the boy and took back his boat that he was holding out towards him.

During the drive home Gage had sat with the soiled boat in his lap as wafts of decaying algae had risen in the heat of the car, making him feel sick. He'd had conflicting feelings towards Megan as on the one hand there was anger when he looked down at his boat and on the other, sympathy, when he looked across at the ugly graze on her small, pale knee.

When they reached home, Gage took his boat and placed it on a shelf in the shed. He knew that he would never take it out to the pond again.

The morning had been productive and Gage had been able to complete everything he had intended to do. Thom had distracted him from thinking about Zoë too much and the radio was playing songs from a year that he particularly liked. As he went back outside to use the equipment that was set up in the garden, he heard a new year of songs begin to play. It was the year that had brought about a change in their lives forever.

Their father, Ben, had been home for a week. Everything about their routine changed when their dad was back. He would drop them off at school in the car, leaving them at the gate instead of walking them to the back entrance like their mum did. It somehow felt incomplete and he missed the conversations they had walking to school together, they'd talk about silly things, but sometimes important things too. Like when his friends had stopped one of the boys in his class playing football at lunchtime because he was no good, they'd said. Gage hadn't known what to do, he felt sorry for the boy, but didn't want to cause trouble for himself by defending him. His mum had talked it through with him while they walked and somehow it seemed less daunting being out in the open, surrounded by the trees and the birds flitting around them and he'd been able to voice his worries without inhibition. It all sorted itself out in the end anyway as one of the other players fell and injured himself, he was replaced by the other boy, who with daily practise improved significantly and was without fuss allowed back into the group.

They would visit relatives when their dad was home too, sometimes straight after school. His parents would pick them both up from the gate and drive the hour or so to his grandparents' house. They'd have their tea there and play in the garden. His grandad would show him things he had made in his workshop and this was where his love of carpentry began. They would return home when it was beginning to get dark and Gage would forget that it was a school night and feel a sense of disorientation when he remembered he had to get up for school the next morning.

His dad loved swimming and would take them to the big pool in the city centre that had a giant snake slide and a wave machine. Rosa hated the chlorine so would sit in the spectators area watching them as they practised their lengths and slid, screaming in delight down the green slide. She would always have a book with her – never a magazine, but it seemed that she would always instinctively look up a crucial moment when either he or Meg was doing something daring or particularly challenging.

Their last trip out together had been on the day before his father was due to return to work, they had all gone to the cinema and then out to eat pizza. As they'd waited at the front entrance of the restaurant to be seated, Gage spotted a girl from his class at school who was sat with her family eating ice-cream from a tall sundae glass. It seemed incongruous seeing her sitting there in her casual clothes with her hair hanging down her back – he hadn't realised it was so long as girls had to have their hair tied back in school at all times. She looked over in his direction and smiled sweetly when she noticed him standing there and he'd smiled awkwardly back at her before quickly looking away. He'd felt a fluttery feeling in his stomach, but hadn't dared to look back again. His parents now had their arms around each other and his father whispered something in his mother's ear that made her laugh loudly. He'd felt a bit annoyed at them for causing attention from others around them. The waiter took them to a table in the far corner which had coloured spotlights hanging down. Gage risked another glance at the girl, but she was showing her mum something in the bag by her side, with the same sweet smile upon her face.

It had been a really great evening. His pizza had been cooked exactly how he liked it and they had all chatted and laughed about the film they had seen. His parents had even let him sit in the front of the car on the way home so he could change gear for his dad when he'd instructed him to do so. He had felt such a thrill as he moved the stick into position and felt the smoothness of the gear change that he and his father instigated together.

That had been the last time that he had seen him. The next morning he'd got ready to go to school, back to the usual routine now as his father had gone back to work. He had proudly walked into his classroom with a model of his fantasy island that his father had helped him finish for his class project. He had asked his mum to save all the cardboard and plastic packaging for weeks and had carefully selected the items that he wanted to create the image he'd held in his mind. The finished item looked amazing and it had sat on the table along with the rest of the classes' efforts for the remainder of the term. When he'd finally got to take it back home, it was dusty, the colours faded from sitting in the sunshine and it had pieces missing from where others had picked it up to inspect it. He put it straight in the dustbin when he got home, not wanting to think about how his father had helped him glue the trickier pieces together, their heads almost touching as they leant over the model under the glare of the light above.

When his mother had collected them from school that day, their grandmother was with her also. Gage thought this was strange but was excited by the prospect of possible further treats that afternoon. This thought quickly dissipated as he and Meg sat in the back of their grandmother's car crawling slowly through the school traffic. His mother had sunglasses on even though it wasn't particularly bright and there was no music playing; his grandmother always had the radio on in the car. Meg and he had exchanged several nervous glances that at one point had turned to grins. To ensure that they did not start laughing they had both quickly turned their faces away from each other and stared out of their side windows. Gage had daren't speak – the tension had been unbearable.

When they eventually arrived back home, their mum had sat them down and told them that their father had been in a car accident on a country lane on the way to the airport. He had died there and then. She had remained still and calm as she told them but then had suddenly let out a screech: *a country lane!! All the times I worried about him on those planes and he gets killed a few miles down the road!*

Gage had been aged thirteen and Meg, ten. They had spent a lot more time with their grandparents for a long while after that day. Gage only felt truly at ease when he was in his grandfather's workshop. The smell of wood and varnish had instantly calmed him as he'd practised his skills on old, rough blocks of wood – chiselling, sandpapering and finally varnishing the pieces until his grandfather was satisfied that he was ready to move on to something more challenging.

One evening a week or so before their first Christmas without their father, thick flakes of snow fell suddenly and unexpectedly from the dark night sky. Gage and his sister had sat with the lights turned out with their heads pressed against their mother's large bedroom window as they watched giant flakes of snow cascade down to the ground below. Tipping their heads back and gazing upwards , it had seemed as though the falling snow was a swarm of bees swooping down and about to land right on top of them. Meg had squealed in delighted terror when Gage had suggested this and then they had both begun to laugh wholeheartedly. The release felt like a long exhalation after holding their breath for too long. Once they had started, they couldn't stop. Neither of them had noticed their mother standing on the landing watching them.

By now the road outside their house had been completely covered with the thickest snow Gage had ever seen. The overhead cables were weighed down by the snow that had settled tenuously on the stretches of wire. Small birds crashed into the branches of the oak tree that stood at the front of their house sending showers of snow to add to the mass below.

A figure dressed in a dark coat suddenly appeared tentatively stepping through the white realm beneath them. Their face was covered by the funnel hood of their parka, but when they turned and looked up to the window and waved two gloved hands at them, Gage realised that the figure was their mother. She beckoned to them using exaggerated arm movements and pointed towards the front door. After racing down the stairs they found that two piles of winter clothing had been left neatly placed by the doormat. It had reminded Gage of the book his mum used to read to him when he was younger, where the shoemaker left out tiny clothes for the elves in return for the help they had given him. Gage never tired of the story of which his favourite part was where the elves found their clothes in the workshop and were then finally free to leave. He let the childish excitement wash over him, everything had been grey those past few months and he had been grateful to feel the unadulterated pleasure of the moment take over him.

They walked through the freshly covered roads together reluctantly disturbing the glistening snow beneath their feet. He felt as if he was cocooned in time. The chunks continued to fall around them with the snow wedging into the grips of his boots making his movements stilted and arduous. Meg and his mother held hands as they walked just behind him and in that moment he had felt important, like an expedition leader guiding them through the white abyss. Their mother hadn't stopped smiling, her mouth appearing too large for her now gaunt face. Her black damp curls had fallen across her eyes after in her excitement she had pulled the hood from her head. Her cheeks that had seemed too sharp and pale of late now had a deep red glow to them.

Although he had known that things would never be the same again, he'd felt that this evening had allowed them to begin their path to some sort of normality where their mother once more began to take an interest in things she had neglected. Books appeared on the arm of her chair, decorated cupcakes were placed in front of them after their meals and the garden returned to the neat state it was accustomed to. He felt the responsibility of constantly watching his mother's actions slowly lift from his shoulders and began to believe things were going to be all right again.

These memories reminded Gage that sometimes you just had to rely on time to do its job. Even though he felt ready to become a parent himself, he would have to wait until Zoë felt the same way and only hoped that it wouldn't take too long.

Arriving home to the comforting smell of baking pastry, Gage headed into the quiet kitchen. For a moment he thought perhaps Zoë was upstairs in the bathroom but as he reached the doorway, he saw her standing with one leg crossed over the other looking out towards the garden. She wore an over-sized fluffy jumper that looked more exaggerated on her petite frame. Both her hands were clasped around a mug holding steaming coffee, its heady aroma interlacing with the pastry as if competing for air space.

'Hey, something smells good,' he went up behind her and kissed her gently on the cheek. He couldn't be sure but he thought he felt her bristle slightly. She didn't turn to look him in the eye but instead averted her gaze towards the items on the side as if suddenly remembering she had preparation to tend to.

'It's just a shop bought quiche and some salad.' She placed her cup down on the worktop beside her and picked up the knife that had been discarded half way through cutting a red pepper.

'Perfect. I'm going to jump in the shower, I won't be long.' Zoë turned away from the job at hand and smiled weakly up at him. He wanted to touch her but for some reason he felt like they were in the first fledgling stage of a relationship where couples were unsure how to read each other's mood. Instead of holding her as he wished to do, he backed out of the kitchen and headed for the bathroom feeling somewhat dejected.

As soon as Gage had gone, Zoë let out a long sigh and massaged the sides of her head. She'd thought that tonight was going to be easier – that she would have an appointment set for the next few days and would have at least a target to aim for. Now it seemed like this anxiety and uncertainty was stretching ahead of her and she could see no end. The thought of having to contain her emotions unnerved her as they seemed to be controlling her instead of the other way around and she was afraid she'd slip up at some point.

Zoë had not laid the table and instead they sat in front of the television eating their slightly charred quiche. Gage didn't question this even though he knew Zoë hated eating in front of the screen usually. She picked at the crust and top layer of her small portion with small, slow movements.

'Made some good headway with the kitchens today, we might just have caught up on the time lost.'

'Yeah? That's good,' she nodded and smiled at him and he felt a slight gap in her defence open briefly.

'How were things at the boutique?'

'Surprisingly busy for a Monday actually, the new stock is really shifting. I'm so relieved.' She hooked a piece of pepper on to her fork, but then let it fall on to the now soft mush of the quiche's innards. 'Actually, I'm going to go up for a bath now. I want to make sure I've got my bag packed and ready for the morning. I'm catching the seven o'clock train, so will have an early night.' She took Gage's empty plate from him and carried both plates away. Scraping the remainder of her food into the bin, she felt a wave of nausea hit her as the smell of cold egg wafted up from the smeared plate. She turned away in disgust and dropped the plates into the now tepid soapy water of the washing up bowl. She felt so tired from all the thoughts and probabilities that plagued her constantly day and night. *What if...? When will...? Who can...?* The thought of lying in a warm bath gave her the impetus to run up the stairs in the hope that she might feel rejuvenated slightly.

Rinsing the plates under hot water Gage again wondered what was happening with Zoë. It was if she had closed herself off from him. Perhaps she was bored or didn't find him attractive any-more? He certainly didn't feel very desirable at the moment. Maybe she had been thinking of finishing it for a while but was unsure if it was what she actually wanted? Was she just buying time until she had come to a decision? His outburst about start-ing a family may have cemented how she felt and now she was trying to find the gentlest way of leaving him. He felt afraid and completely at a loss at what he should do next.

Chapter 6

The already busy train station smelt familiar and safe. People bustled past with eyes averted to the screens above to check the latest developments of their journey. Others were sat on the few available plastic seating areas, reading or drinking coffee from ubiquitous take-away cups. No one was interested in what anybody else was doing. No one was going to ask her questions or watch her because she was acting out of character. She felt a simple relief in this having underestimated how tiring and arduous it would be to conceal her emotions from those around her.

A stooped cleaning attendant passed by her carrying a black refuse sack in one hand and a litter picker in the other. He did not look about him but concentrated his gaze to the ground, collecting each piece of absently dropped food or wrapper and stowing it in the bag. The faded navy blue uniform he wore swamped his slight body, the hems of the trousers gathered in untidy rolls around his ankles and the matching nylon jacket hung rigid where his shoulders should have been. He had an air of apathy towards anyone in his vicinity as if he had long given up making contact with these beings who threw down their rubbish for him to pick up.

Waiting on the platform, a group of six adolescents caught Zoë's eye. They each had a rucksack style bag slung over their shoulder and were huddled around one of the youth's phone.

Their deep laughs echoed around the high canopied roof but were then drowned out by the screeching brakes of the arriving train. Zoë stepped back just enough to let the departing passengers exit but ready to board before others had the chance to push in front of her. She always felt that on the whole, manners seemed to be left at the front doors of a train station.

Comfortably seated she took from her bag the printed email with information regarding the fashion show. Her enthusiasm for the event had waned but she knew that she needed to act as normal as possible by continuing with her planned activities. Cancelling would have definitely sparked questions from Gage and Amber as they both knew how passionate she felt about these events usually. She also needed to fill the hours until she could gain control of her life again. A few days away from everyone could actually give her the space she required to get her head together. She knew that those close to her were getting suspicious of her behaviour and she had to keep it together.

A man came bustling down the centre aisle carrying a heavy looking bag, his breathing was laboured and loud. He settled himself on a seat on the opposite side of the carriage, adjacent to Zoë. As the train began to move Zoë tried to concentrate on the words on the sheet in front of her. She found that she could not as the rasping sound of the man's breathing seemed to grow above the noise of the train. It began to really irritate her and she felt her annoyance showing on her face. She looked about to see if anyone else had noticed. The young woman opposite him had earphones in and was oblivious to the steady rhythmic grating sound. She knew that the earphones that were knotted at the bottom of her own bag were broken and would be of no use to her now. She had meant to replace them but had not got round to it. This she cursed herself for as she felt her hackles rise at the sound of each jarring breath. The book that she had been reading but had remained unopened for days now was wedged in her bag. She took it out and skimmed the last few pages she had read. As she tried to familiarise herself with the plot the thought occurred to her that the last time she had looked at the words on the light buff-coloured pages before her, was before it had happened. Before she had been raped; before he had brutally taken from her, stolen from her, leaving her uncertain of the person she was now. Wishing was foolishly futile – she knew, but it didn't stop her from longing to be able to return to the morning of that day and having the chance to alter her actions.

The train was slowing to a halt and Zoë watched the people waiting outside as they merged forward to position themselves in the best place for the opening doors. The woman with the earphones stood up abruptly and without looking at anybody else, moved with an assertive pace towards the exit. She swiftly hit the button to open the doors and was gone. Zoë gathered up her bags and made to move to the next carriage along, but stopped when she saw how many people were getting on. A harassed looking mother carrying a toddler with long golden curls was edging an older child further down the aisle with her hip. She was awkwardly trying to hold on to the girl's hand who seemed reluctant to release the grip even for a moment. Zoë could hear her uttering encouraging words to keep the little girl moving down the train and as they passed her, the girl raised her eyes from the floor and gave her a shy smile. Unexpectedly, Zoë felt her heart lift with the little girl's small act of kindness and she smiled back at her feeling tears begin to surprisingly prick at her eyes.

Seating herself down in the place that had just been vacated opposite the stertorous breather was a woman who was in the middle of a conversation on her phone. She had a strong pronounced voice and looked out of the window as she spoke, seeing but not seeing what was on the other side of the glass. She had a large frame but looked solid instead of overweight; her dark shoulder length hair had strands of silver grey scattered amongst the thick waves that shimmered in the sunlight. She tilted her head to the side suddenly as if trying to comprehend what had been suggested to her and a slight frown formed around her eyes until the moment was dissipated by her laughing and nodding in agreement to whatever the caller had just said. Her whole face radiated warmth and beauty and her eyes sparkled with joy as she ended the call and tucked the phone into the inside pocket of her jacket. She set up her laptop on the table in front of her and began to skilfully touch type, seemingly unconcerned by the man opposite her as he continued to breathe laboriously. After a while she rummaged in her bag and took out a foil wrapped croissant which she delicately tore at with her fingers as she continued to look at the screen on her laptop. Zoë was suddenly aware that she felt ravenously hungry and couldn't remember the last time that she had eaten properly or finished a meal.

Peeling the unripe banana that she had flung in her bag earlier, she tried to push aside thoughts of French toast, which had been one of her favourite quick meals when she was younger. Occasionally for a Sunday morning brunch treat, she would wake to the unmistakeable smell of the eggs and bread frying in the pan. She would race down to the kitchen and find her father tucking into the first portion as a smile played on his lips – she knew that an early bird joke would always be forthcoming.

Her mother would get the small stool from the cupboard and give Zoë the job of soaking the thick white bread in the mixture of raw egg and milk. She felt ridiculously proud when her mother told her that she was the best helper in the world and that it wouldn't taste as good without her expertise in bread soaking. Eating the first piece, she always felt that her appetite for the honey-coloured slices could never be satiated and would nod enthusiastically when asked if she would like more. Her father would warn her that she would give herself indigestion and that her eyes were bigger than her belly. He was right. She remembered how she would sit at the dining table with an uncomfortable heaviness in her stomach watching the ash burn down on the joss stick that her mother would light to mask the smell of frying. She'd been fascinated to watch the tail of ash gather at the end of the spindly stick until suddenly it curled and collapsed, sprinkling the grey dust on the mat placed underneath. Zoë was never convinced that the aromatic sticks actually served their purpose because she would always be able to detect the smell of frying when they returned home later from wherever they had been.

Wishing that she had picked up something more appetizing this morning, she put the half eaten banana to one side as she was not enjoying it in the least. It held no flavour and the texture was firm and chewy instead of soft and sweet how she liked her bananas to be. Gage would eat them green – never giving the peel a chance to transform into the ripe yellow that Zoë favoured.

At the thought of him, Zoë felt painfully alone. She always eventually shared her worries and concerns with him even if there was nothing that he could really do to help.

This, she knew, she could never share.

The show was taking place in an old disused brewery in East London. It had been transformed into a trendy multi-function venue that was split across several levels. The huge, arched wooden doors were open wide and clusters of people were gathered talking in the entrance. A girl with shocking, white straight hair and full, berry-coloured lips stood to one side holding a cigarette at arm's length from her body. It almost seemed that she wanted to disassociate herself from it, like it disgusted even her. She looked slightly irritated and as if to be in a hurry as she sucked deeply on the cigarette one last time before dropping it into a plastic cup placed next to her foot.

Zoë pulled her overnight bag from her shoulder and rubbed the sore welts that had dug into the delicate skin there. She climbed the metal stairs up to the reception area, her steps adding to the cacophony of others as they ascended and descended the wide coiling staircase. At the top she placed her bag into a locker, glad to be relieved of the weight of it for a while. Her phone tinkled in her hand bag, she reached into the front compartment and took out her phone to read the message: Clarissa was going to be a little late.

When Zoë had been about seventeen, the name Clarissa had begun coming up in conversations between her parents. Her mother had paid a visit to a newly opened boutique on the other side of the city and had instantly found a rapport with the young, free spirited woman named Clarissa. One particularly busy Saturday when Zoë was working in the boutique, the telephone began to ring. On answering it, she heard a small panicked voice asking to speak to Stephanie. Zoë explained that she was busy at the present time and that she would ask her to phone back when she was finished. The woman replied in her broad Norfolk accent that her name was Clarissa and that Stephanie already had her number. When Zoë relayed the message to her mother, she promptly returned the call. Zoë overheard snippets of the conversation during which her mother had been speaking in a gentle, consoling hushed tone that she normally reserved for her. She couldn't help feeling slightly annoyed by this Clarissa who hadn't sounded much older than herself and was obviously taking advantage of her mother's kind nature.

'Oh poor love,' Stephanie had said shaking her head slowly. 'It's so sad, her mother has breast cancer, but they didn't catch it in time and it has now spread. They told Clarissa today that there is nothing more that they can do for her.' Zoë felt instantly ashamed of her unkind thoughts but wondered why her mother had not mentioned it before. When she had questioned her about it, Stephanie had simply replied that she was hoping that the news was going to be positive and that she hadn't wanted to dwell on the worst that could happen. Clarissa's mother was only fifty three; it had all felt too threatening.

Stephanie's own mother had also died from cancer at a relatively young age and all of a sudden thoughts of her own ephemerality had begun to play on her mind. She'd supposed that there was a time in everyone's life when a fear of death hit them more acutely and had wondered if she'd been experiencing some sort of mid-life crisis, although she'd always felt that this term was used all too flippantly for something that could be at the least, a difficult experience and at the most a destructive one.

After Clarissa's mother had died, just a few months after her diagnosis, Stephanie had helped her through her grief. They would meet up once a week for coffee and at first Zoë had felt jealous of the relationship, but as time went on she too became very fond of Clarissa. She was almost like an auntie she'd never had. There being only ten years between them meant that they shared quite a lot of things in common. Other things they learned from each other. Clarissa had a love of indie music and introduced Zoë to the most influential groups in this category whilst Zoë kept Clarissa up to date with changes that were occurring in the late teen scene. The three of them would go on shopping trips together, touting for inspiration from the high street chains to use in their own boutiques.

Zoë walked over to the strip of tables laid out at the back of the room. Each table was draped in a white damask cloth with champagne flutes containing an array of fruit juices placed neatly along the back. In front were silver trays lined with fruit and cheese kebabs, the strawberries stood out like andesine gemstones amongst the display of white. She leant forward and took a glass of cool orange juice, more for something to do with her hands than for need of refreshment. Her eyes took in the huge room where she was standing as she noted the exposed rustic brickwork and steel pillars that were the bare skeleton of the building. The atmosphere was heavy with the history of the place and usually this would have excited her, but today even though she appreciated what she saw, she didn't feel anything.

People had begun to make their way over to the seating area that surrounded the long white catwalk. Zoë sent Clarissa a quick text telling her which side of the room she would be sitting and then placed herself as visible to the main entrance as possible. Looking about her, Zoë could see that copper had been used heavily in the styling of the event – large copper spotlights were hung on overhead beams casting a subtle orange glow on to the white glossy walkway. Letters that had been sculpted out of the russet metal spelt out the name of the show and were placed on both front wings at the top of the runway.

She lifted her face to one of the spotlights that was angled in her direction, feeling drawn to its brilliance as if it were a blood moon in a lunar eclipse. Everything else around her descended into black, as once again, she was there with him in the back room of Her Boutique. The face that she prayed she could forget taunted her from her own memory in an act of cruel betrayal .Every detail of his face seeming to be even sharper than before . . . the open hollows across his cheeks, the tiny spider veins that spread across his nose and worst of all, the look of pure disdain that engulfed his pale blue eyes; his stare that sent a blade of shame ripping through her.

Tearing her eyes away, she dipped her head down as a surge of panic spread over her. The voices around her grew louder and distorted and the thudding of her heart vibrated maniacally in her chest as she tried to reason with herself that she was safe. Her fight to reclaim control was lost, she felt the terrifying narrowing in her windpipe as her own body broke its promise to her and let his presence manipulate her once again.

The hand that gripped her thigh was trembling violently and a veil of sweat encased her rigid body. A malevolent aura held her in its power, feeding off of her fear and goading her body to turn on itself. Feeling as though she was about to faint, she desperately fought the assault as she willed her mind to override the terror that had consumed her. Focusing, she counted to five, looking at each finger as she did so, then she repeated the process again counting back down to zero. She continued until her fingers began to tap along with the counting in her head. The grip in her throat began to abate and she felt some of the tension drain away. Her fingers although still trembling, straightened out and her breathing became calmer, control was returning to her. The conversation between the two women who were sitting behind her became more lucid, she could make out that they were speaking about a particular model that was going to be taking part in the event. Even though she felt sure that those around her would have been able witness her ordeal, when she cautiously raised her head she saw that people were engrossed in their own conversations or that they too had their heads down and were looking at their phones.

After dabbing her face and neck with a tissue she turned her head towards the door and saw a bright red crop of hair. Clarissa had her phone to her ear and was glancing towards the audience and seconds later Zoë's ringtone erupted from her bag.

'Hi Zoë, my eyes aren't what they used to be, can you give me a wave, angel?' Zoë felt a rush of warmth at hearing her friend's familiar soft voice and rose to wave her programme in the air. Clarissa waved back and tottered carefully across the room to meet her.

'Sorry I'm late, I don't know what was going on with the tube but we just sat there for ten minutes not moving anywhere and when it started up again, it was at a snail's pace.' She placed her bag on the chair and swept Zoë into a hug, her sweet perfume wafted up between them from her warm skin.

'It's so good to see you, Rissa. You look gorgeous.'

'I was determined to wear these heels today after walking round London in trainers for the last few days.' She suddenly stopped and peered closer into Zoë's face.

'What have you done to your eye – is that a bruise?'

'Oh it's nothing, I tripped outside the boutique – wasn't even wearing heels! I thought I'd done a good job of covering it up,' she laughed and shook her hair further in front of her face.

'No, it's not really obvious. You just can't help looking into those beautiful eyes though, there's no getting away from it.' Her beatific smile warmed Zoë and at that moment she felt at home being there with Clarissa amongst the others in the room. This was who she was.

There was no time to talk further as a bright flash at the top of the stage momentarily lit up the faces of everyone in the room and signalled the start of the show. A burst of electronic music that Zoë recognised immediately pounded out of the huge speakers. She could feel the vibration beating in her chest as the first set of models made their descent towards the end of the runway. Their heavily shaded eyes were cast straight ahead as they elegantly marched to the thud of the music, every exaggerated movement in time with the beat that rippled around the room. Zoë spotted the girl she had seen smoking outside earlier. She was dressed in a silver asymmetric, cropped corset that looked as if it was made out of metal. As she skilfully stepped to the music with her hands planted on her waist, her body moved beneath the static frame of the garment accentuating the femininity of the look. The skirt she wore was of the same silver and cut in an A line. The spotlights caught her outfit at different angles as she moved and it was almost as if orange sparks were firing from her body. Although the overall effect was dramatic for the sake of the show, Zoë loved the style and ingenuity of this designer. She put a circle around her name in the listing and made a note to check her website when she returned home.

For the rest of the show Zoë let everything wash over her. It felt good not having to think about anything and she let the display and music take over her. She felt in an almost hypnotic state as the she watched the models saunter past. A dark skinned, athletically lean model swept down the centre of the stage wearing a deep red dress. Zoë was uncertain of the fabric but it looked to her to be some sort of cross between silk and satin. It was cut shorter at the front but flared out like a pool of blood skimming the white floor behind her. As the model turned at the end of the stage the back of the dress flew out, highlighting the fluidity of the material. Clarissa turned to Zoë and raised her eyebrows in awe before quickly returning her gaze to the model as she disappeared from view. People in the audience were frantically scribbling notes on pads balanced on their knees barely daring to take their eyes off of the spectacle before them. Now and then they would incline their heads to the side to listen to something said by the person next to them, but nobody wanted to miss a thing.

The show ended with the all the models doing one last lap of the runway followed by all the graduates that had taken part in the event. The delight at being part of such an exciting show was evident in all of their faces as they graciously accepted the applause that was being awarded them. Zoë pointed out the designer that was from Norwich to Clarissa. She looked confident amongst the others on stage with her as she beamed widely into the audience.

Exiting the building was a slow task. They couldn't even really speak to each other as people were all around them, each taking shuffling steps in the same direction. Zoë suddenly felt exhausted as they trudged along and just keeping herself held upright and moving was taking all her energy and focus. Clarissa turned to check that Zoë was still following behind her and seconds later Zoë felt a firm grip on her upper arm and saw Clarissa's concerned face peering down into her own.

'Hey, are you okay? You don't look so good.' Clarissa was frowning slightly with a questioning look in her eyes.

'I do feel a bit dizzy actually,' Zoë breathed. She felt confused, there was an air of surrealism about the moment that made her feel disjointed from everything. Her head sank down as she felt herself being pulled along the sea of bodies by Clarissa.

She couldn't remember how they'd made it through the crowd, or how long it had taken but the next thing she knew, they were both standing by the lockers. Zoë leaned her body against the sturdy metal containers.

'What have you had to eat today, Zoë?' Clarissa was unwrapping a cereal bar as she spoke then without waiting for a reply she thrust it towards Zoë. 'Look at you, you're shaking.'

The effect of the syrupy bar didn't take long to recuperate her somewhat but also left her with a ravenous hunger she had not realised until then.

'Thanks, Rissa. I didn't really get a chance to eat this morning, it was silly of me. Have you got time to get something to eat or have you got to get back to Matt?'

'As much as I love him, I think a couple of hours away from each other will do us good, we've been together twenty four hours a day since Saturday. Anyway, I was planning on taking you for lunch. I have something to tell you.' Her carefully made up face was glowing with joy and excitement. Zoë guessed that she might be pregnant, her and Matt had been trying for a baby for about two years now but as yet had been unsuccessful. She hoped sincerely that this was the case.

'Let's go Italian and get some much needed carbs into you. You're looking a bit on the skinny side if you don't mind me saying, sugar.'

Sitting under the canopy outside the restaurant, Zoë felt the warmth of the sun on her knees. The wider than usual outside seating area had been partitioned off from the main pavement by tall wooden slatted planters, they contained an array of sweet smelling flowers that draped down the sides in an explosion of colour. Potted bay trees with thin plaited stems stood guarding the entrance as if impersonating the foot guards outside the palace. At that moment she felt an optimism that she was going to be able to get past this, that what had happened earlier at the show was just part of the process of burying the whole thing. Feeling more like herself she sipped at the glass of white wine that Clarissa had insisted she have as she watched the waiting staff flit between the tables as deftly as birds to-ing and fro-ing from a nest.

'Come on then, spit it out,' she teased Clarissa as she watched her drain her orange juice.

'Well, as you know, Matt and I have been trying for a baby for some time now, but for whatever reason it seems to be taking longer than we'd expected. I was a bit worried that we'd left it too late but after what happened to Mum I wasn't in the right place to start a family back then. If I'm honest, the thought really frightened me. We've been trying for just over two years now and I don't want to wait any longer.' Zoë waited for her to go on. 'We are going to adopt!'

A moment of confusion flickered on Zoë's face. She realised too late that Clarissa had seen it and rushed to respond.

'Wow, that's great news, how exciting!' She smiled across at her friend and placed her hand on top of hers.

'It is really exciting. I don't think I could be any happier.' She waited a moment and then added: 'Did you think that I was going to say that I was pregnant?' Zoë felt a little uncomfortable and was uncertain of what to say.

'For a moment I did, yes. What, with you drinking orange juice and everything.' Zoë nodded to the empty glass in front of her and laughed. 'But I can tell how happy you are about adopting, there's a real glow about you.'

'That's just it, I am. I don't want people to think that I'm disappointed about not falling pregnant, we're still going to continue trying actually - naturally of course, I don't think we are cut out for the whole IVF thing. And for your information, I'm not having a drink with my lunch because Matt and I are going out tonight. I'm saving myself,' she laughed happily.

'Well I'm really pleased for you both.' Zoë got up and leant across to hug her.

'We have actually started the process and have already asked Steph and Ed to be referees for us. This little break might be the last one with it just being the two of us for a while!' The reference to her parents made Zoë feel a pang of longing to see them, it had been a good four weeks since they had visited last.

Their food arrived and they both enthused about the colour and presentation of the pasta salads placed before them by the cordial waitress. Having not wanting to embarrass herself any further by getting dehydrated on top of the earlier drop in blood sugar, Zoë had ensured that she kept her glass topped up with iced water from the jug sat between them on the table. Getting up from her seat, she apologised to Clarissa as her now swollen bladder demanded to be emptied. She wove her way quickly through the shaded area of the main restaurant. After having being sat outside in the brilliant sunshine it seemed incredibly dull and Zoë wondered why anyone would want to sit inside on such a gorgeous day. She spotted a sign for the toilets towards the back of the room and followed the arrow that pointed the way. Pulling on a heavy dark wooden door that led into a long narrow corridor, she looked for the sign for the ladies'. The first door on her left had a notice which read staff only on it so she continued walking further along. The whooshing sound of a door being pulled open at the end of the corridor startled her. A man of similar age to her came out and confidently made his way towards her. He had a certain air about him that seemed to suggest that he enjoyed making women feel uncomfortable. The type of man that stood too close to a woman on a train or a bus, taking full advantage of being given the benefit of doubt about their understanding of personal space. He slowed down just before he was alongside her and ogled her lasciviously, his eyes not quite focusing from the effects of his alcohol intake. Not wanting to reveal any signs of intimidation Zoë looked him straight in the eye and kept her expression neutral. As he passed her he looked her up and down with a hint of hostility before making his way out back into the restaurant. Hurrying to the ladies' toilet she felt the familiar thudding in her chest and ears. Once inside the brightly lit area she locked herself into a cubicle and leant her back against the door. The wine she had drunk rose up like hot acid in her throat as she felt the floor was shifting beneath her. Propelling herself forwards, she quickly threw her head over the toilet basin and vomited until her stomach was empty and dry. The hand she had pushed up against the cool tiles to support herself began to slip as her arm shook uncontrollably. Cautiously she turned herself round and when she was certain that the sickness had abated she sat and emptied her bladder.

The fear was back – she had been foolish to have believed it had gone away. The girl sat quivering on the toilet was someone Zoë didn't recognise. What was happening to her? She didn't know the answer, but knew she couldn't stay the night in London now. She wanted to be back at home. With this thought in her head she returned to the table.

'Come on, your salad is getting cold.' Clarissa laughed as Zoë sat back in her seat. Zoë gave her a weak smile and then took a sip of water to wash away the sourness in her mouth. Reluctantly she forced a few mouthfuls of pasta into her mouth as she half listened to Clarissa talk about how she and Matt would spend the rest of the week.

Although she knew that Zoë wasn't really paying attention, Clarissa kept on chatting so she could subtly scrutinise her. Something wasn't right. It was as if she kept disappearing into a shadow of herself and she had definitely lost weight since she had last seen her. Even though one eye had slight bruising, it didn't account for the darkness underneath the other one. The subdued expression too, her eyes were clouded with a dullness that Clarissa had never seen in her friend before. Last year she hadn't been able to stop Zoë talking about the fashion show afterwards. She had been so excited and animated about everything they had seen and had a notebook full of ideas. Looking at her now, Clarissa was struck by her apathy. What had happened to her drive?

'Anyway, I think that's enough about me. You've been very quiet, how are things with you? Zoë pushed aside her half empty bowl and straightened her back pushing herself upwards.

She could do it now, open her mouth and let it all spill out on to the table. Relieve herself of the crushing pressure that now tormented her day and night – make Clarissa swear not to tell a soul.

'I'm fine, just a bit tired. Actually, I've decided not to stay the night after all, it would be a little indulgent to spend another day in London really, I could be back at my place instead of looking round other people's boutiques.'

'Well I wouldn't say it was indulgent. It's always good to keep your finger on the pulse on what's going on in the capital. But if you're tired, maybe it would be best to get back.' Frankly Clarissa thought it was for the best that Zoë did go home, she didn't look well. She made a mental note to call Steph later, see if she could pick up on anything from her. Zoë certainly definitely didn't want to divulge anything and she decided not to press her any further on the matter.

They hugged each other goodbye and Zoë promptly left to catch the next train, she could be home by seven if she hurried.

Chapter 7

Tuesday night was curry night, apparently. Gage was surprised by the quantity of curry smeared, steel serving dishes that were sat on the tables waiting to be cleared around them. He and Thom had obviously arrived after a mass exodus of full bellied patrons and he wished that he had been one of them rather than opting for his takeaway of fish and chips. The batter was sitting heavily in his stomach after he'd rushed to meet Thom at the agreed time.

When he'd got home to the empty house after work, he had sat out in the garden with a bottle of beer, listening to the chirping wrens as they hopped along the back fence. Their squat brown bodies flitted backwards and forwards from the bird table that Gage had built last year, collecting morsels of grain and disappearing again with chirrups of delight. With the sun on his face he'd felt the concerns of the day begin to ebb away and he had drifted off for a while. He woke to the excited voices of the children that lived next door as they clattered about in their shed freeing their bikes from the garden paraphernalia that constrained them.

Before leaving the house he called Zoë to see how her day had gone, but it had clicked straight to voicemail, he left her a short message asking her to let him know that she was all right. Even though she was miles away, he still felt as if she was avoiding him. Surely it wouldn't have hurt her to send him a quick text to let him know that she was OK? She usually did, they were both respectful when it came to keeping each other advised on their whereabouts.

'I'll get the first round, what are you having a pint or a bottle?' Thom was already at the bar and was looking at Gage expectantly.

'A pint please, mate.' Gage watched his friend as he made small talk with the Polish-sounding barmaid. She had wide, dark lined eyes and a beautifully sculpted face. Her chocolate coloured hair was pulled into a high plait which hung over her left shoulder, thick like braided rope. He noticed how Thom kept moving his eyes to her peach pigmented lips as she spoke and wondered if she was the reason he was in such a hurry to get the drinks.

'Know her, do you?' Gage smirked as Thom put his pint down in front of him. 'No wonder you went on at me to come out tonight.'

'The perks of being single, my friend. I do know that she works on Tuesdays, Thursdays and Saturdays though,' he laughed as he took a swig of his beer. 'So where has Zoë gone, again?'

'She went to a fashion show today and then tomorrow she's doing some research,' he paused for a moment. 'She's looking round shops in London for inspiration for her window displays.'

'Can't she just google them?' Thom said well humouredly.

'Apparently not,' Gage dead panned back.

They left for another bar just as it had begun to get dark, the temperature seemed to have taken a sudden dip and Gage zipped up his jacket as they walked along. With thoughts of what the next day entailed, he vowed to have just one more drink before heading home.

He heard his phone ripple in his pocket and reached in hoping to see a message from Zoë. It was – a very short message from Zoë letting him know that she was all right and would see him the next night. No details about how her day had gone or an enquiry into how he was. He couldn't help feeling a little put out as he placed the phone back into his jacket pocket.

Amber was beginning to feel comfortable in Theo's presence. He had an unassuming persona that she found attractive and his lack of bravado proved that he was confident without needing to shout about it. The physical attraction was still there too, she had been worried that perhaps the amount of alcohol she had consumed at her party might have clouded her judgement, but he was just as she remembered him. He had made an effort in his choice of clothing. The navy skinny trousers, light coloured shirt and tight fitted waistcoat suited him well, showing off his tall, lean figure. His shoulders were broad but not bulked up by muscle and she had already noticed a few appreciative glances from other women in the bar.

Early on in the evening it had transpired that they shared a love of running. They spent a considerable amount of time discussing races that they had taken part in, comparing distance and time. Theo had raced in Berlin, Dublin and Tuscany as well as other smaller local marathons, Amber felt completely at home as she listened to his description of each event. His eyes shone with fervour as he relived the experiences he'd had and people he had met. She felt relieved that the competitive streak that they shared was forming an easy bond between them and any nerves that she had felt before meeting up had gone.

As he spoke, Amber noticed that he had a habit of rubbing his hand against the closely shaven hair at the back of his head. At the front, the longer pieces were held in place by a strong, pleasant smelling hair product that Amber could smell each time he inclined his head closer to hers.

Then it had happened . . . Theo had rocked back on his stool, laughing at a comment that Amber had made about someone who had been at her party. She had gone the whole date without making any comparisons – comparisons to the man she wished she didn't hold in such high esteem. For the last five years she had watched him and the way he was with Zoë, the small everyday things he did that spoke volumes about how he felt about her. Amber had put him on a pedestal that he had not once fallen from.

The way Theo laughed reminded her of Gage. They both had the same mannerism of throwing back their head and covering their face with their hands. But before this had happened she realised that she hadn't thought about Gage at all. It had become so habitual for her to put Gage and her dates in juxtaposition, the latter competing against the touchstone that was Gage, that she was felt a little disorientated.

'Do you want to go somewhere else?' She looked up into his narrow blue eyes that seemed to be examining her intently. He looked nothing like Gage with his prominent straight nose and high cheek bones.

'Yes, I'd like that very much,' she smiled.

Gage was beginning to regret getting that last round in. He should have called it a night after the last drink but if he was being honest with himself he hadn't wanted to return home to the empty house. Usually this did not concern him at all, he liked being in his own company and took advantage of the time by catching up on programmes that Zoë didn't enjoy. The void that he felt within himself though was unfamiliar to him. He just couldn't shake the feeling that Zoë was hiding something from him. The alcohol, instead of soothing him had only increased his anxiety further. Something was wrong, he felt sure of it.

He flicked on his phone again to check his messages. Nothing more from Zoë since she'd sent a text replying to his missed call. It had been short, curt almost.

The jubilant sounds from the slot machine next to them broke into his thoughts. It whirred and beeped as if to predict an imminent windfall only to suddenly dip down into a long, deep note of forfeiture. Gage turned to look over his shoulder at the two women whose cries of disappointment made them the cynosure of the surrounding area. The one encouraging her friend was facing towards Gage and had her hip leant against the machine. Her black layered hair stood out in spirals and looked to be held in place by a ton of hairspray. One side of her light brown skin was lit up by the manic flashing lights on the fruit machine as they danced up and down in columns on the screen. He watched as she laughed good naturedly at her friend's misfortune, she had a full mouth which was painted with a matte red lipstick that accentuated her large white teeth. She looked straight at him as the laughter left her face and was replaced by a flirtatious timid smile and he noticed that her perfectly defined thick eyebrows framed her black, winged eyes. They both held the gaze longer than was necessary until Gage turned away to take a sip of his drink. When he looked up again she was still staring at him, only now, the smile had left her lips and she was openly taking him in.

'I'd forgotten how much of a magnet you are, Gage!' Thom smirked. Feeling confused by his behaviour, Gage picked up his beer and stood up.

'I think I need some air. Can I cadge a smoke off you?'

Climbing the hill towards one of Amber's favourite pubs, they passed the empty shopping mall. Four bridal dresses were positioned in the wide window with their sequins twinkling alluringly under the security lights. Four perfect dresses for four perfect marriages . . . It wasn't that Amber was anti marriage, she just hated the pretence. Why were people so scared to admit that they had certain difficulties in their relationships? From what she had witnessed, it was hard work. Partners had to constantly remould after the complications of life threw them off track and derailed them from their comfort zones. She felt that there was a noble truth in acknowledging this instead of veiling problems under a display of unblemished sublimity. Amber hadn't yet decided if this was for her. She was not one of those girls who had grown up fantasizing about their big day. If the time came when it felt right then all well and good, but it wasn't something she gave too much thought to.

Theo's wide strides left her struggling to keep up and her heels were only adding to her disadvantage, she could feel her calf muscles straining from the incline of the hill and angle of her heels. He was talking about a recent night out he'd had with a friend as Amber made encouraging noises to show that she was listening. She dared not speak though as this would reveal her difficulty and she was damned if she was going to do that. He slowed as if a thought had occurred to him.

'Sorry, am I walking too quickly?' Amber let out a bout of laughter.

'Now you notice! I didn't want to admit defeat but we're at the top now anyway, so technically it's not a defeat,' she giggled in between heavy breaths. He was smiling as he watched her and she enjoyed the rush that she felt under his gaze.

'You must think I'm such a narcissist, going on about myself and storming ahead. I'm really not though, hopefully you will come to realise that.' Sincerity replaced the humour that had been in his voice.

They approached the side door of the pub and before stepping inside Amber had a quick scour of the outside area to see if she recognised anyone. Stood under the smoking canopy was Gage, she'd know that stance anywhere.

'While the cat's away, hey?' she sniggered as she crept up behind him. He spun round at the sound of her voice and an awkward smile spread across his face. It had taken him a moment to realise that she was actually referring to the fact that he was smoking and not the earlier flirtatious encounter which must have still been playing on his mind. He pushed aside the feeling of unease.

'Hey, you. What are you doing out on a school night?' He enveloped her in a hug before noticing Theo stood a little distance behind her.

'Gage, this is Theo – Theo, this is Gage,' Amber spoke quickly, feeling unusually shy. She watched as they briefly shook hands and then she ushered Theo inside.

Gage felt an overwhelming urge to be at home away from the façade that suddenly appeared more obvious to him. A taxi was pulling up in front of them, he waited a moment to see if anyone else had pre-booked it, but seeing the driver settle in his seat with his head bent over a newspaper, he saw that this was not the case.

'I'm going to call it a night, mate,' he slapped Thom on the back in a farewell gesture and then opened the rear door of the taxi – he was in no mood to talk. Inside, the small space smelt heavy with the scent of a sweet perfume that Gage had noticed in the air all evening. He rested his head back and was glad when the driver drove off without making any small talk.

Sitting in a quieter corner of the pub, Amber watched as Theo leaned over the bar waiting for his turn to be served. It had been a surprise seeing Gage here tonight, she was accustomed to seeing Zoë and him together and it had thrown her slightly. He had looked good in his dark shirt and plaid jacket. She had become so used to seeing him in his work gear recently that she was quite taken aback at his appearance. Although she had only seen him fleetingly she felt that he was distracted and a little sombre. When Zoë returned on Thursday she would try and subtly find out what was going on between them. Zoë had been acting a little odd too. Perhaps she could be pregnant?

A dragging ache clawed at her stomach waking her from her sleep. Remembering where she was, she carefully swung her legs out of the bed and walked over to her bag which was placed on an old wooden chair beside the window. In the inside zip she found a slightly bent wrapped sanitary towel. It would have to do until she got back home.

Zoë pushed the thick floral curtain to one side and a stream of sunlight broke into the small room. The dark grey river looked perfectly still, being shaded from the early morning sunshine it lacked lustre and made Zoë feel cold. Two swans swam regally past leaving the slightest divide in the water behind them. Cars were parked bumper to bumper on the road running horizontally to the guest house that she had stayed in last night. When she had stepped off of the train on to the busy platform, tiredness had engulfed her and the thought of returning home had seemed too great a challenge.

The white bricked guest house that stood on the opposite side of the road to the train station seemed so familiar to her having passed it on her way to and from the city on countless journeys over the years. She was relieved to find that they had one single room remaining and after having a bath in the tired but clean bathroom, she had fallen asleep until having been woken by stomach cramps.

At the small partitioned counter, Zoë vaguely recognised the same genial woman from the night before. Her ample cheeks bunched up as if they each contained two small apricots as she enquired politely about her night's stay. The words slipped from her lips with a rehearsed ease and she tilted her head to one side beaming back at Zoë when she confirmed that everything had been sufficient. Stooping to pick up her bag she winced as a sharp shot of pain squeezed her insides. Thanking the woman she left through the entrance she hardly recalled noticing the evening before.

The sun was facing head on in the small front enclosure and she took a moment to feel its warmth penetrate her unmade face. She felt completely at a loss at what to do next. Inertia seemed to be holding her captive having frozen out the usual proactive side of her. It was if she was waiting for something to happen, something that she had no control over. Until she could get those results she was stuck, waiting. It didn't matter how much she read about statistics or reasoned with herself about *his* life-style. She knew nothing about him, so it was pointless trying to console herself with percentages and predictions.

A new burst of anger gripped her gathering momentum as it surged through her tired body, yet she could find no outlet for the fury that was stoked each time injustice tapped her on the shoulder to remind her of what he had done.

Throwing her bag over her shoulder she started to run along the road that was beginning to build with early morning com-muters. She had to pause at the crossing but enjoying the feeling of her heart pounding in her chest, she carried on running through the suit cladded pedestrians making their way towards the station. She continued past several bus stops until she felt a gush of hot sticky blood spill into the insufficient and now mis-aligned protection in her knickers. Slowing her pace to a fast walk she carried on towards the next stop. There were two boys dressed in school uniform stood waiting as she approached the shelter, they both looked up as she took her place in line behind them, but then quickly bent their heads back towards their phones. Catching a glimpse of her reflection she saw that her cheeks were red and the line of sweat she could feel on her fore-head was glinting in the light. Her hair was damp at the roots and stuck to the sides of her face where the sweat had trailed down. She looked away and following suit took out her phone from her bag. Reading the last message that she had sent to Gage last night, she had little recollection of sending it. The voice-mail he had left her had stirred more guilt about her inability to respond to him in the way she should, but she just didn't know what to say. The less that was said was probably for the best, she couldn't have explained to him why she had stayed away the night before. She couldn't face his questioning and hadn't trusted herself to be around him when she had been feeling so weak.

The bus arrived and Zoë stood at the front holding on to the handrail instead of taking a seat, mainly because she was conscious of any possible leakage from her pad, but also to be ready to jump out as soon as the bus reached her stop.

It didn't take long and she was soon outside her house slightly blighted by the sense of disorientation that had crept up on her. With her hand on the metal gate she stared at the wooden hare that stood majestically in their front window, she remembered the thrill she had felt when Gage had presented her with it on her birthday last year. Knowing that no one else had this spectacular ornament and that it had been made for her by the person she loved made it invaluable. But at that moment she felt as if she shouldn't be there, almost as if the house was surprised by her sudden arrival. She should still be in London devouring the shop windows on Oxford Street and feeding her desire for new innovative concepts for her own boutique. Yet here she was at eight thirty in the morning, stood on her doorstep, a sweaty mess not knowing what to do with herself.

In the hallway Gage's best jacket was hung over the staircase and his going- out shoes left out on the floor beneath. Without touching anything she climbed the stairs to the bathroom, removed all of her clothes and let the hot water scour her body. Smoothing her hair back from her eyes she suddenly knew where she wanted to be and with a new vigour finished up in the bathroom. With her hair still wet she went into the kitchen and swallowed down two paracetamol, the chalky bitterness sat at the back of her throat increasing her ever present nausea further. Passing the fruit bowl as she turned to leave she plucked out a large red apple and hurried out to her car.

Walking along the promenade the air felt cooler, the sea breeze lifted Zoë's hair and she felt a shiver run along her spine. Having at least had the sense to wear a fleece she zipped it up closer to her chin and looked down at the generous sandy shoreline below. Everything still looked exactly the same, as if only a day had passed since she'd last walked there with her mother and father. She would run ahead impatient to get to the sand and fair that had seemed so far down below where they walked. Not being allowed out of sight, she would have to wait for them to catch up with her before running off ahead again willing them to walk faster with every sprightly step she took. They never did though and she would have to stand waiting, jigging on the spot trying to expel some of the built up excitement from her limbs.

The bright coloured beach huts came into view as she turned the corner and made her descent down amongst the greenery of the cliffs. In the distance the proud helter skelter omnipresent at most seaside towns, poked through a gap in the thick over-growth enticing visitors to the foot of its coiled frame with its red and white striped body.

Once she had reached the path that ran along the side of the beach, the wind had dropped and once again the rays of the sun found the exposed parts of her, warming her scalp and face. She removed her trainers and felt the firmness of the recently wet sand under her feet; they hardly left an impression upon its smooth, sleek surface. Walking on without purpose she followed the course of the beach. The sea rhythmically lapped the shoreline leaving a white foamy residue before pulling back on itself again. Seagulls hovered menacingly above her as they watched for signs of food.

It wasn't until she began to feel dizzy that she realised how far she had walked. She had felt at peace, almost in a hypnotic state as the sound of the sea and the gulls filled her ears. Others on the beach had not bothered her – in fact she had not had to look into the face of anyone else for the last hour or so. It seemed quite acceptable to walk with your head down towards the sand or the horizon without having to acknowledge the people that passed you by when at the beach. Again she had made the mistake of not eating properly. Her appetite seemed to have completely disappeared as if her stomach had shrunk to the size of a child's. It felt as though she had something lodged in her throat, a tablet or a piece of food that would not follow the route of her oesophagus and settle in her stomach. She knew that she needed to regain her strength for the walk back, so angling herself towards the pathway she pushed her feet into the drier uneven sand. Her calf muscles felt strained under the effort that the bumpy terrain demanded, suddenly woken into action after the smooth crust she had absently managed.

Stopping at the first food hut she came to she bought a carton of orange juice and a freshly made doughnut. She plucked at the pile of small square napkins sat on the side of the counter and collected her change with her free hand. A patch of grease had already begun to soak through the white paper bag on to her fingers as she walked the short distance to a metal bench set back on the path. The hot dough seemed to melt in her mouth and her body instantly responded to the sugar coated treat. Everything seemed to appear sharper in focus and a stillness returned in her head. She could only manage half of it before the greasiness began a swirling sensation high in her stomach. Wiping her fingers on the course napkin, granules of sugar fell on to her lap and settled on her trousers. Dusting it off, she watched as a young family approached the hut. They looked like the perfect family unit. The father had brown, messy, curly hair and a kind open face. He looked down at his daughter who was hopping from one foot to the other in excitement. Zoë guessed that she was about three years old. She was dressed in black leggings and shiny pink boots. Her miniature denim jacket hung off of one of her shoulders as she pointed towards the ice cream display board. The mother was bent over a small pram rearranging her baby so it could sit further upright. Zoë could see the look of contentment in her eyes as she made exaggerated smiley faces to the wide eyed face that now poked out from the hood of the pram. She felt a sudden jolt when the baby returned its mother's smile, it had a look of complete adoration as it stared back at her.

Her mind drifted back to Amber's party. This is what Gage wanted, she had wanted it too but it had always seemed that they had time to play with. His urgency to start now couldn't have been more badly timed. She didn't know how long she would need to start feeling normal again, but once she had those results she could start afresh and bury everything that had happened.

People did that. Horrible things happened all the time. Burying it away was the only way to get on. What was the point in opening the wound time and time again?

Her thoughts were disturbed when a man appeared by the side of the bench, a Border Collie stood patiently beside him regarding its owner. The man took out a cotton handkerchief and wiped his eyes and nose before folding it slowly and returning it to his trouser pocket.

'You don't mind if I sit, do you?' He half perched above the seat as he looked sideways at Zoë.

'No, not at all.' He smiled kindly in response as he leant back on the flaking metal frame.

They sat in silence for a while, each caught in their own contemplation as the path before them began to build with more buggies, joggers and dog walkers. Zoë was about to leave and return back towards her parked car, when the dog suddenly began to make a high pitched whistling sound. It stared intently at its owner and licked its lips.

'It's all right old boy, shush now.' He leaned over and rubbed behind the dog's ears and pulling its head closer to his own, leant his face against its soft mane. As if sensing her gaze, he looked up at Zoë.

'Cooper and I walk along here every day, rain or shine. On those mornings when putting one foot in front of the other seems impossible, he's always there to get me going.' The deep lines on his face seemed only to enhance his handsome features further and his hazel green eyes displayed compassion and a worldliness of someone befitting his age. Zoë felt strangely soothed by his presence, almost as if she had always known him.

'I've never had a dog. It must be rewarding to feel that loyalty, he's barely taken his eyes off you.' He tightened the lead around his knuckle and then glanced at Zoë before looking back towards the sea.

'He was my daughter's dog.' The sense of sadness hung between them making itself comfortable in the small space that divided them. 'Sara was killed last year in a car accident. She died instantly. Such finality, there was no glimmer of hope to cling on to until our brains had had a chance to process the horror of what had happened.'

'I'm so sorry, that's truly awful.' Zoë felt an ache in her chest for the woman she never knew. The man nodded his head in acceptance of her words of condolence.

'She was about your age; never took anything or anyone for granted, was really kind, you know?'

A small dog walking with a young couple pulled on its extended lead and excitedly ran over to where Cooper was sat and began jumping up and sniffing at him. Cooper twisted round and nuzzled the little dog's belly almost lifting it off of the ground. The owners laughed apologetically as the woman swooped down to pick up her keen pet, she adjusted the length of the lead and placed it back on the pathway. Their laughter and words evaporated as they walked on, leaning into each other with a comfortable ease.

'Are you here on holiday?' he asked.

Something about him reminded Zoë of her father. He radiated composure, even when divulging the horrifying details of his daughter's death. She felt safe and comforted being sat beside him.

'I'm not on holiday, no. I'm not really sure what I'm doing here to be honest. I used to come for days out with my parents when I was young. When I woke this morning I just felt the need to get away and I found myself here.' Again he nodded, this time in understanding.

'Someone hurt me.' The words left her mouth before she had realised that she was going to say them. She covered her mouth with her hand like a child that had spoken out of turn in class. His frown of concern made her eyes sting with the threat of tears. For some time neither of them spoke.

'Are you still in danger, do you need somewhere to go?'

'No, it's nothing like that, but thank you. I'm going to go back home now.' With an overwhelming need to see her mum she got to her feet. She stroked Cooper's soft head and he licked at her hand with his warm tongue.

'Bye, Cooper. It was very nice to meet you.' The man stood too and she felt that she should hug him or at least shake his hand after their intimate conversation. But they just remained facing each other for a moment before she broke the silence.

'It was very nice meeting you too.' This time his nod was accompanied with a small smile.

'And you, perhaps I'll see you walking along here again some time.' The breeze pushed her long fringe into her eyes and sweeping it back, she gave him a tight smile.

'Bye, then.' She left him standing where he was and when she looked over her shoulder a moment later she saw that he was walking away from her in the direction he had come from. Cooper was trotting companionably by his side, his face angled slightly towards his owner. Zoë quickened her step and was grateful that the breeze was now behind her gently pushing her along.

Chapter 8

The city café where she had arranged to meet her mother was heaving with customers. Zoë stood in the open doorway and craned her neck to locate a vacant table. Noticing a couple standing to gather their belongings, she headed over to the side of the café and waited for them to leave. She placed her bag down and sat facing the large window, giving her a vantage point of those passing outside. As she settled herself at the table the vintage wooden chair creaked slightly beneath her as if to remind her of its age. The chair opposite her was similar in size and varnish colour but had a rattan criss-cross seat which dipped in the centre. Zoë and her mother had met here on several occasions as they both enjoyed the atmosphere of the place. From the antique tea cups and saucers to the table and chairs, nothing matched apart from the large, sturdy white coffee cups that held the dark pungent beverage.

Two young mums sat at the table in the window opposite her talked animatedly as their babies slept peacefully in their carriers beside them. As one poured a pale, honey coloured tea from a stout teapot into floral porcelain cups, the other spread butter on to her toasted teacake. She was chatting incessantly as she did so, as if in fear of being imminently interrupted by one of the miniature versions of themselves that, for the moment, slept at their side. It was as if they were cocooned in their own bubble, nothing distracted them from their conversation. Zoë couldn't help but to overhear as they compared experiences about how their offspring slept, fed and cried. They related to each other with such intensity it looked like a kind of desperation. A loose strand of blonde hair required frequent adjustment as one of the women nodded so keenly at what the other was saying that she had to keep tucking it behind her ear. Her eyes were open wide and seemed to act as receptors to the ideas that her friend shared.

From behind her a young child's voice rose over the hissing of the coffee machine and constant chatter of those around. The sound of something being repeatedly beaten upon a table caused Zoë and others to glance in the direction from which the noise came. A small boy with closely shaven brown hair and silver framed round glasses was kneeling on his chair and bashing a plastic toy up and down repeatedly.

'If you don't sit down nicely and eat your sandwich, nanny is going to put you in a baby chair.' The boy stopped and held his action figure in the air whilst he regarded the agitated woman sat beside him.

'I'm not a baby!' he shouted indignantly. Slowly he picked up one of the small wholemeal squares from his plate and took a bite, bobbing his head from side to side as he chewed. His nanny raised her eyebrows at him but couldn't hide her smile as she turned back to the paper splayed out across the table in front of her.

Zoë caught sight of her mother who was outside speaking on her phone whilst trying to see past her own reflection and into the café. She spotted Zoë and rippled her fingers in her usual way of greeting, making Zoë smile.

'Hello my sweetheart.' Zoë rose to hug her mum and was immediately hit by the familiar smell of her perfume. For a moment she didn't think she was going to be able to reply as a sudden lump had formed in her throat. Luckily by the time her mum had released her from her embrace she had managed to swallow it down.

'Hi Mum, sorry I didn't give you much notice, I hope I haven't messed up your day.

'Don't be silly, angel, how could you possibly mess up my day? I was surprised though, I thought you weren't coming back from London until tomorrow,' she unfurled the long, delicate, plum scarf from around her neck and settled herself into the chair.

'I decided to skip the second show; the first one gave me plenty of ideas. You look lovely by the way. That colour is beautiful and really suits you.' Stephanie beamed at her daughter revealing her slightly protruding white, front teeth.

'The timing was perfect actually as I was already coming into the city to take a look in my favourite book shop.' She tapped the hessian bag now sat by her feet. Zoë peered over to see several hardbacks stacked in a neat pile. 'I still love our little library, but there's nothing like having your own book, you can't beat that new-book smell.'

One of the waitresses caught Zoë's eye and approached holding a menu which she placed down on the oval table between them. Zoë ordered a sparkling water for herself and an orange juice for her mother as they scanned the small chalk board that had the specials for that day written in ornate, sage- green chalk. It matched the colour of the logo printed on the front of the premises and on the staff's aprons.

'Super-green spinach soup topped with toasted seeds and a side of rustic bread.' Stephanie read aloud from the board. 'Now that does sound ridiculously healthy, what do you think, should we go for that and then have a ridiculously unhealthy cake for dessert?' She raised her eyes to her daughter's face and in that moment suddenly noticed the discolouration around her eye. Of course she had known that her mother would notice it, but now she had and Zoë had seen the look of concern in her eyes, it felt as if a layer of her resolve was starting to peel away. She put her hand up to her cheek.

'Zoë...?' she almost whispered. The waitress was back holding her pad and looking expectantly between the two of them.

'Two soups, please.' Zoë smiled up at the girl stood beside whose short, blonde ponytail shook as she nodded in response to the order.

It was if her earlier disclosure to the perceptive man she had met that morning, had begun to create a weakness in her resolution. She could feel herself slipping, conscious of the fact that if she gave in and spoke those words to her mother, they could never be taken back. She caught herself just in time as the consequences of disclosing her ugly secret pushed to the front of her mind. The questions that would ensue would just drag it all back to the surface. There would be a need for justice from those who loved and wanted to protect her which could only result in more damage. The boutique would be known locally as, *the shop where the woman was raped.* She couldn't risk that. Everything that she and her parents had worked so hard for would be tainted. She had to stay in control, so again the lie that now sounded believable to her own ears slipped from her lips. She watched as her mother's eyebrows knitted together in concern as she told her about her trip on the cobbles.

'I know that you hate me saying so, but I still think that you're doing too much. Your father and I can't help but worry about all this extra pressure that you're putting on yourself. You look so tired – and you've lost weight.' Stephanie had felt shocked to feel the slightness of her daughter's body when they had hugged. It was if she had lost her softness, she felt all angular and rigid.

'Things have changed Mum! It's not enough to give out a few leaflets, fling open the doors and hope for the best.' Zoë knew immediately that in her irritation she had been unfair and a little cruel and felt instantly remorseful. Stephanie dropped her gaze down to the remnants of the orange juice in her glass; a wounded expression contorted her usual jovial face. Moving her tall glass to one side, Zoë reached across and grabbed her mum's hand.

'I'm sorry Mum, I didn't mean that. I know how much work you put into the boutique. It should all calm down soon as most of the hard work has been done for now.' Stephanie squeezed her hand back and gave her a weak smile.

'You always were a clumsy oaf,' she said with a look of resignation.

Their table jutted suddenly to the side almost sending their glasses over as the little boy with the plastic toy came crashing into it. He looked a little startled as he tried to kick off the strap of Zoë's bag that was twisted around his ankle.

'Oh, hold on, let me help you there,' Zoë stooped to free the little boy's foot and in doing so noticed his bright socks. 'There you are, you're free – I absolutely love your orange socks, by the way.' The boy looked up at her, his large brown eyes magnified further by his tiny metal framed glasses. His expression was unreadable to her as he continued to regard Zoë with his unfaltering gaze.

'Jenson, get back here now and finish your sandwich. You're not going tramlining until it has all gone,' she raised her eyebrows quickly and mouthed the word sorry at Zoë. She smiled back, feeling relieved that the moment had broken some of the tension that had built up between her mother and her.

Turning back to face her, she found her mother watching her and Zoë knew that she could sense her unrest. She would have to work hard now to squash her mother's building concern.

Their soups arrived and they began to eat in an uncomfortable silence that was unfamiliar to them both. Stephanie always had something to say even if Zoë just sat listening.

'Gage has told me that he wants to start a family, but I don't think I'm ready.' Her mother laid the crusty bread that she had broken off back on to her side plate and wiped her mouth on a white napkin.

'I knew that there was something worrying you. Is it causing problems between the two of you?'

'Yes. He seems to have taken it really personally that I don't want to yet. Things have become a little strained, if I'm being honest.' Stephanie nodded her head in understanding and her expression changed to one of acquainted grief as she began to reminisce.

'After the attack and I realised that I wouldn't be able to have any more children, your dad and I went through a very rough period. I didn't actually think that we were going to be able to work it out at one point, we very nearly split up. It was a horrible time for us both.' She took another spoonful of her soup. 'But I think there was so much else going on underneath that, it was easier just to blame it on that one thing.'

Zoë recalled the night when she was six years old and her mother hadn't come home at the expected time from the boutique.

Her mother had asked Ed to collect Zoë from school on this particular afternoon. She thought it would be good for Zoë and her father to have as much time together before the baby was born and had got an extra member of staff in to help her with the stocktake. She had closed the boutique an hour early and was going to deposit the takings in the bank before it closed, as she usually did. In her preoccupation with the stocktake and change in the usual routine, she had completely forgotten about the bag of money sat under the counter, until she went to leave a couple of hours later.

Zoë and her father had spent a lovely afternoon together. Walking home from school, they had stopped off at the corner shop where Zoë had picked out sweets for them all and placed them in individual white paper bags. As they walked the remaining distance home it was almost dark and Zoë could just make out the streams of white that plumed from her father's mouth as they chatted in the cold January air.

When she had got home she went straight up to her bedroom to collect her favourite gel pens, and then sat decorating each paper bag while her father began peeling the potatoes for tea. She had completed her mother and father's bags when she noticed her dad pick up the receiver on the phone. He had a concerned look on his face and kept checking the time on his watch and the clock on the kitchen wall as if one or both were not telling the correct time. She felt a sickly feeling in her tummy and the sweetness escaping from the paper bags suddenly smelt cloying rather than pleasant.

When the telephone eventually rang soon after, her father snatched up the receiver and turned his back on Zoë as he spoke quietly but urgently into the mouthpiece. After a short conversation, he turned back to face her and she was struck to see that his cheeks were white instead of their usual pink. Speaking in a higher pitch than usual, he quickly lifted her up from the chair, knocking some of her gel pens to the floor as he did so.

The rest of the night was a little hazy to Zoë, but she remembered having to go round to their neighbour's house and the kind old lady making her sausages and beans that didn't taste like they did at home. The small brown dog kept jumping up at her thighs as she sat at the table in the kitchen trying to swallow down her food like a good girl. The smell of the dog and the unfamiliar house made her stomach set as though it were full of jelly. Her neighbour's kind face seemed to swim in front of her as she tried to hold back the welled tears in her eyes.

'You have never really told me what happened, Mum,' Zoë said as she pushed her half eaten bowl of soup to one side. As if on cue, the waitress came over and cleared their table. As she deftly balanced the plates on her arm, Stephanie asked for two black Americanos. The waitress nodded and smiled briefly before whisking the items away. Zoë waited while her mother seemed to consider what she was going to say, understanding the discomfort she would be feeling in having to recall something so deeply painful. Just as she was about take back her question, her mother sighed deeply and absently adjusted the bangles on her wrist.

'I've been over that afternoon so many times. How all of our lives would have been so different if I'd remembered to go to the bank earlier. Or if I'd just taken a risk and left the takings in the boutique until the morning like I'd thought about doing.'

Zoë stirred a brown sugar cube into the black coffee that had swiftly arrived as she listened to her mother recall the events of the night that stood out in her own memory like a glowing beacon.

When she had realised her mistake, a little after the closing time at the bank, Stephanie had left the boutique in the darkness of the January late afternoon. She had felt tired and her ankles were swollen from being on her feet all day. The baby had been giving small kicks that made her tummy jolt out and she was keen to get home and show Zoë. She had felt anxious that the pregnancy would unsettle Zoë and so had made a careful effort to include her in everything she could to prepare her for the arrival of her new baby brother or sister.

She had dropped her guard. After locking the front door, she had placed the canvas money bag in a plastic bag, planning to stop off at the bank in the morning. On reflection she still didn't really know why she chose to do this, other than the feeling of safety in knowing where it was.

Feeling secure in her own territory, she never gave a thought to the three adolescents that were smoking in the doorway opposite a few metres down. As she pulled the stiff side door closed, she had to put down the weighted carrier bag to pull the door to her and lock it securely. The kicks from within started up again and she felt an overwhelming surge of happiness. She imagined that her elation had placed itself on a surfing board and was riding the waves of her hormones, travelling around her body to reach every part of her.

The force of the sudden violent push that she felt between her shoulder blades took the breath from her lungs and sent her tumbling forwards straight on to her protruding stomach. She rolled over and curled into the foetal position wrapping her arms around her unborn baby. From behind her she heard some scuffling and the sound of heavy breathing, then footsteps running away. Before she had the chance to process what had happened, she felt a sharp kick to the side of her stomach, and then a singular pair of footsteps fading as they grew in distance from her.

Using the wall to support herself, she was slowly able to stand. She was trembling and her shaking legs could barely hold her body weight. Walking her hands along the wall she managed tiny steps that edged her slowly on to the main pathway. In her small criss-cross bag that was still wrapped round her body, she grappled for her car keys, all her thoughts were of getting back home. Feeling the metal key ring, she managed to hook them out before a sudden vice like sensation gripped her waist and caused her to scream out. The moments that followed held little memory for Stephanie. People seemed to approach from nowhere and were suddenly by her side – unfamiliar bodies lifting and supporting her on both sides. Voices that drifted in and out of her conscience as one phrase played over and over in her mind. *Please let my baby live!* But even as it echoed round her mind she could feel the warm release of blood as it ran down the inside of her trouser leg, like an unstoppable torrent of rain from a broken gutter.

A placental abruption is what the doctor had told them. After having been rushed to hospital in an ambulance, she was temporarily unburdened from the horror that was unfolding as the general anaesthetic blanketed her in its oblivion. Yet once she had learned this devastating fact another was to follow. There had been too much damage and an emergency hysterectomy had had to be carried out. Stephanie had required a blood transfusion and was lucky to be alive.

The unbearable weeks that followed were crammed full of unspoken words and a heavy sense of emptiness. The hollowness in her pelvis felt more profound with each new day. Grey clouds stuck resolutely together refusing to let even a glimmer of sunlight through. These long days stretched into sleepless nights and Stephanie found herself sleeping in a pattern that mimicked a new born. The cruel irony of this taunted her further, dredging up feelings of rage that she had no idea of how to release.

Although Zoë had known about the loss of the baby and the resulting hysterectomy, she had not known about how violent
the attack had been, until now. As a child she remembered hearing the word 'mugging' being used a lot but couldn't really put a
meaning to the word. Of course, she had been shielded from the
true events of that night as her parents had obviously not
wanted to scare their six year old daughter. As fate would have
it, the only daughter they would have.

'Why have we not spoken about this before?' the question had
left Zoë's lips before she could disguise the hurt in her voice.

'Oh darling, it was a time I needed to draw a line under to be
able to function again. The pain of losing our baby and the realisation that the chance to have another had been stolen from
me was unbearable,' she looked across at her daughter's crestfallen expression and reached across for her hand.

'I realised that I had to get past the all the anger, it was destroy-
ing Ed and I. I blamed him you see, for not fighting to save me
from having the hysterectomy. I know that doesn't make sense,
but I felt like all control had been taken from me that night and
he should have been the one to stand up for me.

'And then there was my gorgeous little girl who needed her
mum back,' her whole face softened as the image of Zoë aged six
and dressed in a tartan pinafore ran across her mind. 'I didn't
want to lose any more precious time with you, so I pushed it all
down as far as I could and it was you that helped me do that.'

There was a bustle at the entrance to the café as a family of five
stood looking about for a vacant table and all at once the energy
in the room changed, chairs were scraped back and people were
negotiating their way to the exit or to pay at the till. The clatter
of coins hitting the saucer that was placed on the side for tips
broke into Zoë's thoughts and she looked up to see her mum
looking at her expectantly.

'Are you ok, darling? I said should we go for a wander?'

They began walking the short distance to where Stephanie had parked her car. It was busy and the street opposite where the market stood was full of people of all ages enjoying the end of the Easter break. Zoë wondered fleetingly how things were in the boutique and knew that she would have to call Amber later to make sure everything was all right.

A flight of pigeons rose up in a sudden flutter of activity trying to avoid a small boy who had run shouting into their path. He paused in the now vacant spot and looked up in wonder at the flapping of the hovering birds above him. The smile that played on his lips gave away his satisfaction at this small act of empowerment before his grandmother grabbed his hand and pulled him back on their intended path. He stumbled along the cobbled road turning back every few moments to watch as the pigeons once again settled back to pecking the crumbs left by passers-by. Zoë and Stephanie parted to side-step a milk-shake that had been dropped and left to dry in the warm sunshine. The pink foam had run into the creases of the cobbles and several wasps attracted by the milky sweetness, were hovering, swaying from side to side above the sticky mess.

This new information that she had learned from her mother only seemed to confirm to Zoë that she was right to stay silent about her own attack. She still found it hard to even form the word rape in her mind, wanting to distance herself from the very thought of it. Hadn't her mum found it easier to get on with her life once she'd buried the trauma? That's what she'd said.

She had recognised a similarity in their attacks; Stephanie had not seen the danger in the youths that waited in the alleyway and had felt safe in her own territory. Zoë had felt that also and had been too trusting of the stranger that turned up on her doorstep. She should have locked the door behind her before going to retrieve the bag he had left behind. What a price they had both paid for being too credulous in the goodness of others. She felt so angry with herself and saw that her mother had felt the same way too. But her mother had got past it all and that had given her a renewed hope that she could do the same.

They arrived at her mother's car and Stephanie raised the boot to put away her neat bag of books.

'Just talk to Gage tonight, sweetheart. Don't let things fester, you'll both feel better for getting things out in the open.' She pulled Zoë to her and rubbed her back as they embraced. 'And please make sure that you look after yourself, I wasn't exaggerating when I said that you'd lost weight.'

'I promise, Mum.' Zoë smiled back at her to try and alleviate some of the concern that was telling on her face. They parted with a kiss and Zoë walked back to her car.

Swinging the van into a space just down from their house, Gage noticed that Zoë's car was parked in her usual spot. He hadn't been expecting her home until later and had planned to cook for them both.

The day had passed slowly but together, he and Thom had been able to complete the small jobs that needed attention before the gas engineers arrived to begin their part in the renovation. His mind had felt foggy and he'd been sluggish and unmotivated in his work, the effects of the alcohol had definitely had a negative impact on his day. Thoughts of the woman with the light mahogany skin and full red lips kept resurfacing in his mind. Why had he reacted to her the way he had? Zoë's reticence at having his baby had made him feel insecure and overnight it was like he'd turned into the stereotypical male who'd had his ego dented. He felt ashamed of himself and resolved to make things right with Zoë again.

The bath water was beginning to cool around her causing goose bumps to appear on her arms that were placed at the sides of the bath. She hadn't wanted to move from the sanctuary of it, but on hearing Gage return she had pushed herself up and reached for the towel hanging over the basin. As she did so, she glanced at herself in the long mirror opposite; her mother was right, she had lost weight. In all the excitement of getting new suppliers for the boutique, she had skipped a few meals here and there, but this last week had completely wiped her appetite. Eating was supposed to be pleasurable, but she felt pleasure in nothing at the moment, least of all eating. Her stomach felt in a constant state of saturation, her only need for food was to provide the energy she required to get through each day.

As she stepped out into the hall Gage appeared at the top of the stairs holding a half-eaten chocolate biscuit in his mouth and a heavy looking box in his arms. Zoë felt a surge of affection spread through her at the sight of him. He grinned at her showing his teeth holding the biscuit in place, then turned and quickly placed the box inside their bedroom door. She followed him in securing her towel around herself tightly. The feeling of the sanitary pad in place gave her a ridiculous sense of gratitude, there were be no need for excuses tonight. In the early months of their relationship her period had been no barrier to their sex life, but now they lived together there had been an unspoken agreement that it would be a time to abstain from sex. Making excuses for at least a further week after this though was going to be difficult, but apart from keeping him safe from any potential risk of infection, she couldn't bear the thought of being touched. She had no idea how long this feeling would last – would she ever feel desire in the way she had before?

Gage pushed the other half of the biscuit into his mouth and held out his hand to Zoë.

'You're back nice and early. How did it go?' He pulled her down to sit next to him on the bed and placed his arm around her.

'It was good, I really enjoyed the show. Spent some time with Clarissa afterwards as well and we compared notes on what we had seen. I left early though, didn't do the usual Oxford Street scan.' She neglected to say that she had, in fact, come home last night. There would be no point, it would only provoke questions. He didn't need to know.

'What about you? A little bird told me that you and Thom were out on the town.'

'Would that little bird have long legs and wavy brown hair, by any chance? Gage smiled playfully at her.

'Don't worry – you weren't the main topic of conversation.'

'No?'

'No, Theo was. She seems to really like him. What did you make of him?'

Gage vaguely recalled shaking hands with a tall skinny guy, but he hadn't really taken much notice, the drink had blurred his senses by then and he had been eager to get home and away from the woman inside. He'd been worried that he'd given off the wrong signals and that she would come and try to find him.

'Yeah, he seemed all right. I only saw him briefly just before I left to come home. Anyway, that's enough about Amber and Theo...I missed you,' he turned his body to face her and kissed her gently on the lips. She returned the kiss briefly before getting up to stand.

'I'll get dressed and put some dinner on, is pasta OK with you?'

'Yeah, that will be good. I'll grab a shower then.' Again, he couldn't help feeling slightly rebuffed, it was like she couldn't stand being close to him.

A while later they sat opposite one another at the garden table in the fading light of the sunshine. The bulbs that Zoë had planted when they had first moved in had surfaced again and stood out in a shock of red and yellow amongst the rest of the somewhat unkempt greenery of the garden. A blue tit caught Zoë's eye as it fluttered along the side wall, hopping in and out of the branches of the cherry blossom causing the delicate flowers to quiver slightly before settling back into position.

Gage subtly observed Zoë as she slowly pushed the odd twirl of pasta into her mouth. Her skin had a sallow quality to it and her eyes were clouded as if the sclera was covered by a fine milky film. The grey cotton top she wore hung loosely over one of her shoulders, exposing her clavicle; the smoothness of her skin stretched over the tusk-like bone.

Suddenly she looked at him as if woken rudely from a day-dream.

'You do know that there's nothing I'd like more, than to have a baby with you, don't you?' She held her fork loosely, balanced on the edge of her bowl and didn't seem to notice as a bead of sauce dripped on to the glass table below. There was an urgent tone to her voice, almost as if she were pleading with him and Gage couldn't help feeling a little unnerved. It was almost as if she wanted to say something, but couldn't find the words. A thought crossed his mind; what if she couldn't have children and had known this all along? That would explain the way that she had reacted to his admittedly rash declaration at Amber's party and her subsequent introversion.

'Is there something that you're not telling me, Zo?' He saw just the slightest flinch, but she recovered herself quickly.

'No, of course not, don't be silly.' She hooked her foot around his ankle beneath the table and did the smile that didn't quite reach her eyes. He had noticed that it had returned again re-cently. Having seemed less anxious about the business during the past month, he was concerned that perhaps the stress of managing the boutique had reinstated itself. Had he missed something? He thought back over the last couple of weeks. She had been full of enthusiasm and energy as she'd stocked the boutique with the new clothes range she'd raved about. He'd heard her talking excitedly on the phone to the new contacts she'd made and seemed confident that the boutique was heading in the direction she wanted.

But then she'd had the fall on the afternoon before the party, thinking about it now, this was when he'd first noticed her change of mood. He'd put it all down to their differing views on starting a family, but maybe he had overlooked something? His phone rang breaking his chain of thought and he saw his sister's name flash up on the screen.

'Sorry, I won't be long, it's Meg, she said she'd ring to finalise the details of Mum's birthday,' he stepped away and walked further down the garden.

As Gage was distracted by the call, Zoë picked up their bowls and took them into the kitchen. The acidity of the tomato sauce had stung the inside of her mouth where she had been absent-mindedly biting the soft, pulpy lining and it now felt swollen and tender. She scooped the remains of her bowl into the bin and began washing up, grateful for the opportunity to remove herself from the tense atmosphere that had settled between the two of them outside. She needed to focus and keep her emotions together, but this was proving to be utterly exhausting when all she wanted to do was to hide away from the world, until she was certain that she hadn't been infected by him. The fear had not once left her and the uncertainty that would follow in the days to come, she knew, was only going to test her further.

Chapter 9

A swift breeze that held the early morning coolness lifted Zoë's hair, exposing one side of her neck and allowing a sliver of cold to trace down her back. In the side passage she stood with the key to the boutique held tightly between her fingers. The metallic odour rose up from her clammy hand as she drew courage to place the key into the lock, as she had done countless times before. The cobbles beneath her feet now also held a sinister twist. Her mother too must have had to fight feelings of trepidation every time she'd been positioned in the exact spot that Zoë was now. The knowledge of this helped her to push through her fear. Her mother had not allowed what had happened to her to impact on the future of the boutique and now Zoë had to show the same strength of character.

She placed the laptop on to the table then quickly punched the code into the keypad to disarm the alarm system. Shrugging her jacket from her shoulders she quietly hummed to herself aiming to create a semblance of normality. The silkiness of the lining tickled her bare arms as it slipped effortlessly down her skin. She caught it in one hand and hooked it on the old brass hook beside the door. Turning back to face the room she felt a sudden shift in the atmosphere, as if he were there in the room with her again. All her senses seemed to systematically defy her and she was flooded with the sounds and smells that she now associated with him. She took slow shallow breaths and tried to force his presence out of her mind. Frantically, she grasped for memories to comfort herself: being sat at the table with her parents and munching on digestive biscuits as they talked business - things that did not concern her, as she concentrated on staying within the lines of the picture in her colouring book. Christmases – where the coloured fairy lights that were strung around her bedroom cast a protective glow as she lay in her bed reciting festive poems in her mind.

But these were cruelly over-ridden by the recollection of his dry, rough fingers clawing at the sensitive soft skin of her inner thighs; the sound of his rabid breath in her ear and the look of complete focus and determination in his eyes as he prised her legs apart and inched his body between the space that he had claimed. This was the horrifying moment that she had realised she had no control of what was about to happen. Her nerves had fired like turbulent pistons and her heart had pumped adrenaline, devoid of purpose around her confined body. The futile pleas that she had screamed rang in her ears, intermingled with the vile and vindictive words that had shot from his contorted mouth as he'd showered her with his spit. What was she supposed to do with the impressions that he had left on her? She felt dirty and repulsed, angry with herself for making such a stupid mistake. Her inherent impatience had caused her to allow him into her life resulting in the cataclysmic consequences that now plagued her life. All her hard work in getting her boutique to the place she had set her mind on was being compromised. The years of happy memories that the boutique held for her were at risk of being expunged by that one, horrifying moment.

Hopelessness crept in, the desire to just let it all slip away. The magnitude of the lonely struggle she fought anchored her to the spot where she was standing. She found herself to be in a surrealistic, dreamy state with no urge to move or even think.

A beam of sunshine fell upon the table and the dark room was suddenly blessed with the brightness that bled into it. Her eyes were drawn to a tight knot of wood that she used to run her fingers over as a child, enjoying the coarseness as she circled her soft pads across it over and over again. In her almost hallucinatory state, she stepped forward and gently scraped her fingertips over the calloused wood once again. Somehow it soothed her, to know that something remained the same in a place that she had begun to feel slipping away from her.

The turning of a key in the front door startled her, but she was immediately comforted by the familiar sound of the tread of Amber's heels tapping against the floor.

'Zoë?' Her footsteps grew louder as she approached the back room and then she was there, stood in the doorway with a look of puzzlement on her face.

'Hey, are you all right?' Something seemed amiss to Amber, her friend although perfectly presentable, seemed less polished somehow, like a favoured ornament left under a skin of dust. Her hair lacked its usual sheen and lay flat to her face instead of having the volume and subtle waves that Zoë always maintained.

'Hi. Sorry – yes, I was just deciding what to do first this morning – I'm thinking it really should be admin though as I can't put it off any longer.' Amber's appearance in the room had once again altered the atmosphere. Zoë felt something lift and settle slightly and it gave her the impetus she needed to open the lid of her laptop.

'You didn't really say much about how the show went in your messages, was it worth going?'

'Yes, it was good, I have my eye on one designer in particular but I think we have enough going on for the time being. It's given me a bit of vision for what to concentrate on for the autumn stock though.'

'Oh please don't talk about autumn yet Zo! I'll stick the kettle on and open up then.' Receiving no reply from Zoë, who had begun tapping on her keyboard, Amber filled the kettle and left the room. She realised that now was not the time to broach the subject of how things were between her and Gage.

An hour later, after having dusted and re-stocked the rails, Amber leant against the doorframe and waited for Zoë to look up from her screen. She couldn't put her finger on what she was sensing, but she felt uneasy around Zoë this morning. They were almost like sisters, but she wasn't sure how to be around her right now, it was as if Zoë had completely detached herself from everything and Amber didn't know how to reach her.

'We've not had anyone in yet – I think I'll go mad if I have to dust another rail. How are you getting on?' She pulled a strand of hair between her fingers and inspected it as though looking for hidden answers within the curled tresses.'

'I've nearly finished. If it doesn't pick up we could have a move round of the stock on the side wall ready for tomorrow's delivery, and you can also tell me exactly what happened on your date with Theo.' Amber pulled her hair back from her face with both hands and held them there as if to frame the look of exhilaration that had settled since hearing the sound of his name.

'I thought you'd never ask! Ah Zo, I really like him. I've been on a high ever since Wednesday night. The conversation flowed all evening and there wasn't a moment where I felt awkward or anything. He's also really into sport, running in particular, so that's a bonus. Do you remember him from the night of my party – tall, skinny, blondish short hair?'

'I don't think so, no, sorry, that night is a bit of a blur to be honest, what with feeling rough and everything.' Zoë began picking up the pile of papers that were placed on the table and started pushing them somewhat haphazardly into the concertinaed file at her side. Amber again noted the sudden shift in Zoë's mood.

'Look, just tell me to mind my own business if you want, but is everything all right, Zoë? You seem really quiet and distracted.' Zoë sighed and felt the irritation that she wanted to hide envelope her like an itchy woollen jumper. More questions required more excuses, she felt so tired of it all, but realised that she needed to get Amber off her back. She should have realised that she couldn't conceal her moods from her.

'I've not been sleeping very well. Gage and I are going through a bit of a funny patch, it's nothing serious and we'll sort it out in time, but on top of trying to keep things going here, it's pulling me down a little. Perhaps mum and dad are right, maybe I should take some time off soon?'

'Yes, definitely. It would do you the world of good to get away for a while, you've got to put yourself first for once – otherwise you'll make yourself ill. You know I'm here if you need anything.' She crossed the room and pulled Zoë into a light hug before stepping back to inspect her. 'Look at you – you're like a battered sparrow.' Amber noticed a cluster of bruises on her upper arm that looked unsightly on her otherwise flawless skin.

'Those bruises... how did you get them?' Zoë seemed to flinch and averted her eyes from Amber's gaze.

'It must have been from when I tripped outside. I had my arms full carrying folders and they must have poked into me as I fell, although I always seem to be knocking myself at one time or another in here.' That was two lies in as many minutes that she had told her friend and she was afraid that her body language was betraying her, exposing glimpses of hidden truths. Amber had no time to question her further though as, to Zoë's relief, the sound of the front door opening diffused the moment and she returned to the front of the boutique.

After attending to customers for most of the morning, Amber took advantage of a slower spell and headed out to get some lunch. Zoë was not left alone for long though as three girls brashly entered the shop, pushing the door open wide as they crashed through. The girl in front held a phone to her ear and spoke with obvious irritation to the person at the end of the line. She was quite tall and of heavy build. Her leggings wrinkled at the back of her knees distorting the double white stripe that ran along the outsides of the fabric and making it bulge out slightly. Her thick, red t-shirt rested on her high waistband just covering her rounded stomach. The tips of her hair were blonde and in stark contrast to the chestnut brown of the rest of her head. It looked as though it had been dipped in honey and lay in long straight points down her back. She pulled at folded garments on the table and spoke somewhat disrespectfully to the person on the other end of her mobile. Zoë suspected that it could be the girl's mother from what she had gathered from the tone of the conversation.

The girls that accompanied her were similar looking and Zoë wondered if they were sisters or possibly cousins, they too pulled carelessly at the clothing hung on the rails. She waited a moment to see if any of them would make eye contact with her, but they seemed oblivious to her presence and continued in their mission.

'Hello, feel free to look around and if you need help with anything, please just ask,' Zoë smiled amiably before turning away. One of the girls who wore a cropped pink hoodie that exposed her taut stomach looked at her and nodded before bending to retrieve a delicate blouse that had slipped from its hanger and fallen to the floor. Trying not to show her irritation she returned to her desk as the thought occurred to her that she was pleased her staff understood the importance of keeping the boutique so clean. Members of the public could be so careless when browsing through her stock, but at least the floor and rails were usually free of dirt and dust. Having to sell soiled items at a reduced cost did grate on Zoë a little, but it was one of the downfalls of retail that she had to put up with. All she could do to minimise this occurring was to ensure that the rails were not overloaded and keep the area as clean as possible. On wet days when muddy footsteps and pushchair trails zig-zagged around the shiny wooden flooring Zoë would keep a mop close at hand.

All three girls were now standing at the desk inspecting the jewellery on the stand and the girl with the honey dipped hair had finished her phone call and was pushing a ring on to her finger.

'I like this one. Isla, what do you think – should I get this one or the earrings from the last place?' she pushed the ring, which showed some resistance, further down her reddening finger.

'I really like that, it's different, and the feathers are really pretty.'

'Here, you try it on, Sophie's fingers are more your size.' She passed the ring to her friend.

'You can actually adjust that one – where the feathers meet it can be pulled open to make it bigger or pushed together to tighten it. It's also silver plated.' The girls all lifted their eyes to look at her as if only just noticing her presence for the first time. Up close, Zoë could see that the girl in the red t-shirt had a heart shaped face that was carefully made up. Luminescent streaks of pink highlighter had been applied to the sides of her cheeks and down the ridge of her aquiline nose and her eyelids seemed to droop under the weight of thick false lashes giving her a doe-eyed look.

'Does it come with a box? It's for my sister's birthday and I want it to look nice.'

'Unfortunately it doesn't but I can wrap it in tissue and put it in one of my jewellery bags for you.' Zoë opened the drawer to the desk and showed the girl a silver organza gift bag that she scrutinised for a moment.

'Yeah OK, I'll take it, please.'

Moments later after Zoë had placed the gift into one of her smaller brown boutique bags, the girls left in the same cloud of solipsism that they had entered with as they discussed where to go and eat lunch. Zoë couldn't remember ever showing that kind of confidence and self-assurance at their age, especially around those older than her to whom she had always treated with an air of reverence. Feeling suddenly old, she refolded the pastel coloured tops that had been strewn across the table and stacked them neatly back into their previous positions. Merchandising was one of her favourite aspects of the job, she found it quite therapeutic and rewarding especially when customers purchased items that she had put together.

Feeling thirsty, Zoë made her way towards the back room to get her bottle of water but on reaching the doorway she suddenly stopped as if she had stepped into a spider's sticky web. Anger gripped her again as she recognised the feeling that overwhelmed her, stopping her from acting normally in her own territory. She turned and looked towards the front door which had been left ajar from when the girls had exited moments earlier. As she made her way to the front of the boutique she concentrated on the people that swept past the window in the early afternoon sunshine. She pulled the door open wide and listened to the usual sounds that filled the narrow street at that time. The tables were full in the coffee shop where people were sitting eating baguettes and sipping steaming drinks from oversized cups. Everything was normal and she reasoned with herself that she was safe. She pushed away the feeling of vulnerability and returned to the back. As she reached for the bottle that sat on the table beside her laptop she felt a small moment of victory; she had done it, as distressing as the morning had begun, she had overcome all the negative thoughts that had threatened to pull her under the high tide of emotion that she was tentatively negotiating.

Amber returned carrying two white paper bags and a large bottle of fresh orange juice.

'It's absolutely gorgeous out there now and finally the sun seems to have some heat in it. Here, I bought you a slice of millionaire's shortbread, you look like you could do with it,' she looked at Zoë with a questioning expression. 'Have you been eating properly? I know what you're like when you're on a mission.'

'OK, OK, I can take a hint,' Zoë took the paper bag from her friend and peered in at the marbled topped chocolate square. 'You go and eat your lunch first though – I don't want you going all grumpy on me.'

'When my stomach calls, it has to be listened to Zo, it's not my fault,' she beamed as she carried her hot baguette through to the back, the smell of melted cheese and roasted vegetables trailed after her.

A little later, after she and Amber had spent time condensing the stock on the side wall to accommodate the new arrivals expected the next day; her father appeared in the doorway.

'Hi Dad, it's nice to see you!' she leant in and kissed his smooth cheek. As ever he was immaculately presented, he was dressed in a short sleeved, blue checked shirt which was neatly tucked into his dark trousers. 'You didn't say that you'd be popping in.'

'I was just passing, I've just been to the music shop actually, one of my guitar strings broke last night. It wouldn't surprise me if one of the cats had been playing around with it, they're into absolutely everything. It will be a relief when they can finally go out and let off some steam in the garden.' He smiled good naturedly and the wrinkles that formed around his eyes only accentuated his handsome face further. He bobbed his head to one side to look past Zoë, 'Hello, Amber.'

'Hi, Mr S, can I get you a cup of tea?'

'Have you got time for a quick cup, Zoë? I don't want to hinder you from your work.' The sincere look in his eyes made it impossible for Zoë to turn him down. She would really rather not have to face him at the moment; he was the one person who would make it very difficult for her to be able to disguise the turmoil that she was experiencing. But he was there and it would only seem questionable if she said no, especially as she knew that her mother would have told him about the conversation that they'd had the day before.

'Yes, sure – we've just finished here anyway. It's OK, Amber I'll make it. Come through, Dad.'

As she filled the kettle with water, Ed looked about the small room.

'It could do with a lick of paint in here. I could do it for you if you like? I enjoy painting these days – I find that it can be quite relaxing now that I have more time on my hands.' He stopped surveying the area around him and let his gaze drop to Zoë's face. He realised Steph had not been exaggerating when she had reported to him that Zoë looked tired and strained. They stood looking at each other divided by the large table and neither spoke for a while.

The noise of the kettle rose as it neared boiling point and Zoë busied herself with preparing the tea. Awkward silences were not something that either of them was used to in their relationship. Ed was not someone who wittered unnecessarily and any silences between them were normally comfortable. Zoë had the feeling that in that moment the less she said the better so as not to unconsciously expose any of her anxieties. But it actually felt like it was having the opposite effect. The atmosphere between them felt uncomfortable and her father seemed to be watching her carefully.

Ed had been concerned about his daughter for some time. She seemed unable to unburden herself of problems concerning the boutique and he feared that he had made the wrong decision in passing the business on to her, rather than selling it on. She certainly had the head for business and had already proved this, but she didn't seem able to let things go and he wasn't sure how long that she could continue in this way.

At the time of making the decision though, Zoë had been shocked that the idea of selling was even an option and had begged him to let her take over. But then, the place didn't hold quite the same kind of memories for her as they did for him. It had never felt the same after what had happened to Stephanie.

In recent weeks though he had felt some relief as Zoë had seemed much more satisfied with what she had accomplished and had begun to return to her former character. She had rung him only weeks ago sounding elated at the response to the new stock that she had sourced for the boutique. The call had left him feeling positive and hopeful that things were beginning to settle down. But looking at her now, he felt his concern return. She looked absolutely drained and her usually striking pale, blue eyes lacked any kind of animation or sparkle.

'You would say if things were getting too much here, wouldn't you, my love? It wouldn't be seen as any kind of weakness on your part.' He smiled tentatively at her, unsure of how she would respond to his question, knowing that she hated to acknowledge defeat of any kind. But she said nothing and looked almost to be holding her breath.

The kindness in her father's tone pierced through her stomach and for a moment she could only hold herself completely still so as not to fall apart right there in front of him. If she had to let him think that it was the boutique that was causing her anguish, then that was what she would do. She recognised the irony that now, the one thing that was not worrying her, was the success of the boutique. Her months of research and effort were paying off.

'Give me a few weeks, Dad. I admit that I've been overdoing things and yes, I probably should take some time off, but I just need a few more weeks.' Ed understood that this was the offering of an olive branch from Zoë and he took it gratefully. He knew that pushing her any further on the matter now would not help and that the best solution would be to let her digest what he had said. There had been numerous situations where he had learned this about his daughter, but one occasion stuck in his memory.

They had been walking in a wood on the outskirts of the city. The hidden sky was grey and even though it could only have been early afternoon, the light was low. Zoë had been about eleven years old and they had been collecting conkers that had fallen to the damp ground after the heavy rain the night before. Zoë had been absorbed in the task of searching for the prickly capsules that were buried beneath the soggy leaves. Ed had noticed that she had been withdrawn since returning home from school the previous day. Stephanie had also raised the concern that all did not seem right with their daughter. The walk had been her idea as she was going to have to spend the day in the boutique.

After collecting a significant amount of conkers they passed a fallen tree and Ed suggested that they sat for a while. Zoë placed herself down next to her father and began picking at the shell of one of the tightly closed capsules. When the waxy conker was exposed she held it up and inspected it from different angles. They both agreed that it was a beautiful thing and Zoë slipped it into her pocket. Her father suggested that they should be getting home as he hadn't wanted her to get too cold, but she resisted and suddenly began weeping. Ed remembered feeling absolutely terrified at the prospect of something awful having happened and pressed her gently to tell him what the matter was. After a while she explained that she had been rehearsing for a talent contest that was being held at her school. Her best friend, Beth was not interested in pop music or dancing and so she had entered the contest with another girl in her class. This girl, Rebecca, had not always been kind to Beth and in the past, had taunted her for her choice of clothing and hairstyle. Obviously Beth had felt hurt by the fact that Zoë was spending so much time with Rebecca and in a heated argument had called Zoë a traitor and vowed to never speak to her again. After her tears had subsided Zoë told her father that she had been a bad friend and that she was going to drop out of the contest, even though the dancing made her feel like nothing she'd ever felt before. Ed had tried to offer advice, but ultimately he realised that Zoë had already figured it out for herself and that he was only aware of what had happened because she had sorted it all out in her head and made her decision.

As he took the mug of tea that Zoë held out to him he kissed her lightly on the top of her forehead.

'Please be careful on those cobbles, you're not the first person to come a cropper out there and you certainly won't be the last, but just slow down a bit, hey?' He was pleased to see that she responded with a smile and in that moment he felt that he had got through to her.

After leaving the boutique an hour earlier than was usual, Zoë arrived home to an empty house. Gage had messaged her before she left to say that he would be working late and now as she stood in the kitchen Zoë felt mildly agitated and restless. Throwing down the post she held in her hands, she ran up to the bedroom and quickly changed into her running gear. She had to keep busy to chase away the obsessive thoughts that threatened to pull her under the film of normality that she had established for herself. The familiar day to day activities gave her a sense of security that enabled her to stay buoyant, they bridged the gap that was between the now and after. Once she had confirmation that her body was clear, things would begin to return to normal, she was certain of it.

She kept her pace steady, enjoying the feeling of the air filling her lungs and the rhythmic thudding of her steps on the path below. Thoughts flowed through her mind but nothing that could weigh her down. She ran past the local Chinese takeaway where a queue of people curled round in front of the lightly steamed window. Most, she noticed had their heads down as they flicked idly through their phones as they waited for their brown paper packages. She let the pavement choose her course, too impatient to have to wait to cross busy roads she just kept running and following the curves and turns of the streets. The air was heady with the sweet smell of lilacs that always took her back to her childhood.

It wasn't long before she reached a small cluster of shops that were set back a little from the busy main road. The largest of the three was still a bicycle shop as it had been for as long as she could remember. For her twelfth birthday her parents had taken her there to buy a racer bike that she had longed for. Breathing in the clean rubber smell that made Zoë feel slightly intoxicated, she carefully made her selection from the neat row of bikes in front of her. As she had pushed the pink and cream bike out to the front of the shop, she'd felt excitement in its purest form – nothing could have ruined the moment. She had loved that bike. It had given her all the independence and freedom she'd craved, she had travelled the country lanes that surrounded her home for hours with her friends, marvelling at how brilliant it was to be so far from home without the supervision of her parents.

Outside the narrow gated entrance to the park, a woman was squatting down looking into the face of an obviously distressed little girl. A lead was wound tightly round her wrist securing a small, cream, springy coated dog. Its curious black eyes followed Zoë as she shifted her body sideways to allow her to pass through without disturbing them.

The play area was hustling with children enjoying the warm early evening sunshine. Parents were sat on the benches placed around the perimeter of the brightly painted, panelled fencing that encased the enclosure, able to observe their children but also able to catch up on the events of each other's lives. The metal swings that used to stand in the exact spot where children were playing now were long gone. In their place were rubber framed baskets that toddlers sat safely nestled in as they were pushed by others whose feet sank slightly into the springy, rubber floor beneath them – a gentle reminder that the child was protected. Zoë remembered the sound of the scraping metal as the bar was stiffly pushed upwards to allow access to the scored seat below. One wet Sunday afternoon, her parents had taken her to the park to alleviate the boredom that Zoë had expressed. Dressed in her favourite mustard-coloured rain coat, she had taken one of her larger dolls and positioned her into one of the swings and had begun to happily push her to and fro. Her parents had stood to the side, deep in discussion but with eyes trained towards where Zoë was playing. Bored with just swinging her doll, she had twisted the wet metal chains round and round until they could go no further. She had let go and watched with horror as her doll slipped and began her descent into the puddle below. Without thinking, she lurched to save her from falling into the mud but as a result, she herself slipped and hit her mouth on the metal bar of the swing. Before she had realised what was happening her father had scooped her up and it was only then that she had seen the bright red blood pooling into the creases of her coat. For a moment she had felt no pain, but then was suddenly hit with the stinging and throbbing sensation in her lip. Even now if she stood in a certain light, she could see the faint crooked scar along her bottom lip.

Fatigue seemed to have crept up into her muscles as she reached the edge of the park so after slowing her pace she turned and began retracing her route back home.

Chapter 10

'Looks like it's going to be a busy one!' Aidan strode into the boutique wearing a tight, white T-shirt and tinted aviator style sunglasses. He had a drawstring gym bag slung over one of his shoulders and his damp fringe pushed back from his face. Zoë knew it would only be a matter of time before it was flopping into his eyes again and as always, she couldn't help feeling cheered at the sight of him.

'Morning, Aidan, how's it going?' she indicated to the gym bag that he had now let slip from his shoulder.

'Very well, thank you, I'm pumped up and ready for anything that the day throws at me,' he joined Zoë behind the counter, 'go on, have a feel,' Zoë dutifully squeezed the flexed, lean bicep that he had thrust before her.

'That's very impressive, Aidan,' she laughed feeling lifted by his carefree persona.

'Well I know I'm no Gage, but it's a work in progress,' he chuckled good-naturedly as he went through to the back.

Amber approached the desk holding an armful of clothing as a grave looking woman who appeared to be in her late forties, followed closely behind.

'Are you sure you wouldn't like to try any of these on? The fitting room is empty at the moment.'

'No, thank you, I'm sure they will be absolutely fine, I need to get back home,' she rummaged in her bag as she spoke and pulled out a rather battered looking brown purse which had notes and receipts escaping from the top. Zoë stepped away to give her some privacy as it was obvious that did not want any fuss or conversation. She heard Aidan filling the kettle in the back and went through to join him.

'It's that hot air balloon race today, isn't it? I saw all the traffic heading towards the park on my way in.'

'Oh yes, of course it is – it seems to come round quicker each year.'

'By the way, I actually had to stand up on the bus today, it's an absolute disgrace!' Zoë joined in with his mock dismay and agreed that it was indeed a disgrace.

'I remember the first time I saw the hot air balloons go past above our house when I was younger. It absolutely amazed me – I'd never seen anything like it before. All the different colours and patterns hanging from the sky, it seemed like there were thousands of them. The closest thing to magic that I had ever seen and I still think it's magical now,' said Zoë.

'You should put that on your bucket list: *to ride in a hot air balloon*. You'd never catch me in one though, I like my feet firmly on the ground,' he slopped hot water into three cups leaving a trail of water pooling beneath each one. Zoë tore a sheet of kitchen paper from the roll and placed it in the crook of his arm before heading back out towards the front. She couldn't stand to watch the mess he made of preparing hot drinks and knew that she would later return to the sticky mess of granules of sugar and splashed milk on the small kitchen surface.

As Aidan had predicted, the morning had been busy and now during a slower spell Zoë took a moment to fetch duplicate stock from upstairs. Away from the bustle of the boutique below she searched for the sizes she required.

Monday now seemed like a life time ago, when she had stood shaking as she'd listened to the receptionist telling her that she would have to wait two weeks for an appointment. She took a moment to recognise that she had almost got through one of those weeks, but didn't want to dwell on the fact that it was also a week to the day that he had stepped into her boutique and brought utter turmoil to her life. No amount of wishing could change what had happened, but she still found herself doing it.

Outside, the sound of raised voices interrupted her thoughts. She crossed over to the sash window and peered out at the people milling past each other in the narrow street below. Zoë pinpointed where the disturbance had come from; a bald man with a kind, round face was shouting over to someone he recognised on the opposite side. As he enthusiastically gesticulated and strained his neck in an attempt to see past the shoppers walking between them, his T-shirt rode up exposing a white belly that hung over the top of his jeans. He didn't look to be more than in his late twenties and Zoë couldn't help but to feel charmed by his hedonistic manner. Suddenly he looked up and caught her watching him. He paused for a moment, and then gave her a comical grin followed by an exaggerated wave. Feeling self-conscious she stepped back out of view before laughing to herself. In that moment, she realised that today, she had felt more like her old self and not so much like the victim she hardly recognised.

Amber turned to see Zoë coming through from the back, efficiently carrying an array of clothes in her arms. Her face looked less strained today, she noticed, and she definitely seemed more relaxed than she had done on Thursday. Amber had tried to bring up the topic of her and Gage, but Zoë had batted away her concern and swiftly changed the subject by asking questions about her date with Theo. She was pleased to see that her drive had returned after seeming stilted since her return from London.

'Here, give me the tops and trousers. You can fold the knitwear, you'll only re-do my handiwork if I do them anyway,' Amber teased Zoë.

'Ah, come on, I don't do that!' Zoë laughed. Amber tilted her head to the side and raised her eyebrows at her. 'OK, I do *sometimes*, but only *sometimes*,' she admitted sheepishly.

A woman with sleek, short blonde hair stepped into the boutique, she removed her large sunglasses and looked about, as if adjusting her eyes to the light inside. Behind her followed a younger woman with slightly darker hair which fell in loose curls around her shoulders. Zoë greeted them with a smile which they both returned, before they moved over to the wall that displayed the occasional wear. They spoke quietly to each other and Zoë left them for a while, discreetly gauging the correct time to approach. They looked as though they could possibly be mother and daughter or aunt and niece and the elder of the two had selected two dresses which she was holding up next to each other.

'Those are both from the new collection that we've introduced here, they've only been in for a week or so,' Zoë said as she hung some clothes up nearby. The woman dropped the dresses down slightly and averted her eyes to her. Zoë noticed how startlingly blue her irises were and briefly wondered if they were contact lenses.

'I bought a dress from here a few months ago and like the fact that your clothes are a bit different – different from the high street, I mean. I'm looking for a dress for my daughter's wedding,' she indicated her head towards the woman beside her, 'and I'd really like something that won't be duplicated, if you know what I mean,' her laugh had a slightly wheezy edge to it and Zoë felt instantly warmed to her.

'I know exactly what you mean,' Zoë smiled. 'You are Mother of the Bride after all. There is a jacket in a slightly darker shade that goes beautifully with this dress.'

'Yes, I noticed that, but because of my height, I didn't know if I would look lost in it.'

'I have exactly the same problem,' Zoë sympathised. 'Why don't you take a selection to try on? I know an excellent seamstress; she often alters clothing for me and charges very reasonably prices.'

Zoë spent the best part of the next hour advising and discussing options with the women. The mother finally settled on an oyster coloured dress that would be altered to fall just at the knee and the slightly darker jacket that Zoë had suggested earlier. It too would require a little alteration, but the woman couldn't thank Zoë enough for her help in finding the right outfit. The daughter had also bought a deep red halter-neck dress for her hen do. Zoë watched them leave the boutique carrying their purchases which she had wrapped in grey tissue and placed in the *Her Boutique* brown paper bags. She felt overcome with a feeling of pride and relished in the satisfaction that serving the two women had given her. This was what all her hard work had been about and she wasn't going to let anyone destroy what she had built.

'If it's OK with you, Zo, I'm just going to grab something for lunch?'

'Yes, of course it's OK, Amber.'

'Do you want anything, either of you?' she looked form Zoë to Aidan.

'Could you get me a chicken salad sandwich? I'll pay you when you get back – oh, and some plain crisps!' Aidan smiled mischievously at Amber.

'Hmmm, I've heard that one before. How about you, Zo?'

'Actually, yes, I'll have the same, please.' She grabbed a ten pound note out of her purse and thrust it at Amber who had begun to walk away but stopped suddenly just outside the door and turned her head to the sky.

'Oh look, the race has started – back in a bit,' she called over her shoulder.

In her efforts to help the mother and daughter, she had forgotten all about the balloon race. Outside she could see that many passers-by had either slowed or stopped to appraise the magnificent spectacle above them. *Her Boutique* was empty of all customers now, so Aidan and Zoë both went to stand in the doorway and watch the vividly patterned balloons as they drifted serenely across the backdrop of the azure sky. Above the exclamations and general chatter of the shoppers passing by,

Zoë could hear the gentle rumble of the burners as they propelled their heat up into the balloons. She felt a moment of envy towards the travellers who stood in their baskets looking down on them as they floated past. The experience must be so invigorating that it would be almost impossible to carry any worries along with you. As soon as the thought had come to her, she disregarded it – knowing all too well that some things weighed so heavily on the mind it seemed impossible to let them go, even for a short while.

'Not sure about that ensemble,' Aidan muttered under his breath. Zoë was momentarily confused before she realised that Aidan was no longer looking upwards, as she had been. His attention was focused on a man to their right who was wearing a stiff collared shirt with flimsy knee- length shorts and brown brogue style shoes over white towelling socks. 'That's the most exaggerated form of smart-casual that I've ever seen. I don't know if he should be playing tennis, swimming or heading in for a day at the office.' Zoë couldn't help laughing at Aidan's wit even though she felt guilty at laughing at the man's expense. She reasoned with herself that he probably wouldn't care as style didn't seem to be of importance to him and clothing was probably just a necessity. She wondered what it was that he had an interest in – everybody had to have something that gave them those flickers of joy, or what was the point?

'Trust you! There is this amazing event happening above us and you're more interested in checking out the dress sense of some poor guy,' she giggled.

'I know, but come *on*, that is something else,' he deadpanned. Zoë turned to see the object of their attention bend down to retrieve the bag that was placed on the floor between his legs. In the clearing above him, Zoë spotted a young girl who was sitting up on a man's shoulders. Her burnt orange hair was tied in short pig-tails that stuck out on either side of her head and she was squealing in delight and pointing her tiny finger up to the balloon-filled sky. Suddenly she bobbed her head down and wrapped her arms around the man's neck placing a kiss on his bearded cheek. Zoë smiled at the simple act of affection and felt a pleasant heaviness in her chest before it was replaced with the feeling of complete and utter horror.

There he stood. He wasn't looking up like most others around him, but down at his feet. For a moment Zoë couldn't move, the sounds around her were muted, it was as if her brain had lost the ability to receive all sensory input. After a moment she saw that Amanda was beside him, talking with another woman. Her face looked more severe due to her silky hair being pulled back from her face in a pony-tail. The crowd shifted and Zoë lost sight of them both. *What were they doing here? They were supposed to be on holiday!*

Almost too afraid, but needing confirmation that her mind was not playing a cruel trick on her, Zoë craned her neck to the side in an effort to see past those now obstructing her view. The face that had tormented her for the past week was now framed between the little girl's delighted face and the back of a by-stander's head; the high forehead and neat hairline exactly how she remembered them to be.

The physical effect of seeing him again was an immediate assault on her body, from the threatening burning bile in her stomach to the loss of power in her legs, but she needed to get away from him. Trying to conceal her panicked state from Aidan, she steadied herself on the window behind her and backed into the boutique.

'I'm going to do some work upstairs, Aidan.' Not waiting for a response she walked as quickly as her legs, in their weakened state would allow, through to the back room.

Out of view leant against a wall by the doorway, she tried to control the vibrations that shook her body. In her peripheral vision bright colours pulsed in time to the beating of her erratic heart. Confusion flooded her mind, *why hadn't they gone away? They were supposed to be away!*

The distant sound of Aidan's voice began to grow louder as she heard him walk through the boutique. This was followed by the soft, even voice of Amanda. 'I absolutely love them, but they're just a tiny bit too long, and I think if I had them altered it would ruin the shape.' Zoë recognised the crumpling sound of one of the boutique bags. 'I don't suppose they come in a shorter length, do they?'

'No, they don't, I'm afraid. I can show you some other styles, but not in white, unfortunately.'

'I did actually buy a few pieces last week, a blonde woman helped me choose some last minute holiday pieces – we were supposed to have flown out on Monday, but had to cancel at the last minute due to my husband being unwell.'

'That would have been Zoë, the owner. It's a shame about your holiday, how disappointing for you – well, if I could just have your receipt, I'll do a refund for you.' The familiar sound of the card terminal purred in the background as Aidan chatted amiably. 'I'm a bit miffed at missing out on this gorgeous sunshine today, it rained all day yesterday when I was off. I just hope it stays nice for this evening.' Zoë heard Aidan tear off the receipt, 'If you could just pop your name and address at the bottom, please.' It went quiet for a moment and Zoë heard the whooshing of blood in her ears.

'Yes, if only you could depend on the weather. I've booked a boat trip on the broads next weekend for my husband's birthday.'

'Oh, anywhere near Wroxham? My parents live there.'

'Yes, actually – we'll be using the boatyard at Ludham as a base.'

'We used to go there a lot when I was younger - lots of trees to get lost in. My brother and I were forever scaring our parents, we'd hide for ages!'

'That's an idea – perhaps I could lose my husband, Toby, in

there!'

Zoë barely registered their laughter, Toby – that was his name? That couldn't be right... Toby was a name for small dogs or little boys, not fitting for the savage bastard that had attacked her. It felt strange to even accept that he had a name and Zoë had never even considered it before now.

At the sound of footsteps approaching, Zoë impulsively flattened herself up against the wall. The door opened and Amber walked in carrying the requested lunch items in her arms. The smile slipped from her lips when she saw her friend. 'What the ...?' she stopped in acknowledgement of Zoë's terrified expression and brief shake of her head.

'Speaking of Toby, I'd better go - he's waiting for me outside.' After she and Aidan had said goodbye, Zoë waited to hear Amanda leave the boutique, she couldn't detect the sound of her footsteps though, so shakily, she inched herself sideways and peered around through the gap in the door. Amanda's back was almost touching the outside window as she stood rummaging in the bag placed in the crook of her arm. In the tight opening between the door and frame Zoë could hear her shallow breaths begin to quicken as she watched him appear into view. From the other side of the path, he wove his way through the still crowded area and stopped in front of his wife.

He looked different. His face held an impassive expression as if he had all the time in the world to wait for Amanda to finish whatever it was that she was doing. People brushed past him, blissfully unaware of the violent streak that bubbled below the cool exterior. Despite her instinct warning her to move away before his presence could terrorize her further, her feet remained planted to the spot. Then, with just the slightest movement of his head, he was looking straight at her. She felt as if he could sense her fear and was enjoying the power that he held, even from the position of where he was standing now. Realistically it was impossible that he could actually see her, but it didn't matter – she had again been beaten by him and now realised that this threat was never going to go away.

'Zoë . . . ,' she felt Amber touch her arm lightly, 'what's going on?' she whispered. Unable to look away until she was certain that they had gone, she gave no response until she saw them walking away and begin to merge into the bodies around them. She closed her eyes and when she re-opened them, there was somebody else positioned in the place he had been.

Very slowly, Zoë turned her body, and without speaking began climbing the steps to the stockroom. Terrified at what she was about to discover, Amber followed her up and found her stood in the centre of the room facing the window. Her small frame was trembling despite the stuffy warmth surrounding them.

'I'm so tired,' she murmured, 'I thought if I just kept it all in, that it would just go away – but it's not going away, I was wrong.' Amber gently gripped Zoë's shoulders and dipped her head to look into her unfocused eyes.

'Who was that woman, Zo?' Seconds passed in which questions flashed through Amber's mind as she watched for clues in Zoë's vacant expression. Could she be in some kind of financial trouble? Was she being blackmailed, perhaps?

'Her husband, he raped me.' Amber pulled back as if she had been slapped. Zoë remained completely still with a slight look of confusion on her face. 'He raped me here, in the boutique, exactly one week ago. And today he came back.' Without warning a violent choke erupted from her throat and then she was crying. Hot tears coursed down her cheeks as if suddenly released from a levee and then she felt the warm skin of Amber's arm pressed against her damp face as she held her in a tight embrace.

Amber waited for the sobbing to subside before she released Zoë from her hold. If the occasion had allowed, they would have both found humour in the trail of tears that had been deposited on Amber's arm and were now running down toward her elbow.

'I'm guessing that you haven't told Gage yet?' Zoë sniffed and wiped her face quickly with both hands.

'No, and I'm not planning to either.'

'Zoë, you can't possibly keep this from him, you need his support,' Amber pleaded.

'I don't know how to. It's too late now, anyway.'

'Of course it isn't, I could be there, if you like?' Zoë moved towards the window, agitation beginning to sweep over her like a heat rash.

'I can't say anything at the moment - we've got his mum's birthday lunch tomorrow, all the family are coming over.' At the thought of having to face everyone she covered her eyes, 'Oh God, I don't know how I'm going to cope.'

Amber realised that there was nothing she could say that would be of use to her friend at that moment. She was still trying to absorb the shocking news herself. How had Zoë kept this from them all? Reaching forward she tentatively took Zoë's fingers in her own, 'What can I do to help?' she had meant to sound confident and assuring but the words somehow got caught in her throat and became more beseeching. Zoë was watching the last solitary balloon drift out of view and noted sadly how empty the sky looked now.

'I really don't know,' she replied as a surge of lassitude engulfed her.

A rhythmic thudding greeted her when she returned home. Outside, Gage was repairing the fence that had been damaged during one of the winter storms. From the kitchen window she watched him work. As ever his technique was methodical, each strike of the sledgehammer was equal in deliverance and his tools lay in a neat line at his feet. A majestic bouquet of flowers dominated the small kitchen table with fiery reds and golden yellows that erupted from the delicate tissue paper that enveloped them. Their sweet fragrance was mingled with the toxic odour of paint and hung densely in the warm air accentuating Zoë's nausea further. She moved towards the back door breathing steadily, desperately trying to control the waves in her gut.

Gage turned round to pick up a wooden post on the grass behind him and in doing so, noticed Zoë, the lines between his brows softened from their knot of concentration as he smiled at her.

'You OK?' The compassion in his simple question triggered an ache deep within her. He tucked a piece of stray hair behind his ear and stepped closer to her, bringing his hand up to stroke her face. In response she tilted her head too and let her cheek rest on his palm.

'Careful, you'll be covered in green paint,' he grinned. Looking into his genial eyes she was suddenly overwhelmed with the need to tell him everything, the thought of carrying the secret a moment longer seemed impossible to bear. But she knew, those words, once uttered could never be taken back and her mind seemed too resolute on keeping them contained.

'You look tired, come and sit down. I've made a salad, thought we could have it with some tuna and rice.' She followed him into the kitchen.

'That sounds great,' she enthused, watching him dip his head into the fridge.

'Can I see the card you got for Mum?' She hung her head and pressed her eyes shut tightly together. She had meant to nip out during the afternoon to the little card shop a few doors down from the boutique. Its collection included cards made by local artists offering unique designs that could not be found anywhere else, and Zoë had offered to choose one for his mother.

'Gage, I'm so sorry, it got busy this afternoon and it just went right out of my head.' The disappointed look on his face felt like a tear to her skin.

'Right, well I don't want to leave it until the morning as I'm not sure what time Meg and Dale will be arriving – I'd better go and get one now.' As he grabbed his keys they made a scraping sound on the kitchen worktop that seemed to echo in Zoë's ears long after the front door had closed behind him.

Chapter 11

The proud daffodils dipped and raised their fluted heads as the warm breeze caught them on the edge of the river bank. In contrast, the pub inside felt dark and cool and the air was stale with smell of yesterday's food. Zoë imagined that the heavily patterned carpet that stretched through the room would be masking a plethora of stains.

A delighted shriek from Jack brought her back to the moment. The table where they were all sat was brimming with discarded wrapping paper, envelopes and cardboard. In the middle, partially obscuring Zoë's view of Rosa was the huge bouquet that Gage had bought – a symbol of his disappointment in her, she felt.

After he had returned the night before with the generic birthday card held loosely in his hand, she had again tried to apologise, but he had dismissed her saying that it didn't matter. She had been relieved that when he had finished his food he'd gone straight back outside to finish his work and she was able to scrape the remains of her food away unseen.

When she had finished her bath and gone downstairs to tell Gage that she was having an early night, he'd hardly batted an eyelid and even when she leant over to kiss him, he'd hardly moved his eyes from the television screen.

She sipped at her wine, the acidity burning her already sensitive stomach. Meg who was sat between Dale and Rosa, made exaggerated animated faces across at her son who was happily gurgling next to Gage. His chubby fists thumped excitely at the tray of his high chair knocking the chunky wooden car that Gage had made for him, on to the floor.

'I hear things are going really well in the boutique, Zoë, you must be so pleased.' Rosa had tilted her head to one side to enable herself a better view of Zoë.

'Yes, the new stock is selling very well – even better than I'd hoped actually.' Even to her ears her response sounded stilted, but she really didn't want to think about the boutique right now. The image of his face as he looked through the window yesterday was just too raw. 'Excuse me, I'm just going to nip to the toilet.'

'Oh, I'll come with you – before our food arrives.' Zoë smiled briefly while she waited for Rosa to make her way round from her seat, she tried to quell the irrational feeling of irritation that crept up her spine like a hot spike of mercury.

It was beginning to get busier and they had to weave their way through a large party of people who were waiting at the bar. Zoë was grateful for the distraction and for the fact that they were forced to walk in single file, preventing any chance of conversation.

Staring at her reflection in the garishly lit toilet, the circles beneath her eyes appeared to look even darker. However, the powder blue dress that she wore fortunately seemed to enhance her irises which she hoped, would mask her tiredness. She had taken care in applying her make-up that morning, mostly so as to avoid Gage, but also to try and prevent any further comments about her appearance – she was aware that she looked tired and didn't need reminding of that fact.

Last night she had lain awake listening to the familiar sounds of Gage moving about the house, dipping in and out of fretful sleep. Not only did she have to try and control her own emotions, but now she had the added pressure of Amber knowing. Part of her had felt relieved at first, but having loosened the grip on her control, it felt that she could come completely undone at any moment.

The toilet flushed and Rosa came out of her cubicle and stood beside Zoë to wash her hands.

'Your dress is lovely, Zoë, is it from Her Boutique?'

'Yes, it's one from last year – I got it to wear to a wedding and only wore it once. You look great – as always.' Rosa had an elegant style and Zoë couldn't recall a time when she'd ever seen her looking unkempt.

'Thank you,' she placed her tan handbag on the edge of the basin and began carefully retouching the caramel colour to her lips as Zoë needlessly adjusted the strap of her shoe.

'Zoë, I hope you don't mind me saying, but you seem awfully quiet. I know that Gage has been worried about you working too hard, and I understand that it must be tiring having the boutique to think about all the time, but you are taking care of yourself, aren't you?' Zoë couldn't risk a moment's hesitation,

'I'm fine – really, but thanks for asking, Rosa. Gage and I will probably have a holiday soon, he deserves a break too.' In her haste to dampen Rosa's concern the words had slipped from her mouth before she'd had time to think.

'Oh that's good to hear, have you anywhere in mind?' Zoë was beginning to realise that lies only brought more questions and she felt exhausted with trying to keep up the façade.

'Not yet, we'll probably do a last minute booking, you can get some really good bargains if you leave it until the last minute.' Rosa nodded her head in an unconvincing fashion before pulling open the door to leave. They retraced their footsteps back to their table.

Typically, their food had arrived in their absence. The table had been cleared of all the birthday paraphernalia and everyone was sat with an air of anticipation as Zoë and Rosa returned.

'Oh, you needn't have waited, it will be getting cold,' Rosa exclaimed.

Apart from a few appreciative comments about the food, it went quiet as everyone began eating. Zoë looked down at her deep bowl of salad; the roasted peppers glistened amongst the deep green of the spinach leaves and the goats' cheese emanated its alluring, strong tangy aroma, yet she knew that she would not be able to eat a bite. Picking up her cutlery, she began cutting into the rounds of cheese and moving them around her bowl, mimicking her actions as a child when she didn't want to eat a certain food. She pushed a small amount of salad into her mouth and continued hiding the cheese under a layer of leaves as she made pretence of enjoying her mouthful.

Her phone rang, suddenly breaking out into the first few bars of one of her favourite songs. Gage turned his head as he was putting a forkful of pie into his mouth; a small frown appeared on his face as he glanced towards her phone in front of her. She snatched it up, apologising to everyone as she did so and turned away to speak. 'Hi Amber, I can't talk right now.'

'It's OK, I just wanted to check that you're alright? You didn't answer any of my texts.'

'I'll phone you later,' she ended the call and apologised directly to Rosa.

'Is everything alright? Gage asked.

'It's fine – just Amber, I'll speak to her later.' A shriek from Jack distracted the attention away from her. He was beginning to get restless and all the placatory advances from Meg and Dale were being resisted, his cries quickly progressing into body-wracking sobs.

'It's his nap time, I'll have to put him in his pushchair and try and rock him to sleep.' Meg gently eased his rigid body from the constraints of the high chair unperturbed by his frantic cry and flailing fists.

'Here, let me,' Zoë interjected. She got up and grabbed the handles of his pushchair before anyone could intercept.

'Are you sure, Zoë? – you haven't finished your food,' Meg looked uncertain as she strapped Jack into position.

'It's fine I've only got salad. Your quiche will definitely get cold though – please, I want to, I've hardly seen the little guy – it will give him a chance to get to know his auntie.' Meg hesitated slightly before giving in and without looking back at anyone else Zoë pushed the chair through the patio doors and out into the sunshine.

It didn't take long for Jack's crying to subside, but Zoë continued to walk along the river watching the ducks and swans as they scavenged for food on the water. Inertia stirred within her as thoughts of Monday loomed. She couldn't picture herself engaging in her usual routine; getting dressed for work, opening up the boutique and putting on the act that everything was fine, when it was anything but.

She knew that she wouldn't be able to do it.

The sharp click of her heeled sandals echoed around the underside of the bridge as she passed beneath it. Here the stench of the river seemed more concentrated and she found herself holding her breath until she reached the other side. Stooping over, she checked that Jack was still comfortable and saw that he was fast asleep with his full red lips pressed into a tiny pout. Afraid that the sun would burn his skin, she rearranged the angle of the cotton umbrella until she was satisfied that he was amply shaded. The thought crossed her mind that she should turn back, but she disregarded it before it could fully take shape in her mind and she walked on.

The humming of a boat caught her attention as it came towards her; she could hear the distant jubilant voices of the passengers aboard. As it drew closer she saw a group of about eight people of a similar age to herself, sitting on the deck drinking from fluted glasses. The boat was brilliant white with a thin blue trim that ran all the way round the middle and it had the name 'Lucille' painted in ornate writing along the rear side. She absently wondered who Lucille was before a twist of resentment pulled at her insides.

Having absorbed the humiliation and pain that his vile act had caused her, she had struggled alone to put her life back into some semblance of order. Had tried to convince herself that it would, with time, become easier and that the feelings of degradation, powerlessness and fear would fade. He though, seemed to be continuing with his life completely impervious to the devastation that he had caused. He probably had no more to worry about than his upcoming pathetic boat trip, she thought bitterly to herself.

A memory of a conversation she had had with her mother popped into her mind. When Zoë was about ten years old, she had been complaining to Stephanie about some small injustice involving a group of her friends. On having finished the rant saying that it was not fair, her mother had simply, but not unkindly stated that, life was not fair and that she would need to get used to the fact. It had completely shocked her as she'd been expecting her mother to offer some resolution that would rebalance the scales in her mind. But no, she had confirmed that equity was not going to be an ever-present and deserved right in life. It took her some time to accept this concept, but once she had, she found that it actually made things a little easier for her; that she could just brush away concerns with the mantra that life wasn't fair, instead of having to find reasonable solutions every time.

Was this something that she could just brush aside though? She had been trying to protect herself from the repercussions that divulging the ugly truth would cause, but it was so hard. Every day it seemed like another weight was being cruelly dropped on to her resolve and she felt that she had entered into another phase of unfairness – like her nose was being rubbed in it.

Jack began making low moaning sounds and looking about her Zoë realised that she had walked much further than she had intended. She crouched down in front of him and stroked his plump cheek, his eyes focused on hers and he looked at her for a few seconds before his mouth turned down and he broke into a heart-rending whimper. She hastily turned the pushchair around and began to walk as quickly as her heels allowed back in the direction from which she had come. Her mind felt muddled, she had no idea how long she had been walking the stretch of river. Her phone remained on the table alongside her uneaten salad and she didn't have her watch on. The unmistakeable smell of a dirty nappy wafted under her nose as she began to clumsily run along the uneven path.

In the distance she caught sight of Gage coming towards her. His gait was unmistakeable even though he was some way off, and his bright purple shirt stood out in the muted colours around him. It seemed that he'd seen her too because he picked up his pace and was soon by her side.

'Where the hell have you been? Everyone is really worried – you've been gone for almost an hour!' he stooped down and began undoing the straps constraining Jack. 'We thought you'd just gone out the back. Meg was frantic when we realised you were nowhere to be seen.'

'I'm so sorry, I didn't mean to worry anyone, I didn't realise how far I'd walked.' Jack seemed to sense the tension between them and his crying increased in volume and intensity.

'Come here, little man, it's alright, let's get you back to your mummy.' Gage held Jack up to his chest grimacing slightly as the stench of his dirty nappy hit him square on. He looked so small in Gage's arms and Zoë felt ashamed of her carelessness. Of course they would have been worried; Jack was still so reliant on his parents. Gage was right to be so angry with her . . . what had she been thinking? The noises around her seemed to mag- nify in volume as she suddenly felt as if she was viewing herself from a different aspect. It was like seeing her garden from a friend's bedroom window when she was younger; some of the features looked familiar but it looked so different to the view from her own window. The conscientious, reliable and diligent qualities she possessed were giving way to attributes she didn't recognise.

The taxi moved slowly through the mid-afternoon Sunday traffic as Zoë and Gage sat at either end of the back seat, both looking anywhere but at each other. Gage had been left with a dull ache in his head after the soothing effects of the alcohol had been replaced with tension following Zoë's thoughtless behaviour. He had felt so embarrassed and helpless when they had realised that Zoë had disappeared. His mother had questioned why she had left her phone behind, then added more quietly so only Gage could hear, that perhaps she had been taken ill.

The waitress had removed their plates, pausing at Zoë's place uncertain as to whether she should remove the untouched dish or not. By the time she had returned with the dessert menu, Meg had once again stepped outside to see if she could locate Zoë. A discussion about the possible reasons for her absence had ensued with Rosa and Dale agreeing that it was out of character for Zoë to behave this way. Gage had tried to diffuse the tension by reasoning that Jack would be in safe hands with his auntie, but he could tell that they still found the situation a little odd.

Zoë closed the front door behind her and went through to the lounge where Gage stood facing away from her with his hands planted on his hips.

'Gage,' she began, but the ferocity with which he turned to face her stopped her in her tracks.

'I just don't understand why you would do that – disappear without a word to anyone,' he shouted. She couldn't remember a time when he had been so angry with her and it made her shrink into herself, leaving her feeling detached from the situation. She felt as though a thick layer of cotton wool had been wedged beneath her skin inducing a remoteness of her senses. Gage watched her incredulously, waiting for an explanation that she could not give.

'OK, so this is what I think. I think that I'm not enough for you anymore, that you are pushing me away and extracting yourself from this relationship.' He spoke quietly now and his eyes exuded the pain that was evident in his voice. 'You haven't touched me in days and when I try to get close to you, you make some excuse to get as far away from me as possible.

'I thought we'd worked through the worst of the concerns with the boutique – you seemed happier. But this is just too much, I don't know who you are anymore, you've become selfish and today, well that was just another example of that.'

Still she felt no impetus to speak despite the tears that slipped steadily down her cheeks.

'Don't you have *anything* to say? Or have you just completely given up?' He dropped his head down unable to look at Zoë's impassive expression any longer.

'I'm going to stay at Thom's tonight – perhaps it will give us both a chance to think.' As he moved past her, his elbow gently brushed her arm and it felt absurdly intimate to her in that moment. She heard him thumping about upstairs and then he was gone. Just the faintest smell of his aftershave remained in the hallway as she pulled herself up the stairs to the bedroom. Without removing her dress, she got into bed and pulled the cover over herself. Moments later she had fallen into a deep sleep.

Voices outside woke her suddenly. The shrill, excited shouts of girls from the garden next door felt like an intrusion of her personal space.

The room was weakly lit by the remnants of daylight but Zoë had no idea what time it was. She pushed back her pillow to read the time on her bedside clock. It was almost eight-thirty and she needed to get in contact with Amber and Sian before she could bury herself under the covers again. Reluctantly she made her way downstairs to the kitchen.

Her dry mouth reminded her that she hadn't had a drink for hours. She filled a tall glass with water and drank it down in one go. Her stomach turned in revolt and she had to wait for the nausea to pass before she could make her call. She didn't want to have to speak to Sian and so sent her a message which was quickly answered.

Amber would not be so easy. She would have questions but the fog that had descended upon her was making it impossible to think clearly. The phone rang twice before Amber picked up, 'Zoë – at last, I've been ringing you for hours! How did it go with Gage?'

'Amber, I can't really talk now, but I need to ask you a favour – could you cover me tomorrow?'

'Yes, of course, but what's going on with you two?' Zoë let out a long sigh.

'It didn't go to plan, Amber. I wasn't able to tell him and we had a bit of an argument so he's gone to stay at Thom's for the night.'

'What? So you're on your own? I'm coming over – '

'No, please Amber. I just need to sleep . . . Gage and I can talk tomorrow, but I need to know that you can take care of things in the shop, please.'

'Yes, yes. Stop worrying about the bloody boutique – you need to take care of yourself right now, I'll deal with it.'

'Thanks, Amber. Sian will be in at ten.'

'OK, just rest and I'll phone you tomorrow. Promise me you'll let me know if you need anything?'

'I will. Speak later.' She switched off her phone and placed it on the side. As she walked through to the lounge she picked up her work bag that she had left in the corner, partially hidden by the chair.

The crumpled piece of paper grazed her fingers as she slipped her hand into the side pocket. She'd almost half expected it to have mysteriously vanished, but no, it was there in her hand.

Peering at the hastily written address that she had copied down before she'd left on Saturday, she formed a mental image in her mind. She knew the area and had once been to a friend's house nearby, for tea many years ago. The smell of furniture polish came back to her now; a gleaming piano had dominated the small back room where sunshine spilled in and shone a spotlight on the wood, waxy and coloured like a conker. Zoë could not remember anything else about the afternoon, what her friend's bedroom had looked like or what they'd eaten for tea – just the regal piano and scent of polish.

Setting her laptop on the kitchen table she typed in the address. Within minutes she was staring at his house. It had light coloured brick work with a large bay fronted window and potted spiky plants in the paved front garden. She adjusted the angle to the side of the house that was enclosed by a brick wall the same colour as the house. A huge conservatory had been built on to the back and she could just see the top of a cream-coloured parasol poking out above the top of the wall, the rest of the garden was dense with trees and greenery.

In her mind she saw him sitting in the dimly lit conservatory sipping on a tumbler of whisky while Amanda occupied the bedroom, reading or watching television. His life remained unaffected, whilst hers was gradually falling to pieces around her. All her efforts to stop it from caving in, she realised now, had been futile. It was happening anyway.

Anger swelled within her, pushing up through her body with a violent force that required an urgent outlet.

Jumping up, she swiped the laptop across the table sending it crashing to the floor. Rage circulated around her body as her heart pumped adrenaline filled blood to each of her organs, pushing her nearer to the edge. Yanking the handle of the back door she threw it open and ran into the garden – the voices next door barely registered with her now.

She picked up a spade that Gage had left leaning up against a fence and lifting it above her head, speared it into the thick stem of the nearest plant. The tough bark splintered slightly revealing its lime coloured innards, she hit it again and again, its sharp thorns scratched at her arms and legs but she continued to pound at it repeatedly. Her bare feet dug into the dry earth providing sturdy support as she successfully tore branches from the calloused trunk. Sweat began to pool in the hollow between her breasts dampening the fabric of her dress. Each jab of the spade sent a juddering sensation up through her forearms which seemed to ricochet in her head.

Finally, her energy expended, she threw down the spade and stared down at the destruction she'd caused. Her limbs felt stiff and heavy as she dragged herself back inside.

Standing under the shower, the angry scratches stung like a thousand shards of glass beneath her skin. She lifted up her arms away from the force of the water in an attempt to alleviate some of the discomfort, but the cuts around her calves and feet continued to smart.

Too tired to move, she let the water cascade down her aching muscles. Her foggy state of mind was beginning to return, but something had shifted, she felt different.

Now she was certain of one thing; quiescence was no longer an option. She was tired of being held captive to the feeling of injustice. She needed him to know what he'd done to her . . . then perhaps she could find some peace.

Chapter 12

As Gage lifted his head the effects of sleeping on Thom's sofa became apparent. His neck was stiff and sore on one side and his body ached as if he'd had a heavy weights session the day before.

The room felt cold with none of the morning's sun to warm the shaded room. From under the gap of the kitchen door a sliver of sunlight bled on to the laminated floor, which was the only indication to Gage that it was actually morning. The house was still silent around him. He picked up his phone and winced as the bright screen flashed before him. They had another hour before they'd have to leave for work and Gage knew that Thom would not appear until the very last moment.

From the plate that they'd used as an ashtray the night before, a tower of discarded, curled butts emitted their now stale odour. Easing himself up slowly, Gage picked it up and took it through to the kitchen. He looked about, but seeing no obvious signs of a bin, left it on the side furthest away from him.

An image of Zoë first thing in the morning played on his mind. Her unmade face that always looked younger and more vulnerable somehow. Her soft skin exposed in the cute vest and shorts sets she always wore to sleep in. He felt a moment's remorse at the way he had spoken to her last night, but was all too quickly reminded of the way that she'd been taking him for granted lately. The mediocre state in which their relationship had seemed to slip into overnight could not be ignored. But that didn't stop the sharp ache that he felt in his chest from hurting any less.

He made himself a cup of tea and waited for Thom to get up. They had a deadline to meet today and Gage would need to focus all his attention on that.

The house looked slightly altered from the image she had seen last night. The driveway looked more expansive in real-life and in it now, was parked a black car. A deep magenta clematis climbed the wall beside the door and several ceramic pots were dotted along the pathway, bursting with resplendent blooms.

Zoë was parked beneath one of the large trees that lined the road. Their heavily blossomed branches danced in the breeze and drooped on to the roofs of cars beneath them. The light drizzle which had been mostly constant since her arrival a few hours before, had sent a steady stream of tiny, fine white petals to fall on to her windscreen. With her view impeded, she had been forced to wind her window down a little which had allowed regular sprays of rain to shower her face.

Fortunately though, the weather had provided the perfect excuse for her to be wearing her waterproof coat. She had the fur-edged hood pulled up, which felt both comforting and also had the added benefit of partially hiding her features.

All her windows had become fogged over due to the amount of time she had sat watching the house; she felt cocooned, safe. Here, at least, she knew where he was and even felt an air of superiority over him – he had no idea that she knew where he lived, let alone the fact that, at that moment she was sat outside his property.

Muted voices reached her as a woman wearing a mustard-coloured padded jacket walked by the car. She was pushing a stroller and a young boy walked alongside her holding on to the handle, his red cap and school bag stood out as the blurred images passed by.

Transferring her attention back to the house she saw that the front door was ajar. Instantly on alert, she adjusted her position to look through the small gap in the window.

There he was. Her muscles tightened in shock and she gripped the base of her padded jacket as if waiting for the sting of a needle in the gum at the dentist.

He had dipped his head into a silver car that was parked up a few metres from the house, then quickly reappeared holding something that Zoë couldn't identify from where she was. Without looking about, he went back inside, slamming the door behind him.

On high alert now, Zoë felt poised as if waiting with her toe against the line of a race track for the sound of the gun to fire.

She didn't have to wait very long before he re-emerged, this time holding onto a lead at the end of which an excited Springer Spaniel sniffed the air before shaking its head frantically. She watched, trance-like until realising that they had turned down the road alongside their back garden and were quickly disappearing from view.

Not giving herself time to think it through, she got out of her car and began to follow. She had to jog a little to shorten the distance between them, but was careful not to get too close.

At the end of the road he turned left and continued down a very similar looking street. Beneath her the white petals that covered her car also stuck to the wet pavement she walked. Her trainers made no sound as she followed behind him, although she noticed, that he had not looked about him at all, even when the dog had stopped to intensely sniff the ground or pull itself up to look over a low wall. He seemed completely withdrawn and absorbed in himself.

The Spaniel suddenly turned leading him down a passageway that if she had not been following him, she would not have seen. As she neared the opening she hesitated – what if this was a trap? Maybe he'd known that she was there the whole time and was waiting for her around the corner?

But if it wasn't a trap, she was going to lose him. Taking a deep breath, she pulled her hood down further over one side of her face as if to protect herself from the rain. She stepped forward and walked on as though she were continuing straight. As she reached the passageway she turned her head briefly. Her ears filled with the sound of her thumping heart beat as her mind played tricks on her, but in reality, there was no one there. Relief flooded her as she darted down the narrow overgrown path.

Under the sanctuary of the wooded area from where she stood, she watched him. As the Spaniel ran in rings around the perimeter of the playing field, he just stayed where he was – completely still. He had his hands sunk into the pockets of his jeans and his eyes were cast downwards, every now and then he would swing the lead around his wrist as if suddenly remembering it was there.

A torrid twist of anger assaulted her. Here was the man, who, just over a week ago had held her down and forced his way into her, taking from her not only physically, but also stealing her identity and purpose. His impassive demeanour only infuriated her further. He seemed completely unconcerned – by anything. She had heard Amanda tell Aidan that he had been too unwell to go on holiday, which seemed strange because he looked fine, physically.

A break in the clouds revealed the rays of the hidden sun and the rain had all but stopped. Zoë felt suddenly conspicuous with her hood pulled up and having satisfied her curiosity for the moment, felt the need to get out of the field before he did.

She moved quickly without looking back and retraced her steps back to where she'd parked her car hours earlier.

Only when she was safely sat in her seat did she lower her hood. The sun was now out fully, quickly warming the air around her. She reached her hand into her bag for her sunglasses, but they weren't there. Keeping her eyes on the path that ran alongside his garden, she placed her key into the ignition. Just as she was about to make the turn, she saw the cream and brown dog reappear on its extended lead.

From where she sat, she knew that there was a chance that he could possibly spot her. This time he would be facing towards her before he made the turn towards his front door.

Not daring to breathe, she watched him turn the corner, walk across his driveway and disappear back inside his house. Without a moment's hesitation, she started her car and pulled away.

Perhaps if she had given more than just a glance in her rear-view mirror, she would have seen who was following a little way behind her.

After Zoë had failed to answer her phone for the fourth time, Amber began to feel agitated. Why was she not taking picking up?

She had left regular intervals between her calls to allow Zoë to get back to her; she'd told herself that perhaps Zoë was sleeping or busy – but she couldn't ignore the uneasy feeling that had built throughout the day any longer. Looking at the clock, she made her decision – if she hadn't reached her by half-past three, she would phone Gage. As much as she hated the idea of interfering, she did not want to risk making the same mistake she had made with Caitlin, all those years before. If her gut told her that something was wrong, this time she would listen.

It was their shared love of sports that had brought them together in high school. Caitlin could not be beaten in the hundred metre sprint and Amber was the queen of long distance. Living within walking distance of one another, they were always in and out of each other's houses. If they wanted privacy to discuss the details of their latest crush or the wonders of their ever-changing bodies, perhaps, then Amber's house would be the place to go as both her parents were often at work. If, on the other hand they wanted to watch videos or sit outside, it would be Caitlin's house they chose. Her mother loved baking and stayed at home to look after Caitlin's younger brother. She would bring them delicious cakes to devour whilst they sunbathed or sat watching films from the columns of cases stacked high in the spare room.

They had shared everything, from the food on their plates, to the changes in breast size.

Then, in their last few months spent at school, Caitlin's behaviour changed suddenly. She began to make excuses when Amber tried to make arrangements for them to meet up. At school she no longer sat with Amber in the school hall at lunch, saying that she'd eaten a sandwich out on the field or in the library whilst she revised.

Amber missed the closeness they'd shared but assumed it was the pressure of exams and that things would return to normal when they were all over. She herself was swept up in the change of timetables and revision periods that occurred in the run up to their exams. She would see Caitlin fleetingly as they passed each other in the corridor or across the room in some lessons they shared, but they rarely had time to speak, it seemed.

A party was being held to mark the end of their exams and Amber was relieved when Caitlin had called her to let her know what time her father would pick her up. Amber had suggested that they meet up that afternoon, but Caitlin had declined saying that she had a training session. Although she had felt a little stung at being left out again, she was looking forward to the party and spent the afternoon flicking through magazines looking for hair and beauty ideas.

When Caitlin arrived at her door the next evening, Amber was shocked at what she saw.

It was the first time in a while that she had seen her friend dressed in anything other than her school uniform or baggy running gear. What had struck her first were her arms; they looked so thin. She wore a light grey skater style jersey dress with capped sleeves, but her arms seemed too long, her elbows too pointed and wrists too sharp.

She'd had her hair cut into a sleek bob, which as she standing at the door, blew across her protruding cheek bones. For a moment Amber had just stood and stared, it wasn't until her mother pushed past her to speak to Caitlin's father who was sat waiting in his car, that she followed on behind.

She knew from the start that it was wrong. Whenever Amber tried to broach the subject of Caitlin's weight loss, she would quickly change the subject. Caitlin had a way of making Amber feel silly for showing concern, as if it were she who had a problem and that she was being over-bearing. Caitlin assured her time and time again that she was fine, sometimes she could be quite sharp, or she would shut-down and they would sit watching the small screen in an uncomfortable silence.

They spent less and less time together that summer, partly because Amber had begun to feel uncomfortable in Caitlin's presence and partly because she felt that she could no longer reach her friend, it was as if she was speaking to a robot. When she did go round to her house, her mother still offered her the beautifully iced cakes, but she found that she was eating them alone and somehow the icing just seemed to get clogged in her throat.

The summer passed and Amber started college, while Caitlin began work at her father's company. They gradually lost contact with each other, although Amber would sometimes see Caitlin run past her house on a Saturday morning. She would duck down below her bedroom window, even though she knew that Caitlin would probably never look up from the path in front of her.

Three days before Christmas, they got a phone call. Her mother answered and Amber knew immediately from the grave tone of her voice that something bad had happened.

Caitlin had collapsed whilst out running. Somebody walking

their dog had found her and called for an ambulance.

The guilt that Amber had felt over-shadowed the whole festive period. She knew that she could have done more, been more insistent, listened to the voice in her head, the feeling in her gut.

But she hadn't. It had been easier to let it go.

Caitlin began her long road to recovery. Amber visited her weekly until she was strong enough to go back to work. Then their paths had eventually split and they were each just a memory to one another, tucked away in a corner of their minds.

It was done. She had rung Gage immediately after her last call had yet again gone to voicemail.

Gage had sounded surprised when she had asked him to meet her at her house, but he must have heard something in her voice because he agreed to leave as soon as he'd packed away his work gear.

Amber had closed the boutique early, apologising to a woman as she ushered her out of the door, citing a family emergency.

Unable to keep still, she tidied the front room and washed up the dishes that Hannah and Claire had left in the sink. She was thankful that they were both on the same shift at the hospital and she had the house to herself for the moment.

Perhaps she wouldn't have to actually tell him? If she could persuade him to go home and speak to Zoë, it would clarify that she was alright and then Zoë would be able to tell him herself as she had planned to do yesterday.

The loud knock jolted her from her thoughts. She took a calming breath and then stepped forward to open the door. Even to her admiring eye, she could see that he looked rough. His face bore the puffy features of someone that had not slept well and his movements were deliberate and slow.

Neither of them went to greet the other with their usual

friendly hug, instead, Gage slipped past Amber and sank into the nearest chair. He brought his hands up to his face and held them up across his nose as if in prayer, before letting out a long sigh.

'So, what's this about, Amber?' he spoke gently, but she could hear a slight edge laced beneath his mild tone.

'Are you going home now?'

He released another sigh.

'At the moment, I really don't know what I'm going to do.'

'I really think you need to go and speak to her, Gage.'

'What's the point? I think she's made it perfectly clear that I'm the last person she wants to see right now.'

'No, Gage you've got it all wrong! Zoë really needs you right now – please just go home and see her!'

'I don't know what she's told you, Amber, but I think it would be better if I gave her a bit of space – give her time to decide what she actually wants.' Gage mistook Amber's silence as acceptance of what he had said. 'Ever since I brought up the idea of starting a family, she seems to have withdrawn into her own world. I don't think I'm what she wants anymore – maybe she has outgrown me or something.'

'Gage, just stop!' her outburst visually startled him, but then it seemed as though he was about to continue and she knew she couldn't waste any more time. 'Zoë was raped!' her voice shook with the enormity of what she had said, but she had to go on, 'the afternoon of my party, a man raped her in the back room of the boutique.'

The silence that followed was even more unbearable than being forced to release the words she just had.

Gage tried to swallow the painful lump that had formed in his throat and blinked away the sting of tears from his eyes. He stood up abruptly and clasped his hands behind his head.

'Who?'

'I hardly know anything, Gage, I only found out myself on Saturday. She said that she was going to tell you when you got back from having lunch with your family. I've been trying to ring her all day, but she's not answering.'

'What? You mean that you haven't seen her today?' his face creased with confusion as he stared back at Amber. Panic began to grip hold of her as she explained to Gage about how Zoë had asked her to look after the boutique. He listened but she could see that he was already forming a plan in his head.

Without another word, he fled from the room almost knocking into Amber as he did so. The front door slammed behind him and only then did Amber let out the breath that she had been holding – there was nothing more that she could do for the time being, it was up to Gage now.

He never drove carelessly; Zoë often teased him about his precise attitude to driving and said that it was like travelling with a person who had just passed their test the day before, being in a car with him.

He couldn't think of anything but getting back home to Zoë and his tension mounted with every traffic light that seemed to take an eternity to change in his favour. He was perspiring heavily, not only from the sudden appearance of the sun, but from the shock of the news that was beginning to pervade his brain.

His Zoë. Raped. A word that he'd heard on countless occasions during news reports and seen printed in papers time after time, but had only ever skimmed the surface of his conscience, until now. Now it had rudely intruded into their lives inciting its damage before he had even been aware of its presence. Like a sharp knife effortlessly cutting through the delicate layers of their relationship, leaving them weak and exposed.

Why had she not told him straight away? The thought of her going about her usual daily tasks while all the time she had been holding on to this shocking secret was too much for him to comprehend. He wiped his face angrily across his arm dispelling the tears that threatened to spill down his cheeks; it would be OK, now he knew, they could sort it out together.

As he approached their house, his heart sank as he saw that Zoë's car was not parked in her usual spot. He pulled into a space further down and scanned the road to see if he could see it parked nearby. He couldn't.

Bursting into the house, he looked for clues of her possible whereabouts. Perhaps she had gone food shopping or to get her hair cut? These thoughts were soon dispelled as he entered the kitchen.

Her laptop was on the floor in the corner; the screen black and cracked. Mud was trailed on the floor and matted foot marks stood out on the otherwise shiny lengths of laminate. A glass was placed on the side beside the kettle, it had a tiny dribble of water left at the bottom and Gage could just make out the faint trace of where Zoë's mouth had been. He touched the kettle then the toaster, hoping for recent signs of activity, but they were both cold.

Pulling out his phone his opened the recent calls file and tried her number. No answer.

Just as he was about to go and check the bedroom, he noticed that one of the kitchen chairs was sticking out as if someone had left in a hurry without tucking it back under the table. Beneath it was a screwed up piece of paper. He bent down and as he did so, he recognised the *Her* Boutique logo slightly distorted within the creases. He unravelled it quickly and saw an address written in Zoë's handwriting. He was familiar with the road, but neither of them knew anyone who lived there.

Grapping his keys, he left the house. He could be there in ten minutes if he missed the tea-time traffic.

Slowing down to scan the visible house numbers, Gage realised that he was nearing the vicinity of the house that he was looking for. He pulled over into the next available space behind a dark red Mini and got out. He didn't have to walk very far before he spotted Zoë's car parked just a few cars down from him. Ducking down to peer through the back window, he saw that it was empty. Even though he'd known that this would probably be the case, a thud of disappointment dropped like a stone in his stomach. Looking about him, he crossed over the road to check the house adjacent to where her car was positioned. It was heavily concealed by hedging, but fortunately also had a large slate plaque on the wall beside the door on which the number was engraved. It was two digits off from the one written on the crumpled piece of paper he held in his hand.

He looked across the road beside it that separated the two houses and saw a sand coloured, weathered edged brick wall that ran along the edge of a garden. Gage could tell that it had been recently built and when he ran his eye over the property he suspected that the owner was not short of cash. Not knowing the reason for Zoë's interest though, he fought the urge to knock on the door and returned to his van, he daren't risk causing any harm by turning up unannounced.

As he waited, alone with his thoughts, he finally had to surrender to the truth that he had been trying to ignore – he hadn't been able to protect her. She had suffered a brutal attack and then afterwards, hadn't even been able to tell him. Why hadn't he been able to tell that something was drastically wrong? The more he thought about it, the more he realised that he'd missed signs that now seemed glaringly obvious. The bruise around her eye, the secrecy – they never locked doors in the house, but on numerous occasions recently, he had found himself talking to her through a closed door. Then there was her extreme sullenness, not only around him, but others too. The meal had been a perfect example of that and now he couldn't help feeling that he had let her down.

Too wrapped up in his own ideas about where their relationship should be heading next, he'd accepted the excuses that Zoë had fed him. He'd sulked and withdrawn from her a little when she hadn't reacted as he'd hoped.

His timing, he could see now, couldn't have been worse and this realisation sparked feelings of regret that sat buoyant in the acid that lay in his stomach.

A group of young school children walked towards the van each holding an ice-cream, through his open window the sound of their excited chatter grew louder as they passed by. Following behind them were two women, and a man carrying a sleeping baby in his arms. They walked at a leisurely pace, enjoying the afternoon sunshine and momentary pause before getting back home and continuing with the chores that would be waiting for them.

None of them glanced in Gage's direction. He suddenly felt a strange sensation of being present but totally cut off from those around him as the children's voices gradually faded into the distance. Leaning forward for a moment, he rested his head on the steering wheel to try and stop the spinning in his head. He had so many questions that he wanted to ask Zoë, but he knew that he could not rush her, he would need to tread very carefully and take everything at her pace.

With his eyes trained on the house, he noticed a figure suddenly come into view. She was walking at some speed along the pavement beside the walled garden.

It took him a moment to realise that it was Zoë. She had a thick padded jacket on that she wore in winter sometimes when the rain fell heavily – the hood was pulled up over her head. Her actions were quick and precise and she did not pause before unlocking her car and getting in. He held his hand on his key ready to follow as soon as she moved, but the car remained where it was.

Torn between getting out and going over to her or just waiting to see what she did next, he found that he could bear it no longer. Just as he placed his fingers on the door latch, he saw another figure approaching from the same place Zoë had just come from. A dog scurried ahead of him and Gage only managed a short glance at him before he turned the corner and walked into the house. He was tall, and looked to be in his mid-forties. His short dark hair was set back revealing a high forehead and thick eyebrows that had been knitted together under the glare of the sun.

Any sound around Gage instantly deadened.

It was him.

His ears filled with the noise of rushing blood as a malevolent presence overcame him. He opened his arms to the feeling of pure hatred that he felt for this man whom he had not known had existed until moments before.

Zoë was leaving. He snapped back to attention and began following her a little way behind. He waited for her eyes to meet his in her rear view mirror, but they didn't once, apart from the customary required looks, left and right, she stared straight ahead all the way home.

Exhausted now, Zoë planned to have a bath and prepare what she needed to do for tomorrow. She knew that she would have to go back to work, but after, she would return to the house. Being there, she knew where he was. She was the one who held the power over him. How and when she would make her move, she didn't know yet, but she had to build up a resistance to the physical effect he had on her before she could face him. She would not show weakness again.

Lifting her muted phone out of her bag, she saw the multiple notifications spread along the top of the status bar.

Amber answered on the second ring, 'Zoë – are you OK?

'Yes, look I'm sorry I didn't get back to you earlier – there was something that I needed to do.'

'Is Gage with you?'

'Gage? – what do you mean?'

'Zo, he's knows . . . I told him. I'm so sorry,' before Zoë could respond, she heard the sound of a key turning in the front door.

Gage's frame partially obscured the sunlight that had been flooding through the front window until his arrival.

They stood facing each other as they had done only the afternoon before, but now everything had changed. Zoë could not bring herself to speak first. Gage looked physically pained as if he had been involved in a violent altercation. She dropped her eyes to the floor, unable to hold his gaze any longer.

'Zoë, I'm so sorry,' the words that had meant to follow were denied him due to the painful spasms that were constricting his throat. He bent his head down in an effort to restore his composure, but it didn't come. Instead tears began to run down the side of his nose, they dropped on to his dusty boots below creating little splash marks on the weathered leather.

At the sight of his distress, her heart felt as if it was being dragged from her chest, but still she couldn't move. Using his thumb, he pushed away the remains of his tears and then reached out for her hand. Gently, he pulled her to him and she let her head rest against his chest. She could feel the vibrations of his thumping heart and for a short while, felt the tension leave her body.

'It's going to be alright. Once you've told the police everything, they'll catch the bastard and -- 'she pulled herself out of his grasp and suddenly found her voice again.

'The police? No Gage, there is no way that I'm going to the

police!'

'But Zoë, you have to,' he tried to step closer to tighten the gap she'd created.

'No, I don't have to! This is exactly the reason I didn't tell you!' she shouted back. All the frustration she'd had to solely endure bubbled to the surface and exploded, ripping the lid from her self-control.

'There is no way – NO way that I'm going to put myself through that – the judgement, the questions, all the surmising and whispering. I won't do it!

And as for the business – everything I've worked so hard for will be wiped out because *Her* Boutique will be forever labelled as *the shop where the girl was raped!*' Anger spewed out of her distorting her usually mild features into hard lines that Gage didn't recognise.

'It's not like that anymore, Zo. They have special units, trained specialists who'll look after you. He can't just get away with it – he needs to pay for what he's done to you!'

Tears of exasperation billowed from her eyes as she lurched forward and struck Gage on the side of his arm.

'Yes Gage, what he did to me! Don't you see? – It's not your decision!' she spat, 'It's mine – and not you nor anybody else is going to tell me how to deal with this!'

Finally her enfeebled body gave way to the suppressed feelings of despair as her legs folded beneath her and she crumpled to the floor. Gage grabbed her arms, breaking her fall and squatted down before her, pulling her up slightly so she could lean into him. When her sobs had subsided and he felt that some of the tension had left her muscles, he lifted her chin so she was facing him. Her beautiful soft, blue eyes slowly emerged from their swollen lids as she blinked away her last few tears and looked up at him. A fervid feeling of unconditional love temporarily stopped the breath in his lungs.

'It's going to be alright, you don't have to do anything you don't want to,' he paused in an attempt to find the right words in order not to upset or threaten her again, 'but we do have a bit of a dilemma, Zoë.' He rose and reached into his pocket pulling out the crumpled piece of paper that he wished never existed. 'You see, I know where he lives too, and I can't just let him get away with what he's done to you . . . I just can't.'

Chapter 13

It seemed as though the full moon had positioned itself exclusively to illuminate the kitchen table where she had been sat for the past few minutes.

She still felt afraid – but now the fear stemmed from a different source. She felt relieved that she no longer had to maintain a pretence in front of Gage, but his knowing had come at a price.

The control that she had briefly tasted yesterday, as she waited outside the house had been snatched away. Her undeveloped plan to somehow initiate Toby's understanding of the trauma he had caused would remain undeveloped. Now there was a new plan.

When she was certain that she'd told Gage everything she knew about Toby and Amanda Kempson she had gone up to take a long bath. After having to stay silent for what felt like an eternity, the sudden exposure of her secret instigated a release of the tension that had wrapped itself around her muscles and tendons like insidious bindweed.

On leaving the bathroom the smell of egg bread flooded her nostrils. Gage had sat her down and made her eat two slices of her favourite comfort food before leaving her alone to have a shower himself. It was the first time in over a week that she had actually been able to enjoy food. Her stomach had at first resisted the heavy invasion, but she had persisted under the watchful eye of Gage and eventually managed the two slices that he had insisted were to be finished.

Later that evening they had sat down together on the sofa. He'd sat at one end leaving a space between them, but had gathered her legs up on to his lap and gently stroked her skin as she spoke. She had tentatively begun to disclose some of the details of that day, beginning with the mix up that had led her to be alone in the first place. As she progressed to divulging how

Toby had tricked her into allowing him in, she had moved her legs away from Gage and sat leaning forward on the edge of the sofa. She could not bring herself to look at him as she re-lived the minutes that had irrevocably changed not only her life, but her outlook also.

Her eyes had stayed fixated on the candle that was positioned on the hearth as she continued her disturbing monologue. The flame occasionally waned as it sank down into the surrounding pool of wax, only to re-emerge again licking the sides of its glass holder as if in victory.

She found herself looking down on the act as she spoke, as if watching it happen to somebody else.

When she had finished, the silence that had filled the room had felt stilted and oppressive, she didn't know what Gage could say, but she needed him to say something. After a moment she'd taken a deep inhalation and held the air in her expanded lungs until her body forced her to release it again. She hadn't cried whilst she'd been speaking, it had almost felt as if she'd been under the influence of a numbing drug or a spell. But when she'd allowed herself to look over at Gage, she saw that his face was swollen with tears.

Pulling herself over to him, she had used the pads of her thumbs to wipe away the tears beneath his eyes and again, he'd made the promise to her that he wouldn't let the bastard get away with what he'd done.

Then he'd asked her the question she knew would come: what had been caught on CCTV?

Monitors were only positioned in the actual boutique, so there would be the footage of him entering, locking the door behind him and following her through to the back and then leaving again sometime after. She hadn't been able to actually watch it, but she had it. The factor that was in her favour was that Toby was not to know that she did not have cameras anywhere else –

and she planned to exploit this.

Together they initiated the seeds of a plan, now they would just have to wait until the weekend to put them into fruition.

She had eventually fallen asleep, but when her alarm woke her the next morning she did not feel rested. Gage was already dressed and had eaten breakfast when she entered the kitchen.

'I wish I didn't have to go in today,' he said as he reached over and took her fingers in his.

'No, it's good. It will take our minds off things for a while.' As she spoke a thought entered her mind. 'Gage, you won't do anything silly – will you?'

'What do you mean?' He knew exactly what she meant. He'd already had to talk himself down from going over to the house today and pummelling Toby to a mush.

'Remember that we need to do this together, please don't do anything to jeopardise the plan.' He dropped his eyes from hers.

'I won't.'

Satisfied with his reply, she kissed him and went back to her usual weekday routine before heading off to the boutique.

Entering the car park, Zoë noticed Amber's car positioned in her preferred spot. For a moment she feared that she'd forgotten to inform her that she would be in today, but checking her phone she saw that her last message confirmed she had.

The radio was playing as Zoë walked through the side entrance; it injected a cheerful feel to the back room that the grey morning failed to provide and this, she was extremely grateful for.

'Hey, how are you?' Amber came through from the front, holding the open, stock folder in her hands.

'Yeah, not bad – tired, but I'm OK.'

'Zo, I'm so sorry. When you didn't answer your phone, I panicked and then Gage was talking as though you and he were going to split up and I just didn't know what to do!' Zoë held up her hands in protest.

'Firstly, you have absolutely nothing to be sorry for. You've been brilliant, Amber, I can't thank you enough,' she saw the relief in her face and so continued. 'I went to the house, just sat outside watching for hours. I saw him, followed him when he took his dog for a walk.' Amber's eyes widened in shock as she absorbed what Zoë had said.

'Zoë, he could have seen you or anything! What were you thinking?'

'I had to! I can't really explain, but being there helped a little. To see that he is just a man, who walks his dog, empties the bin, well it helped take away some of the fear that had built up in my mind. I don't want to feel afraid anymore.' Amber nodded in sympathetic understanding.

'What happened with Gage?' she asked tentatively.

'We talked for hours, I'm actually glad that it is all out in the open – but it's going to take time for us both to adjust. But we will.' Amber placed down the folder that she'd been holding on to and pulled Zoë into a hug. Moving away she self-consciously placed her hand over her mouth.

'Sorry, I probably stink of onions, Theo came over last night and we had Indian take-out,' she smiled sheepishly.

'Indian?! Well I guess that there are still some things he needs to learn about you then?'

'I know, but I didn't have the heart to tell him – I had to scrape my plate into the bin when he went up to the bathroom!' They both laughed.

'Ah well, it must be serious then,' Zoë teased. 'Right, I think I'd better get things organised for the new delivery, it should hopefully be with us this morning.' She felt a bubble of excitement at the thought of setting up the new displays. At least for now, her work would provide a much needed distraction from thinking about Sunday.

Sleep had not been forthcoming for either her or Gage. She had kept going over the different possible scenarios that could be a result of their actions today. Most important to her was that Toby would show shame and guilt for what he had done. She needed him to understand the mental and physical pain that he had inflicted upon her before she could begin to accept what had happened. He needed to see the ugly consequences of his actions.

But also she simply needed to know why? The word had repeatedly played over in her mind trapping her beneath a net of shame and self-doubt.

Sitting at the kitchen table she watched the branches of the tree swaying in the light breeze. The strengthening sunlight played in between the gaps in the leaves as they shimmied against the backdrop of the pink- washed sky. It created a kaleidoscopic effect that evoked memories from a particular Christmas. She had been entranced by the cylindrical shaped wonder that she had unwrapped early; the sky had still been dark and the tree lights in the garden had twinkled with the promise of what the day would hold. When she placed the colourful tube to her eye it cast a mirage of colourful jewels that danced exclusively for her.

Dropping her mug into the bowl as she passed, she went up to do her hair and make-up. It was her parents' anniversary and they were going to have lunch at the house, Steph had phoned the night before and had spoken to Gage whilst Zoë was in the shower. Clarissa was going to be there too, but Zoë's usual excitement at the prospect of spending time with her parents was overshadowed by the uncertainty of what would happen after.

'We're in the garden,' Steph called out unnecessarily. As soon as Gage had turned off the engine, the sound of reggae music had filtered through to them, replacing the overly-cheerful voice of the radio presenter that neither of them had been listening to.

Stephanie came jogging towards them, her movements exaggerated as she carefully positioned her bejewelled sandaled feet on the stony drive to greet them. The light chiffon material of her ankle length dress caught in the warm breeze and billowed out to the side momentarily stilting her effort. On reaching Zoë she wrapped her arms around her neck and rocked her from side to side.

'Hello, my baby,' she breathed into her hair, before turning to Gage. 'Hello, Gage.'

'Happy anniversary, Mum – you look as though you may have started celebrating already,' Zoë teased.

'I most definitely have – I'm not going to waste a moment of this gorgeous weather. Come on – let me get you both a drink.'

They followed her round into the garden where Ed was sat beneath a parasol sipping a glass of beer. Beside him was a large square shaped wooden enclosure that she had never seen before.

'Happy anni, Dad,' she dipped down to kiss his cheek and then peered over the edge of one of the sides. 'Aww, hello, you two!'

'Didn't want them to miss out on the fun – they've just been neutered, so thought that this was the best way to keep them out of harm's way.

'He made it himself – honestly at one point I thought that he

197

was going to paint the outside with cartoon animals – a bit like he did with your bedroom wall, Zo, do you remember?'

'Of course I remember, I absolutely loved that wall.' She rummaged in her bag and pulled out a large envelope, 'We really didn't know what to get you, so I'm sorry, but we went for the unimaginative gift voucher in the end,' she handed the envelope to her mother, who touched her shoulder before taking it.

'You shouldn't have got us anything, your being here is a gift in itself, but thank you, darlings. Now what are you having to drink? Zoë, are you having a glass of wine?'

'Er no thanks, Mum – I'll just have lemonade, actually.'

'Oh, OK. Gage, what about you?'

'I'll have the same, please, Steph.' Zoë could see that her mother was a little surprised, but she just nodded and turned towards the house, where Zoë followed her inside.

The unmistakeable aroma of her mother's freshly baked bread greeted her as she entered the cool kitchen. On the table, a Victoria sponge sat regally beneath a glass dome. Strawberry and kiwi segments decorated the lightly dusted top and its jam and cream centre spilled out of the edges as if to tantalise anyone that regarded it.

'So tell me, Angel – how have you been? Have the two of you been able to work things out?' A cloud of concern had spread across her mother's face as she handed Zoë a tall sugar-rimmed glass of lemonade. A piece of lime was wedged on the edge and a slice of cucumber floated on top of the bubbles. Zoë couldn't help but smile at her mother's extravagance.

'Yes, we really have. I feel so much better, and so does Gage – you were right, we just needed to make time for each other and talk things through.'

'Well that's a relief, I'm so pleased,' she beamed.

'Actually, I hope you don't mind, but we thought we would

leave a little earlier than planned this afternoon. We are going to take a walk by the broads – Gage likes looking at the boats.' She didn't know why she had felt the need to add that, Gage wasn't especially interested in boats.

Stephanie had picked up on the note of discomfort in her daughter's voice and wasn't sure if it was from fear of offending herself and Ed, or from something else.

'Of course not, it's a great idea. We can still have a bit of lunch together, it will be perfect,' she kissed Zoë on the cheek, then hastily wiped away the residue of her lipstick away before picking up Gage's similarly dressed drink.

'Look who's here,' Ed called as they returned to the garden.

'Rissa, it's lovely to see you – thanks so much for coming,' Stephanie reached for her hand and pulled her into a hug.

'Good to see you too, Steph, happy anniversary,' she presented Stephanie with a huge bouquet of lilies and then greeted Zoë with a hug also. 'How have you been?' she whispered in her ear, 'No more dizzy spells, I hope?' Zoë subtly shook her head and they went over to join the others at the table.

As Clarissa spoke about the details of the adoption procedure, Zoë was grateful that she was there to detract some attention away from herself. She listened as Clarissa explained that she and Matt were due to visit a young family next week, when Matt returned from his overseas business trip. The family were not in a suitable position to provide for another baby, the mother was already struggling with the three young children she had. It had been deemed by all concerned that this baby would only add pressure to an already difficult situation. The mother, she told them, had agreed to have a sterilisation as soon as the baby had been born.

Zoë reached across to pick up her drink, as she did so she felt Gage looking at her and lifted her eyes to meet his. His gaze was unfaltering as if he was trying to convey something unspoken to her, then his face broke into a sad smile.

'So I've been looking at some of the websites of the designers we saw, Zoë. Did you tell Steph about that fabulous red dress with the long train?'

'No, she certainly did not,' Steph interjected.

'It was amazing, looked really dramatic against the white shiny floor too. Are you going to buy from any of them then?' Zoë asked.

'Yes, I'm thinking about it. How's your new stock selling?'

'Really well and I'm also selling quite a bit online.'

Ed went inside to bring out the food that Stephanie had prepared for lunch. As they ate, Clarissa and Stephanie began discussing a mutual acquaintance. Zoë was relieved that the opportunity enabled her to fade out of any conversation for the time being. She pulled at a sinewy piece of cold chicken on her plate and forced herself to swallow it down before sipping at her lemonade. Fortunately it seemed that any ambivalence Gage may have been feeling, had not affected his appetite, she saw her mother smile at him as he re-filled his plate.

'Zoë, you don't seem to have had very much to eat, and to think, you used to love my bread!' After her spell of neutrality, suddenly all eyes were on her. She felt as if she had been caught with a banned substance at an exclusive function.

'Ah Steph, that's probably my fault – I was up early this morning and made pancakes for breakfast, I have to admit , they were a little heavy on the stomach – even for me!' he rubbed his stomach as he laughed. Zoë sent him a look of gratitude.

'Well, as long as you're eating something – even if it is Gage's stodgy pancakes!' Stephanie playfully swiped Gage on the arm, to which he feigned incredulity.

The sun disappeared behind a lone cloud, temporarily stealing the warmth from Zoë's skin and causing her to shiver unexpectedly. A sickening grip of melancholy encompassed her submerging her in a state of paralysis. Her stomach juices felt hot and animated and she knew that she needed to move before completely making a show of herself. Without saying a word she got up and walked quickly towards the house, concentrating on every breath she took as she did so. Once inside the bathroom she threw herself over the toilet, stopped fighting her reflexes and violently vomited into the pristine, white china bowl.

Descending the stairs moments later, she paused as her father appeared in the hallway at the bottom. He placed his hand on the bannister and looked up at Zoë as if waiting for her to pass. She quickened her pace, but when she drew level with him, he pointed to one of the framed photographs hung on the wall.

'Things were so much easier then,' he chuckled. In the image Zoë was aged about three and was standing in front of a rose bush holding a yellow watering can in one hand and a trowel in the other. The camera had caught her brilliant smile and preserved the moment and memory from that day to this. 'I think that's the hardest part about being a parent – accepting that you can't always make things better for your children.' His doleful expression sliced right through her.

'On the plus side though, your roses are no longer in any danger.' She hugged him briefly then released him before the tears that threatened, had a chance to spill.

Stephanie had wrapped up some cake and placed it in a cool bag for them to take home with them, as Gage took the bag from her fingers, she grabbed his hand.

'She looks too thin, Gage,' she whispered. 'I don't know if it's the fact that she's been working too hard – or something else, but I can't help worrying.' Gage glanced at Zoë who was sat in the passenger's seat.

'I know that you're worried, but we are working things out. Everything will be fine,' he rubbed her shoulder in what he hoped was a reassuring gesture. He had been about to add that he would never let anything bad happen to Zoë, but stopped himself as he realised that this was not a statement that could be upheld.

The car park was full. Gage drove round several times on the look-out for somebody vacating their space, but eventually he gave up and drove towards a lane that was a few minutes' walk from the boatyard.

Before getting out of the car, Zoë pulled on the black cap and sunglasses that she had left in the foot well. Now that she was there she felt strangely more composed and able to use her nervous energy to her advantage.

Gage's face was set with a look of hard determination as he held out his hand to her. They began walking down the lane that was shaded by the trees on either side and so gave the impression of it being a cloudy day, Zoë shivered slightly, in the car the sun had been shining directly on to her dark blue shorts and now she felt bereft of its attention.

She turned to look up at Gage but he kept his eyes straight ahead as above them in the trees the crows cawed out their warning.

When they reached the car park they were once again under the full glare of the sun and Zoë could feel the delicate skin on her feet burning between the straps of her sandals as they crossed the stony expanse.

Families were gathered outside the small tourist shop clutching ice-creams and bottled drinks. As they neared the path that ran alongside the water they were met with a pack of male youths who all appeared to be holding an alcoholic drink of some sort. It sounded as though they were all speaking over each other and they seemed oblivious to the stares that they attracted from those around them. A couple of them had removed their t-shirts and Zoë saw that one exceptionally tall lad, who had his t-shirt wrapped around this neck, had a painful looking splash of sunburn across his pale chest. As they reached Gage and Zoë they split into two groups and walked around them without registering their presence at all.

As they continued walking, they passed a row of unoccupied boats that were partially covered with frayed blue tarpaulin. Their pointed bows faced away from the pathway as if in anticipation of their next trip out.

Zoë loosened her hand from Gage's hold and folded it against her body. He didn't speak but gave her a questioning look to which she responded to by turning up the corners of her mouth, in a gesture of reassurance.

The concrete paving ended abruptly and became a dusty, well-trodden track through the grass. A brace of ducks crossed a little way in front of them, quickening their pace as they did so to ensure a suitable space was kept between bird and human. They pecked at the grass beneath a recently vacated picnic table looking for remnants of carelessly left food.

The sound of an excited dog barking drew her attention to a boat further down the line. Before she even saw the brown and cream Spaniel she knew it was their dog. Her foot kicked up a dust of dry dirt as she stopped suddenly and put her hand out to touch Gage's arm.

'It's them,' she said. Gage nodded and grabbed her hand pulling her towards a large weeping willow that stood facing the canal on the edge of a heavily wooded area. They wove their way through several picnic tables, where families were enjoying the unusually hot weather and over-indulgent treats that they would probably later regret.

When they reached a spot that Gage was happy with, he pulled out the tartan blanket that accompanied them on all their walks and picnics and laid it down on the ground. The grass was longer and more uneven due to the trailing willow that would have impeded the keeper of the grounds. Gage smoothed the blanket over the lumps and pulled Zoë down beside him.

They had the perfect view of the boat.

Amanda was standing at the back talking to a couple who were of similar age to her. The man before her held himself bolt upright with his hands placed on his hips as if mimicking an action hero. He gave off an impression of superiority. The woman had large black sunglasses on that hid her features, but she held one hand up to the strap of her shoulder bag, almost in anticipation of making an imminent retreat.

A radio close by was emitting a tenuous sound of tinny music. Zoë turned her head in the direction from which it came and saw that it was placed on a table occupied by an elderly couple a few metres from them.

The man had a sprightliness about him and was bouncing his knees up and down to the music. His knee-length shorts were a light blue shade, similar to that of a nurse's tunic and his short-sleeved shirt was unbuttoned slightly, exposing his thin white chest. Sat beside him was a less animated heavy-set lady, whose surprisingly white hair was starting to curl in the heat at the nape of her neck. She held a wafer cone that was liberally filled with soft, whipped, white ice-cream. As she lifted it to her mouth, the cuff of her pink blouse dug into the flesh of her upper arm causing the skin to bulge out around it. She jerked suddenly as a blob of melted ice-cream fell into the lap of her floral skirt. Whooping with laughter, she grabbed the arm of the man beside her who shook his head slowly in mock disbelief. With a grin spreading across his face he reached into his breast pocket and produced a handkerchief which he used to wipe her skirt.

Gage's fingers gently tapping her forearm brought her back to the moment. She twisted her head back round to face him, but his eyes remained fixed ahead. The vein at the side of his temple was protruding and pulsing rapidly and his eyes were brimming with malevolent intensity.

She wanted to stall and turn her attention back to the couple beside them whose contentment stirred a sense of equilibrium within her. Instead though, she forced herself to look ahead and for the second time that week, secretly watched her attacker.

Immediately, Zoë could see that something wasn't quite right. This did not look like the idyllic image that Amanda had described to Aidan the day she had returned to the boutique. The friends that she had spoken of didn't look to be having a particularly good time. Their departure looked a little uncomfortable – awkward even. The couple each hugged Amanda. As the man stepped out of the stiff embrace, he seemed to drop his guard somewhat and held on to the side of Amanda's arm in a gesture of reassurance. She dipped her head and smiled uneasily.

Slowly he turned around to face Toby who was bent over the dog, clumsily trying to attach its lead to the collar. He held a bottle of beer between his teeth and was swaying slightly on the stationary boat. His friend was attempting to draw his attention, but whatever he had said to him seemed to fall on deaf ears as Toby continued with his seemingly arduous task. Accepting defeat, the couple left, leaving Amanda and Toby alone.

She snatched the lead out of his hands and pulled the dog to her side. Toby straightened and tipped his head back, draining the remains of the bottle before dropping it into a crate in the corner. Amanda was shaking her head as she said something to him, to which he responded with a shout that visibly startled her. Zoë felt her own muscles tighten in the mounting tension.

Around them, people were briefly distracted from their own concerns and turned towards the couple on the boat. After a moment's contemplation, everyone seemed satisfied that there was nothing more to see and returned to their own business.

Beside her, she felt Gage brush against her as he got to his feet. His eyes remained centred on Toby, who was clumsily exiting the boat as he held on to the excited dog.

It suddenly felt too dangerous – she didn't feel ready, but as she watched Gage absently stuffing the blanket into his bag, she knew that there could be no going back now.

Before she knew it, they were back on the dusty path, only this time, Toby was stumbling ahead of them. In her head she frantically tried to recall what she had planned to say, but now the words seemed hollow and lacking in vehemence. Uncertainty confidently curled itself around her allowing doubt to nestle in the cracks it formed. As if sensing her hesitancy, Gage squeezed her hand and pulled it up closer to his body so she automatically had to step nearer to him.

The pathway became more secluded as the grassy area ran into a copse of trees that grew into a heavily wooded section behind. There was only enough space for two people to walk side by side and Zoë and Gage had to stop to allow another couple to pass. As they did so, Zoë saw that the woman was pregnant. She wore a long, tight, khaki jersey dress that showed off her neat bump like a photo displayed in a frame. Her eyes sparkled with warmth and amity as she walked by giving them both a full smile. Zoë was glad that the coldness in her own was hidden by her sunglasses and could not be projected on to this vision of happiness.

Ahead, Toby had paused to let the dog off the lead. Gage pulled Zoë along to tighten the gap between themselves and him. Although Toby had not once turned to look back, Zoë felt uneasy now that they were only a few metres behind him, certain that he would see her and somehow manage to escape them.

All of a sudden, he stopped and stooped down. Gage slowed a little, tightening the gap further. He stood upright again holding a stick in the air, which he threw rather clumsily into some bushes.

'Oh shit! Lester, here boy, get the stick,' he slurred. The dog came bounding out of the bushes, triumphantly holding the stick in his mouth. He threw it again and it landed not much more successfully in a divide between the trees. They were almost in touching distance of Toby now and Zoë felt sure that he would hear their footsteps and suddenly swing round.

He stopped again, this time turning slightly so that he was facing the trees to the side of them. From his shirt pocket he pulled out a roll-up and then fumbled around in the pocket of his shorts before obtaining his lighter. Before he had a chance to flick the flame Gage pounced.

He was so quick that it took Zoë a moment to process what had happened. Gage had taken advantage of Toby's preoccupied state and had grabbed him by the shoulders marching him into the clearing that Lester had just disappeared into. Zoë followed them in.

Once inside the small clearing Gage shoved Toby away from him as if he could no longer stand their physical closeness. Toby lurched forward landing at the foot of a tree that broke his fall, but also scraped his cheek in the process.

'What the fuck . . .?' he rolled on to his side and looked up at them.

Lester came leaping out of the long grass behind them and dropped the stick by Toby's leg, barking excitedly. He began spinning in circles and then then jumped on to Toby's stomach demanding attention. Gage picked up a stick from the ground and hurled it into the grass, sending Lester bounding after it.

Using the tree to support himself, Toby got to his feet. In an instant Gage was there again pinning against the bark.

'If it was up to me I'd rip your fucking dick off,' he hissed between his teeth. Zoë felt shocked and unnerved by the sudden violent atmosphere and hardly recognised Gage as the lividity displayed on his face distorted his features completely.

She hardly felt the ground beneath her feet as she moved towards them. It felt as if she was floating rather than walking and everything around her dulled into a distant haze. Stunned by the belligerent force that emanated from the two of them, she felt unable to reach out and touch Gage as she had wanted to do.

'Gage,' she whispered. She saw him slowly loosen his grip and release Toby before stepping back a little way.

Lester was back, this time holding a much larger piece of bark between his teeth. He dropped it to the ground, looking pleased with himself, but also a little confused at the situation. He gave his owner a questioning look, before crouching down, panting in the heat.

Zoë removed her sunglasses. She needed to look him in the eyes one more time to see him as he had seen her; weak and vulnerable.

Toby let out an impertinent breath of air through his nose and turned his head away. The skin around the scratch on his cheek had swollen and looked angry and sore.

'You need to know what you did to me,' she began. He looked back at her, arrogance shining in his eyes. 'What you took from me. . .' the words she wanted to say were stuck in a void somewhere between her brain and mouth. 'You repulse me . . . I despise you – you are a pathetic excuse of a man.'

'Well, that's obviously not what you thought when you let me into your shop,' he sneered.

In a flash Gage was there again, he knocked Toby off of his feet and sent him thudding to the ground. Lester jumped up unsure if it was a game or not and started barking furiously.

Before he had a chance to cover himself Gage and Zoë both saw it. Toby's shirt had torn, partially revealing one side of his chest and shoulder. Even though it felt wrong, Zoë could not take her eyes away. His skin there was puckered and pink and resembled the texture of old leather. The permanent welts looked as though they had been hastily stitched on to the healthy surrounding skin, where hair was still present.

'Well I hope you both enjoyed the show,' Toby jeered. Wrapping his shirt angrily around his chest, he picked himself up and then reached into his pocket for Lester's lead. The dog had stopped barking now and sat still as Toby reattached the lead, without any difficulty this time, to his collar.

None of them had noticed Amanda arrive.

'Toby? What happened?' she looked at them each in turn. Her confusion was evident in the small frown that played on her face. 'I know you, you own the boutique,' she said quietly.

Realising that in order to get away she would need to placate Amanda, she turned to her and smiled, 'Yes I do, hello again. We were just walking past when we heard a dog barking, it sounded quite distressed so we came to see if it was alright and found your husband on the floor.' She knew from the expression on Amanda's face that she had said enough.

'Well, thank you so much for your help – I'll help him back to our boat now.' She smiled at them amiably and walked towards Toby who was staring at the ground.

'Right then, we should be getting back,' Zoë looked to Gage who had already begun walking towards her and without looking back they hastily made their retreat.

Chapter 14

The clinic was at the end of a side road, tucked away behind a small music shop. As Zoë killed time waiting for her appointment, she couldn't help casting a critical eye over the shop front. It was such a crucial introduction to a business, and yet this seemed to show little thought to the impression it gave and blended into the overall drabness of the area. Tatty paper adverts giving notice of past and future events were haphazardly stuck in the window which had a fine, grainy coating of dust on the outside. Beyond this though, sat three acoustic guitars which were placed parallel to one another, each displaying their beautiful contours. In the middle, a bourbon-coloured jumbo took centre stage proudly showing its glossy curved body to the observer.

She thought of her father and how his passion for music would probably outweigh any concerns about the aesthetics of the shop itself. There was probably no need for clever displays when your customers looked beyond the exterior and were only concerned with the products inside.

In the distance the bells of a church chimed, Zoë checked her phone and saw that they were premature by two minutes.

Making her way to the entrance of the clinic, she felt no nerves, now that she was actually there she felt that she was being proactive and after all the waiting, was grateful that the day was finally here.

The vertically slatted blinds gave nothing away as she approached the glass doorway. Pulling on the handle, she felt resistance as the door rattled noisily in its frame. Feeling slightly disconcerted, she stepped back and then noticed a buzzer at the side, just above her eye-level. She pressed it and immediately a woman appeared and let her in. She directed Zoë to sit in one of the grey plastic chairs that were lined up in front of the reception desk and then handed her a clipboard to fill in a form.

The blinds gently moved and tapped against the window in

the small breeze that came through from the open gap at the top. Zoë hadn't really known what to expect of the clinic and although it looked like any other medical waiting room, there was definitely a different air to any other she had been to. Because of the way the chairs were positioned, anyone needing to pass by would require Zoë to pull her legs in slightly to permit them to go by without breaking the unspoken personal space gap. No one had given her eye-contact, which had seemed absurd, but after a while she found herself doing the same – somehow it was just easier.

When at last she found herself sitting opposite the doctor, she lost her nerve. She had planned on being honest, knowing that anything she did say would be honoured by the confidentiality clause, but she just couldn't bear to say it out loud again. The doctor was tall and slim with thinning hair and a long angular face. His eyes shone with credibility from behind his round glasses. His affability should have made it easier for her to tell him but it seemed only to enhance her shame that radiated from her like some sort of tainted aura.

'My partner and I are starting a family, so I thought it would be best to get myself checked out before we do so.'

'A sensible course to take,' he smiled, 'is there a particular reason that brings you here today?'

'Perhaps,' she answered flatly, leaving the question of infidelity hanging in the air.

'Well, we can do all the usual tests for you. An HIV test can be done by taking a small drop of blood from your finger and we will have the results in about thirty minutes. Would you like me to arrange this?'

'Yes, please.' The doctor nodded and turned to his screen.

Back in the waiting area, she let out a long breath. Just the physical side of the ordeal remained now and although she knew that it wouldn't be pleasant, it was somehow less daunting than the consultation she had just had.

When later that afternoon she arrived home, Gage was sat in the garden gulping water from a large bottle, he had his feet resting on an upturned barrel plant pot and when he noticed her he lowered the bottle and wiped his mouth with the back of his hand.

'Good day?' he stared up at her with his eyes screwed up against the glare of the sun. Zoë dropped a kiss on his lips and then stood in front of him shielding him from the brightness.

'I went to the STI clinic this morning.' Gage placed his feet on the ground and sat forward in his chair.

'Why didn't you say anything? I would have come with you,' she heard the hurt tone in his voice.

'I just wanted to get it done without having to think about it too much. It probably doesn't make sense to you, but I felt it was for the best,' she smiled to reassure him that she had not meant to shut him out. 'If I don't hear anything within two weeks, then I'm all clear.' Tears sprang from nowhere and she let them fall before continuing, 'It looks like there is no chance of having contracted HIV though, they did a test there and then.' Gage leant forward and took hold of her hands, bringing them up to his mouth where he kissed each in turn. Zoë felt his mouth trembling against her knuckles as he held on to her. Twisting her body round, she sat down on to his lap and brought her head to his so that their foreheads were touching.

Her breathing gradually began to return to normal and as she lifted her head away she let out a loud sniff. All of a sudden she was laughing and the recent tension that had caused complicated knots and loops in her muscles began to unravel as though slick with oil. Gage watched her with an uncertain grin playing on his lips and even though she felt a little ridiculous, she let the laughter rip through her until the contractions in her diaphragm were too much to bear.

'What shall we have for tea then, crazy girl?' Zoë flicked away the tears from beneath her eyes and pushed her hair behind her ears.

'Let's get take-away; I don't mind what we get as long as it's quick as I'm starving.' Gage had taken his phone from his pocket before she'd even finished the sentence.

Having eaten as much as her stomach would allow, Zoë took their plates over to the sink and began to run the hot tap.

'Here, let me do that – you go and sit down.' Gage took the sponge from her hand and gently nudged her out of the way with his hip. She stepped backwards and perched on the edge of the table watching him he hunched over the sink. She noticed that he had caught the sun on his arms and on the back of his neck. His hair had grown longer than he usually liked, he had it tucked in place behind his ears as he washed their plates with the meticulous care he applied to everything he did.

Becoming aware of her scrutiny, he turned his head and smiled at her.

'What?' he smirked

'Nothing . . .' she pushed herself away from the table and slid her arms around his waist, resting the side of her cheek on his back. Feeling comforted by his density and warmth, she tightened her grip until she felt as though she were an extension of him.

'It seems like ages since you've done that,' he spoke softly, holding his hands still in the water as if the slightest movement would break the moment, 'touched me first, I mean. I really thought that I was going to lose you.' Zoë let her hands fall to his hips and twisted his body round to face her before tenderly pulling his neck down to kiss him. She felt the words that he had been unable to say in the urgency of the way that his mouth pressed against hers.

They moved upstairs to the bedroom where the warmth of the sun had clung to the bedding emitting the soft scent of fabric conditioner alongside traces of their own unique fragrance. They lay facing each other and although he didn't say anything, Zoë could sense him wondering.

'Soon,' she whispered.

Her mind turned to the faint bruising that still remained on the inside of her thighs. It seemed that the soft, sensitive area that was unused to such violent handling was showing resistance in letting her heal. She could not let Gage see, it would only set them back further again.

'I wasn't trying – ' she held her finger up to his lips.

'I know.'

Outside, the sounds of everyday life blew in from their open window; an intense one-sided conversation, birds chirping as they flitted from tree to tree and the chiming of an ice-cream van that somehow always evoked a wave of melancholy in her. She closed her eyes and let it all wash over, but somewhere in a small corner of mind something was unwilling to settle. Like a restless child distracting its fellow classmates, it became active, niggling at her when she tried to clear her mind of thoughts: their plan had failed.

After she had tried to make him understand just what it was that he had done to her, she had planned to plant the idea of the CCTV footage in his mind and hopefully wipe the arrogant look from his face. But she had been denied that tiny sense of victory by the arrival of Amanda. She and Gage had actually achieved nothing other than witnessing his moment of humiliation at them seeing his scarred chest . . . what was she going to do now?

Beside her, Gage stared up at the ceiling, deafened to the sounds of the world outside by the mantra that chanted in his head: *the bastard had to suffer.*

The week so far, had been a busy one in the boutique with people being attracted to the area by a food market that was taking place close by. Zoë had taken a moment to watch the stall-holders as they set up that morning. The 'Around the World' theme was a spectacular visual treat of colour and vibrancy. As she had made her way through the centre of the stands, smoke had flared in front of her from the hissing meats that cooked on the griddles.

Beneath a pink and white striped parasol, a petite young woman with striking titanium grey hair had been delicately placing colourful macarons into neat, coordinated rows. The mix of pastel and jewel hues had drawn her eyes so powerfully that she had found herself approaching the stall as if spellbound. The woman had smiled at her knowingly which had left Zoë in no doubt that she was accustomed to the delighted reaction her confectionary treats induced. Zoë had cast her gaze across the hard-shelled beds of colour; each perfectly complemented by a glimpse of ganache filling, that gently enticed the onlooker. Her eyes had settled on the pastel shades that evoked the memory of the sweet peas that had grown in cane wigwams in the garden of her childhood. The distinct sweet aroma of the fragile flower had filled her nostrils as if an actual bouquet had been placed in her hand.

The effect that the short-lived, unexpected experience had brought remained with her as she had begun her usual morning routine. A small bubble of excitement had re-ignited every time she thought of the candy-pink striped box that contained her hand-picked delights. She couldn't wait to present them to Gage later that evening as his sweet tooth would definitely appreciate the almond biscuits even if his eyes failed to recognise their charm.

As Amber had taken a few days off, Zoë had got Sian into cover for her. Having obtained her Business and Management degree, she had worked intermittently for Zoë during the past year. The arrangement had proven to be beneficial to them both as Zoë could only offer Sian hours when she required cover for holidays or sickness and Sian, being on a gap-year was away travelling for regular stretches.

Sian had arrived this morning looking every inch the business woman, wearing a coral pencil skirt and ribbed short-sleeved cream top. Her long blonde hair was pulled into a top knot as was typical of her when she was working. Zoë had only ever seen her hair down in photographs taken in the various countries she had visited, that Sian had shown her on her phone. But one thing that was always present was the bright red lipstick that stained her full, plump lips and always reminded Zoë of plush velvet cushions. On the counter she had placed a single macaron that the titanium-haired stall holder had wrapped in a paper bag and tied with raffia straw ribbon. It matched the cherry-red of her lips perfectly.

Now it was lunch time, the constant stream of customers that had kept Zoë and Sian busy for the entire morning had disappeared and they were alone in the boutique for the first time that day. Zoë adjusted her blouse where it had become untucked from her waistband. The silky material felt a little damp as her fingers ran along the inside of her skirt – proof of the ardent duty she had shown to her customers, and yet as the sun had blazed through *Her* Boutique's windows, Sian had remained her usual vision of serenity and grace. Zoë had never seen anything faze her and found herself to be slightly jealous of this attribute.

'Well that was pretty intense – I can't ever remember it being that busy on a week day before.' Sian towered over Zoë with her hands placed on her hips, the only hint of exertion on her part being a strand of hair that had escaped from her perfect bun.

'It was – I could do with there being a food market here every week,' Zoë laughed.

'I might go and have my cake now, replenish my energy levels in case we have another surge.'

'Good idea, could you stick the kettle on while you're there? I'm just going to re-stock, while it's quiet.'

Zoë moved deftly around the boutique, straightening the clothes on the rails and filling up where necessary. One of the mannequins in the window stood naked after having been stripped of its dress in the rush. She chose a new outfit to replace it and carried it over to the window. As she placed the clothes on the model, carefully pinning the items where needed, she could feel the fierce heat of the sun on her back. It had been reported that the dry spell was coming to an end and that more showery weather would follow, but for now she had decided to keep the window in summer mode.

She had recently been sent details from a new company specialising in bespoke- style umbrellas. The website had been impressive and she had not needed much encouragement to place her order of the quirky and unique patterned pieces. It could be a small item of luxury that she felt sure her customers would appreciate; a possible add-on sale or an item bought when the purchaser's budget would not stretch to an item of clothing, but would still provide the thrill of a purchase. A small rush of excitement rose up in her like the sprinkling of a water fountain.

Outside, she faced the window and assessed her work, checking for any minor flaws that would spoil the over-all look. She tilted her head to the side in deliberation of which items she could use accessorise the display, and in that moment caught sight of a face reflected back at her over her shoulder.

Amanda.

Her breath caught in her throat, before driven by compulsion she turned around and faced her. For a short time neither of them moved as a steady trail of people passed between them, but as if suddenly having made a decision, Amanda ran her hand over the strap of her bag and walked towards Zoë.

'It's Zoë, isn't it?

'Yes.'

'I wondered if you would be able to spare me a moment of your time, perhaps get a drink somewhere.' Zoë looked about her, stalling for time but also as an excuse to avert her eyes away from the keen scrutiny of the woman before her. It was still considerably busier than a usual weekday, but Zoë knew that Sian could cope perfectly well alone in the boutique for a short while.

'I can't go too far, in case I'm needed back here.'

'No, of course not – how about the pub on the corner? Zoë had assumed that when Amanda had suggested a drink she had meant in a coffee shop, but curious to know her motive for coming and eager get the ordeal over with, she agreed.

'Let me just get my bag.'

They walked the short distance to the pub in silence, each using the excuse of dodging customers to remain quiet and Zoë, suddenly conscious of the absurdity of the situation, wondered if it was too late to back out.

When they entered the heavily air-conditioned bar Zoë felt the coolness sweep across her heated skin inducing a small shiver to slice through her. Although not particularly busy, the long bar area was lined with lunch time drinkers that were either sat or stood in groups.

Zoë looked for the nearest available table and went over to place down her bag on the bucket style seat.

'What would you like to drink?'

'Just a mineral water, please.' Amanda looked as though she were about to comment, but then nodded her head and turned away.

As she sat waiting, she caught snippets of people's conversations as they passed by the open door. Although she wanted to keep half an eye on Amanda she daren't be caught doing so – it was important that she stay composed and just let Amanda say what she came to say. She couldn't risk arousing any kind of suspicion because she, herself, hadn't decided on what she was going to do next.

Two men were walking down a wide set of stairs in front of her and she fixated on them as a way of distraction. They were both dressed in tailored fitted shirts and trousers and were deliberating the details of a future event or function. Both looked to be the shining example of the millennial male who drank homemade smoothies for breakfast before lifting weights in the gym. The shorter of the two men held the confident tone of a sales manager who had perfected his pitch and used it time after time.

The building itself was much larger than Zoë had expected from the outside and it was obvious that it had been recently renovated. Everything still had that shiny new edge to it and Zoë wondered how long it would be before signs of wear and tear would become evident.

The two men were shaking hands, somewhat zealously and then their conversation came to a close as the taller man swept his eyes over Zoë and put on his sunglasses before disappearing out of the door. The other man, that Zoë assumed to be the manager or supervisor, rubbed his hands together in an exaggerated fashion as he headed over to the bar; his tight trousers only just managing to contain the cheeks of his protruding muscular backside.

Amanda approached balancing the drinks vice-like between her fingers, she leant over and put down the glass bottle of mineral water first and then placed the empty glass in front of Zoë. As she settled herself down in her seat she glanced towards the door as if expecting to see somebody standing there. Seeming satisfied she took a large mouthful of her wine and shifted her weight from side to side.

'I just wanted to thank you, really – for helping Toby that afternoon.' Zoë nodded and let her gaze fall to the table.

'It's unnecessary – we hardly did anything.' She was only too well aware that this was the point where she was supposed to ask after him, but the silence grew and in her discomfort Zoë frantically scrambled for something to say. Amanda saved her the bother.

'Is there something that you're not telling me? I mean, was Toby rude to either of you or anything?' The directness of the question took Zoë by surprise – Amanda had gone from expressing gratitude to touching on dangerous ground in a matter of seconds. She seemed to take Zoë's hesitancy as confirmation. 'He'd been drinking, you see, for most of the day actually. To be honest with you, it caused a bit of tension between Toby and our friends and they ended up leaving earlier than planned. He'd stormed off when they left – so he probably wasn't in the best of moods when you saw him.'

'Look, you really don't have to explain, it's absolutely none of my business.' Zoë was desperately regretting her decision to see her, what had she been thinking? She didn't owe Amanda anything and should have just told her that she was too busy. 'I'd better be getting back actually.' Zoë shifted in her chair slightly in an effort to show that she was about to leave. It seemed that Amanda had not heard her though and instead of responding with the awkward farewell platitudes that Zoë had expected, she sat with her shoulders down staring at a spot on the wall behind her.

'And now he's disappeared – I waited up for him last night, but he didn't come home. I knew that something had been bothering him – he'd been drinking more than usual and was acting completely irrationally.' Zoë could not believe that this deflated, weak looking woman was the same person that she had assisted in her boutique only a month ago.

'I have to go, Amanda,' Zoë repeated more urgently. Suddenly stirred, Amanda picked up her glass and took another swig, draining it completely.

'He wasn't always like this, you know. When he was in the army he was a totally different man – confident, driven, and when he would come home on leave, he was always so happy to see me. We did things together. It didn't matter if it was just being out tidying the garden or away on holiday, we always seemed to be content and happy.' She paused and spun the stem of her glass between her fingers. 'And then the explosion happened.' The pink welts that Zoë had seen on Toby's chest flashed before her eyes. 'He was lucky to have been saved, most of his platoon died right there and then, but it's like he is too bitter to appreciate that now.'

The small waves of uncertainty that Zoë had experienced on first arriving had now increased in ferocity. Something was very wrong.

Amanda continued to talk about how, in the months after the explosion, Toby had seemed to slowly heal, both physically and mentally. They grew closer and he seemed grateful for all the hours she put into nursing and nurturing him, of course he'd still had bad days, but he always managed to lift himself out of the despair he felt.

But then he had suddenly stopped taking his medication and had begun looking for work. Amanda had expressed her concerns, but he had assured her that it was what he needed and that he couldn't stay on anti-depressants forever – he had to find something that would fill the gap that his departure from the army had left.

Things changed for the worse when Toby was turned down for a position he felt he was far too good for. He began to show signs of bitterness and would disappear for hours without telling Amanda where he was, often returning home drunk and aggressive. He'd begun regularly taking his frustration out on her and had even broken her arm on one occasion.

She had started making excuses for him and at first friends and family had been understanding, but as the months crept into years, this fell by the wayside and she was left alone to clean up the mess that he caused.

Her narrative abruptly stopped and she looked Zoë directly in the eye.

'You didn't just *bump* into Toby – did you?' her features hardened and she seemed to rise up as if a pole had been suddenly inserted into her spine. Zoë was held to the spot by her piercing gaze – a look so cold that she feared she might actually physically shudder and therefore reveal her alarm. 'You see, Zoë, I've been thinking about it and there are just too many coincidences when it comes to you,' she held up her index finger to indicate her first point, 'Toby refusing to go on holiday, or to even move out of his chair, on the day after we came to your boutique. I had assumed that he was having another one of his meltdowns, but then a week later when I returned my trousers, he wouldn't step foot inside the shop, despite the fact that he'd been complaining about the heat outside.' The middle and ring fingers were now also held up and Zoë waited for the last piece of damning evidence to be spoken. 'And then there you were at the boatyard the other week . . . did you really think that I would believe that ridiculous story you gave me, or that I wouldn't notice the thick tension that made it almost impossible to breathe in that wooded enclosure?' she dropped her hand slightly and rested her chin on her fingers as she waited for Zoë's response. 'What happened?' she prompted, as though speaking to a small child after a playground spat.

Zoë's only concern was to get away, she knew that it was highly unlikely that she could convince Amanda that she had it all wrong, but she had to try.

'I'm so sorry that you have suffered, but this really doesn't have anything to do with me – I think that you have misread the situation and perhaps convinced yourself of this theory you have come up with. I really do have to be getting back now,' she stood and picked up her bag from the solid oak floor, 'under the circumstances though, I think it's for the best that neither you nor your husband come to my boutique again.'

'Wait, don't go yet – just tell me ... is there something going on between you and my husband?' Zoë felt her whole body stiffen at what the question implied.

'No, absolutely not!' She swept out of the door with her heart thumping erratically in her chest, before Amanda could add anything further.

As she hurried back to the boutique, she misplaced her footing a little in the ridges between the cobbles and was sent off balance momentarily which only increased her feeling of unease. Every few seconds she turned her head to make sure that Amanda had not followed her.

By the time she reached the entrance to the boutique her cheeks were flushed and a light film of sweat had dampened her hairline. Sian was standing with her head poking through the curtain of the changing room advising a customer, when she heard Zoë's footsteps she swung her neck back and smiled brightly.

'Everything OK?' Zoë asked.

'Yes, fine.'

'Sorry, I was longer than I expected. When you've finished there, feel free to take your break.'

'Ah it's fine – that macaron kept me going, but I do just need to pop out to the chemist.' Zoë nodded and went through to the back. As she put her bag away, she knocked the candy-striped box with her arm and sent it tumbling to the floor. She reached down to retrieve it and as she did so heard the grainy sound of smashed meringue as it rattled at the bottom of the box. With a heavy sigh she placed them further back on the side.

The remainder of the afternoon passed steadily, with just the right amount of customers to keep her from dwelling on her earlier conversation too much. Just after four o'clock when the boutique was empty, Sian came down from the stockroom carrying a bulging bag of rubbish.

'I've given it a good going over up there – most things are now hung on the rails, so they should be easier to find and I've given the floor a good sweep too.' Zoë couldn't help feeling embarrassed as normally this was something she kept on top of. Sian must be thinking that Zoë was letting her standards drop.

'Thank you, Sian, that's really good of you – what with my trip to London and the shop being busy most days, I just haven't had time.'

'No worries, I actually enjoyed it,' she beamed.

'You may as well get off – there's not much going on here now.'

'OK, if you're sure? I'll go out the back and get rid of this. See you tomorrow then.' Zoë locked the door behind her and grabbed the brush that Sian had left leaning up against the wall. With the boutique still empty, she pulled the rail nearest the door to one side and swept the dust that had collected beneath the fixture, it never failed to amaze her how dirty the place could get in just a couple of days.

Now that she was alone, she could no longer stop thoughts of Amanda and what she'd disclosed from pushing to the forefront of her mind. She had half expected her to show up again but as the afternoon had worn on that threat seemed less likely.

The thought occurred to her that she should be feeling at least a small sense of satisfaction; he was suffering. Perhaps not for what he had done to her, but suffering all the same. But instead she felt an air of unrest as though having been given notice of an imminent attack expected in the area. Also the fact still remained that he had not taken responsibility for what he'd done, that was obvious from the way he'd reacted on Sunday. It was as though it were a game to him and her feelings were an irrelevance, she now started to doubt whether the threat of the CCTV would actually even have an effect on him – he didn't seem to care about anything.

Amanda's controlled voice rang in her ears again: *what happened?* The certainty with which she had spoken had astonished her – she seemed convinced that Zoë was somehow involved with Toby and was to blame for his current behaviour. It was this insight that had frightened her, Amanda seemed dangerous and she had temporarily been blind-sided by her need to protect herself. But now she realised the source of her concern was not only for herself, but also for Amanda. From what she had told Zoë today, she had already spent years being a victim of Toby's mental and physical abuse and now that she had connected his deterioration to her, it could only cause more trouble. This was not something she could ignore by burying her head in the sand.

Amanda's crestfallen expression as Zoë had made her demands about them staying away, replayed in her mind. It was such a disparate image from the one she had displayed earlier when she had risen up and confronted Zoë. She recognised that look; it was one of absolute resignation, she had given up.

Zoë couldn't help feeling that Amanda was in some kind of danger.

She closed and locked the front door and went through to the back having made a decision. Punching the code in to unlock her phone she felt her hand trembling, 'Gage – can you come and pick me up?'

Chapter 15

Sat outside the house once again, she was hit by how much stronger she felt compared to the week before when she had followed Toby. Even if she and Gage had not achieved what they had first set out to do, it had at least given her this. Any apprehension she felt now was overridden by her sense of purpose – she had to speak to Amanda again.

'What are we going to do if he's there?'

'I don't know – I'm hoping that if he is, he'll be too inebriated to know what's going on . . . that's what I'm counting on anyway.'

'Are you sure that you want to do this?'

'Yes, definitely – I won't be able to rest until I've spoken to her, then perhaps we can put this behind us.' Zoë had filled Gage in with the details of what had happened at lunch time whilst they had driven across the city to the house. 'And I have to see for myself that she is all right. The way that she was acting today – well, it was just really odd.'

'Don't take this the wrong way, but what if she is OK now and it was just the drink talking, how are you going to explain us turning up on her doorstep?'

'Then I will try and convince her that she is wrong about there being some sort of connection between me and *him*. That it *was* just a coincidence that we were there that Sunday. I'll admit that you pushed him because, in his drunken state he had become aggressive towards us after I'd petted their dog.' Gage shook his head slowly.

'This is not your responsibility, Zo – you don't owe her a damn thing, this could all be a way of her drawing you into their problems, have you thought of that? I think we should just go home and let things settle – he's even more fucked up than we first thought'

'Gage, you didn't see her – she really seemed on the edge. I mean what if she tried to do something stupid? I have to make sure she's OK.' He sighed and reached for her hand.

'Come on then, let's get this over with so we can go home.'

As Zoë pushed open the gate it let out a long moan as if to signal their arrival to anyone inside. Now outside the door, she got the impression that in fact, there wasn't anybody present to have heard it, despite the parked car in the driveway. All the windows were closed and the house had an air of stillness about it. She pulled back the door knocker and gave three short raps. Immediately, they were answered by the shrill, urgent barks of Lester. It fell silent again for a few seconds and then he appeared at the window with his breath forming little clouds of condensation on the glass. Gage cupped his hands by the side of his head and leant on the window to peer into the lounge.

'Doesn't look like there's anyone here.'

'Maybe when she went out earlier she left the car here, she was drinking, after all,' Zoë suggested. Lester began scraping his paws up and down the glass, his pads making a faint thudding sound as they bounced against it. They both turned their attention to him.

'Wait – is that . . .?' Before she could finish her sentence, Gage was pushing her back towards the gate, his face set as it had been on the day that they had confronted Toby.

'Just stay here a minute – let me go and have a look.' Back at the window Lester's barking had intensified, but as Gage moved back to face him, he jumped down and disappeared through a door connecting to the room behind. Within seconds he was back, in his mouth he was carrying a man's slipper which he dropped on to the grey rug in the centre of the room. He then bounced back up on to the dark leather chair and stood upright regarding Gage as his cream patterned paws pressed into the edge of the chair.

This time Gage was left in no doubt – it was definitely blood. The sides of his two front paws were matted with crimson as if he had stepped in a puddle of red paint, and on the glass his prints had left a dry, smeared impression.

Gage lurched back to the door and banged his fist against it, the dull dogged raps echoing their note of intensity along the road. Next door an elderly woman peered cautiously over the wall.

'What's going on?' she called across to Gage.

'I'm sorry to disturb you, but could you tell me if you have seen your neighbours today?' Zoë moved closer to Gage in an effort to try and reassure the woman of his credibility. She looked warily from one to the other as if trying to determine the legitimacy of each of their characters.

'Have you seen Amanda today, by any chance?' Zoë asked. Seemingly satisfied, the woman nodded her head.

'I saw her go out at about eleven o'clock when my carer was leaving.'

'Did you notice if she took her car,' Zoë added.

'No, she didn't, she walked.'

'Thank you, you've been really helpful.' The woman nodded but instead of going back inside her house, she watched them walk round to the side gate. Zoë looked about nervously as Gage tried the latch. It rattled noisily but the gate remained firmly closed.

'Follow me,' Gage urged. He deftly unclipped the ladder from the roof of his van and slid it back feeding the rungs through his hands.

'I don't like this, Gage, shouldn't we call the police?'

'I just want to see if there is anything obvious round the back. For all we know, the dog could have caught a mole in the garden.'

'But what if a neighbour sees us and calls them?'

'I think that we have to take that chance, Zoë, hopefully they will think I'm on a job, we really don't want to get them involved unless we have to.'

'Come on then, let's get this over with,' she relented.

Gage set the ladder against the side wall and climbed a few steps. Once his legs drew level with the top of the gate he used the post furthest from him to swing himself over. She heard the neat thud of his feet as they hit the ground on the other side and then the gate was pulled open revealing an immaculately kept garden – the garden that belonged to her attacker.

Gage held up his palm to Zoë motioning her to stay where she was and then followed the pathway round to the back of the house. Straight away she could tell from his body language that he had seen something. She recognised the nervous gesture as he ran his hand down the side of his jeans before he tapped lightly on the conservatory window.

'Amanda.' No response came from within, other than the return of Lester's barks. Zoë could no longer remain stationary and went to stand beside Gage.

On the other side of the glass Amanda was sat completely still with her back to them. Placed on the table in front of her an empty bottle of wine glinted under a beam of sunlight beside a large vase of pink peonies. The sense of foreboding that had brought her to the house increased further. Something felt very wrong.

Behind them, the fluttering wings of a sparrow darting from one hedgerow to another, startled Zoë and she grabbed hold of Gage making him jump also. After regaining her composure she tapped on the glass.

'Amanda, we just want to know that you're OK, and then we'll leave,' she shouted. Lester paced from room to room as if unaware of Amanda's presence. 'Amanda, please – just show me that you're not hurt.' The slightest jerk of her head gave Zoë encouragement and so she persevered in her coaxing tone, 'I meant to tell you something earlier – please come out and speak to me.' A moment of relief washed over her as she watched Amanda turn her neck to look at them – but this was to be short-lived.

She stared at them with wide, glassy eyes and on her cheek, the splattering of red that adorned her ashen skin stood out like a flare in the night sky.

Zoë and Gage remained motionless for a moment as if confronted by a wild animal protecting its young. Possible scenarios played out in Zoë's mind as she felt Gage's hand on her arm, slowly pulling her back.

'See if you can keep her there while I call for help,' he whispered.

Amanda's eyes stayed fixed on Zoë as Gage discreetly turned away and pulled his phone from his pocket. With an air of possession, she rose from her chair as if pulled up by an invisible force. Her stained arms hung limply by her side, where in the warmth of the sun the blood had dried and now looked like flaking paint on a neglected wall.

Despite the trembling that threatened to overpower her, she reached out her hand to touch the glass.

'Can you open the door?' Zoë saw Amanda's lips move but her

words were swallowed up by a drawn out whine from Lester. 'Please open the door, Amanda, let me help you.' A flicker of understanding ignited in her eyes and as if Zoë had spoken the correct code into an intercom, Amanda lifted her arm and turned the key in the lock. Zoë gave her a small smile of encouragement to which she responded to by pulling the door open.

Lester flew out, brushing her leg with his fur as he rushed by. He lapped the garden once, pausing to jump up at Gage who was by the gate, and then disappeared back inside as Amanda tentatively stepped on to the path. So as not to startle her, Zoë kept as much distance as possible between them as she placed her hands on Amanda's upper arms and gently ushered her away from the house. She dropped her head forward and her hair fell around her face casting a protective cover. They were now standing beside a heavily foliaged archway where wisteria hung like huge drop earrings from the greenery. The lavender tubs that were sat on either side, emanated the age-old scent that Zoë always associated with her grandparents' garden, but now it fought for supremacy over the sickly metallic odour that covered Amanda.

Zoë felt her arm muscles beginning to strain as Amanda seemed to surrender her whole body weight over to her, but she feared that if she took her hands away Amanda would fold in on herself.

'I'm so tired,' she murmured.

Gage slipped behind them and charged into the conservatory. The air inside was dry and stagnant from being closed up in the heat, it caught in his throat as he skirted the table and headed towards the open door in front of him.

For a moment he thought he had conjured the image from the darkest corner of his mind, but then Lester was there nudging his owner's bare foot with his nose and Gage heard the raspy, laboured breath sounds that came from Toby's mouth. He was slumped upright against a heavy oak sideboard, his chest was covered with blood and his eyes were half- closed as if he were barely holding on to consciousness. Gage could feel all the signs of adrenaline storming his body in preparation for him to react to the shocking situation.

But he didn't. He stood with his legs planted to the spot as Toby fought for breath in front of him.

From the doorway he heard Zoë gasp and then the sound of her panting as though having run a great distance to get there. 'Gage! For fuck's sake – do something! Call an ambulance!'

Neither of them could face going straight home after they had finished speaking to the police. Gage had told the detective who had taken his statement that he had dropped by to discuss a job that Amanda had approached him about. Zoë had explained that she vaguely knew Amanda from her being a customer in the boutique. She had given her Gage's number and that was how they had found themselves there this afternoon.

The paramedics that had attended the scene had told them that if they had not arrived when they did, Toby would surely have bled to death.

Zoë's intuition had saved not Amanda, but Toby.

Together they ambled along the vaulted walkway of the cathedral cloisters. Each arch that they passed framed a live image of the different activities that were taking place in the grassy area at the front. School children still dressed in their summer uniforms, practised a range of songs led by a man with round spectacles who played along with his guitar. A couple, whose American accents sounded quick and sharp above the usual slow drawn-out timbre of the locals were gazing up towards the spire with their hands cupped above their eyes.

They had hardly spoken to each other since they had arrived, both had been absorbed in thought and they had respected each other's need for quiet contemplation in the cool surroundings. It had been Zoë's idea to come though, Gage had suggested that they go for a drink, but Zoë had felt that the brash atmosphere of a bar would be too imposing on her mood somehow. She had yearned for the serenity that was constant in the historic limestone cathedral.

Her eyes swept across the green and gold of the roof bosses that decorated the ceiling overhead as they continued walking. When faced with the head of an ugly, devilish carving she stopped and inspected it with a kind of morbid curiosity. It was the terrifying expression that held her attention more than anything else – the cold penetrative stare and derogatory sneer filled her with a kind of childish terror, she let her eyes drop and turned back to face the activities outside.

She assumed that she must be in some sort of a state of shock as her mind kept replaying the moment that she first saw Toby's bloodied body splayed across the stone floor, she had never seen so much blood and had felt certain that he would die. She didn't know how she felt about the fact that he was going to live, she felt no closure.

The speed in which she had become embroiled in their complicated and messed- up relationship had astounded her and she wished more than anything that she could change the events of the day that had brought Toby into her life. A futile act, she knew, but it didn't stop her from imagining herself locking the door and going to retrieve the forgotten bag alone, then passing it through a gap in the door and him leaving to return to his troubled life without ever involving her.

In reality though, the consequences of that day had drastically changed her and she and Gage would need to find a way to cope with that fact.

She reached for Gage's hand and felt him give a gentle squeeze of assurance as if he knew what she had been thinking. Perhaps it really would be over now and she could begin to heal.

The sound of evensong began to pour out from the heart of the cathedral. Zoë felt instantly soothed by the reverberations that drifted along the passages and as the soprano voices soared she felt herself rise up with them. It seemed as though she was not alone in this sense as outside she saw that everyone had turned towards the direction from which the music came.

In the second week of June the temperature had dropped and it seemed that any signs of summer that they had experienced in the previous month would be all that they could expect that summer. But today as Zoë and Gage sat on the grassy dunes over-looking the beach, they felt the hazy sunshine begin to warm their faces.

With it being a Sunday the beach was busy and families had ar-rived early to set up windbreakers and blankets in order to se-cure their expanse of the sand for the day. Zoë was carefully manoeuvring her tongue along the velvety contours of her ice-cream whilst idly watching events unfold before her. A group of teenagers had set up a volleyball net in a space that could argu-ably be claimed was too tight for the activity and therefore pro-ceeded to annoy everyone in the vicinity, all but for a small Jack Russell. It was secured on a lead to a beach chair beneath its owner and was intensely following every rise and fall of the fluorescent coloured ball, ready to pounce in the event of it roll-ing in its direction.

Gage ran his hand down the length of Zoë's shin and smiled freely when she turned to him. They were slowly adjusting to aftermath that followed their findings at the house although they had not discussed it in any detail since the night that they returned home from the cathedral.

'Oh my goodness – have you finished yours already?!' Gage con-tinued pushing the remains of the cone into his mouth and crunched noisily on the wafer as he laughed.

'You can't buy me the smallest ice-cream available to man and then expect me to make it last for hours like you do!'

'I'm just keeping an eye on your sugar intake . . . and of course it doesn't help that you've dropped thirty percent of it down your t-shirt,' she inclined her head towards his chest and gave him a self-satisfied smile.

'Oh yeah, that's a shame.' He wiped unsuccessfully at the drying yellow stain as Zoë playfully shook her head at him.

Although she had been desperately relieved to receive the news that all her test results had come back clear, it had not culminated in the closure that she had naively and optimistically hoped for. Looking back now, she realised that she had been clinging to a false hope to get her through the initial shock and trauma and in reality the process of healing would be a long one.

'We should be getting back soon, I've got some emails to reply to and some orders to complete before dinner tonight.' They had arranged to meet up with Amber and Theo at a new Italian restaurant that had recently opened in the city centre, it would be the first time that they had gone out in a foursome together and Zoë was really looking forward to it.

Gage nodded as he drew his knees up to his chest and wrapped his arms around them. He kept his face trained towards the sea, his eyes crinkling at the sides in an automatic response to the brightness.

Their private enclosure was suddenly disturbed when they were descended upon by a small group of children running down the hill behind them. Their squeals of delight carried the absolute joy and abandonment that once you pass a certain age cannot again be replicated. As they flew down the dune their small feet displaced the sand spraying Zoë and Gage in the process which caused them both to sharply turn their heads away. When they looked round again they noticed a vivid-pink hair band lying in the sand beside them. Gage got to his feet and plucked it up. As he was shaking the excess grains from the stretchy material, a little girl appeared before them with her blonde fringe hanging down over her eyes.

'Is this yours?' Gage proffered the band towards the girl, who looked back at him uncertainly. 'You won't be able to see where you're going without it,' he stepped forward smiling brightly. As if this reminded her of the fact she made a quick sweeping motion across her forehead with her hand and then smiled shyly back at Gage before gingerly taking it from him.

'Thank you,' she said in a tiny voice before turning and bellowing after the group for them to wait for her. They watched her re-join the others who were waiting for her at the bottom of the hill. In the silence that followed, Zoë could feel Gage's sorrow that had been evoked by the impromptu encounter that had just occurred. He had been aware that he wouldn't be able to conceal it from her and so had turned away.

'Gage – we need to talk about this.' He raised his arms up and rested them on the back of his head as if he was under arrest and even though it could not have been more inappropriate, she began to laugh. His look of disbelief unhinged her further and her laughter began to verge on the hysterical until she saw the hurt expression on his face.

'I'm so sorry, I'm not sure where that came from, please forgive me. I just feel that I don't want to carry on living in fear anymore ... fear of failure, of making the wrong decisions, of imperfection and ... most of all, fear that someone else could hurt me like he did.' She felt the beginnings of tears pushing from behind her eyes but needed to finish what she had to say. 'I could wait until I felt it was the right time to have a baby – but when would that be? I'm never going to fully *get over* what happened and the boutique is never going to get easier to manage, so I will just have to learn to take things step by step.' She paused and waited for Gage to respond realising that he had gone very quiet.

'When Amber first told me about the rape, I felt pain that I hadn't imagined was possible. I suppose I thought that with my father dying when I was so young, I'd already experienced the kind of life-changing hurt that happens and stupidly thought I'd be able to cope with anything else that life threw at me. I couldn't have been more wrong. Anyway what I'm trying to explain to you is that I don't *need* anything more, you don't have to feel that I am waiting for you to decide that you're ready – I already have everything I want.' The wind whipped Zoë's hair up into her eyes distracting her for a moment and she shook her head from side to side before scooping her hair into a hand-held ponytail.

'Well it's a good job that I don't need a baby either – but I do want one and I'm not going to let anything stop me from moving on with my life – our life.' She gently nudged him forwards with the side of her body, 'Come on, we've got work to do.' Gage stared at her with a hint of doubt before allowing her words to sink in.

From below they heard the astonished cries as the Jack Russell, having escaped from its restraint, had run off with the fluorescent ball and now had a trail of people chasing after it.

'A dog though, is absolutely out of the question,' Zoë gave Gage a sideways look and he held his hands up in protest.

'The thought has never entered my head,' he grabbed her hand and pulled her down the dune. She felt the cool sand flick the back of her calves as they ran with abandonment to the bottom of the mound, just as the children had done moments before. In the seconds that it took them to get there she had felt completely weightless with her mind empty of everything but the thrill of the moment.

38455342R00141

Printed in Poland
by Amazon Fulfillment
Poland Sp. z o.o., Wrocław